TRAITS & TRAITORS

THE INTELLIGENCERS · BOOK TWO

BY

JANE GLATT

TRAITS

&

TRAITORS

THE INTELLIGENCERS  BOOK TWO

BY
JANE GLATT

TYCHE BOOKS LTD.

Traits & Traitors
Copyright © 2019 Jane Glatt

This is a work of fiction. All of the characters, organizations and events portrayed in this story are either the product of the author's imagination or are used fictitiously.

Any resemblance to persons living or dead would be really cool, but is purely coincidental.

Published by Tyche Books Ltd.
Calgary, Alberta, Canada
www.TycheBooks.com

Cover Design by Indigo Chick Designs
Interior Layout by Ryah Deines
Editorial by Karley Hauser

First Tyche Books Ltd Edition 2019
Print ISBN: 978-1-928025-99-3
Ebook ISBN: 978-1-989407-00-4

Author photograph: Eugene Choi
Echo1 Photography

This book was funded in part by a grant from the Alberta Media Fund.

For the ladies who lunch, Doreen and Heather.

And for Dorothy, who we miss terribly.

I was editing this book when the Yonge Street van attack happened, steps from where Dorothy lived. She was running an errand on a sunny spring day and didn't make it home. I miss your practical outspokenness and sense of humour. And of course, your shortbread cookies. Goodbye, Dorothy. I will remember you and not the way your life was taken from you.

Chapter 1

"Go right," Dag called out softly, and Calder pushed the tiller to starboard, forcing the small boat to turn to port, following the direction of Dag's outstretched hand.

Solvig had found them this sailboat and had told Calder and Dag to take whatever they wanted from her place and leave immediately for Tarklee: the Fair Seas Treaty Alliance needed to know what was happening on Lavais Island.

He'd grabbed a small fishing net that he'd mended, and Dag had filled two waterskins. Then they'd sailed away, leaving Solvig and her neighbours to defend their small settlement against the pirates.

Now, dark clouds blocked the moon, and Dag was the only one who could safely steer them away from Lavais Island. In such a small boat, staying close to the coast was the safest way to travel, but it could take them as long as three or four days to reach Tarklee. And that was assuming the winds held.

The sail billowed out comfortingly, and he stared past Dag, trying to see beyond her in the dark. No one lived along this coast. There would be no lights from villages or a lone fisherman's cottage amongst the tangled mass of the Blighted Woods; nothing to help him keep clear of the dead trees and submerged rocks that littered the coast. Nothing except Dag's Trait.

"Left," Dag called out. Then a moment later, "Right."

Calder swung the tiller, and the little boat ploughed through the sea in response. The boat lifted and fell as a wave swept past them. They were getting closer to shore; maybe even close enough for him to see—

Lights flickered on his right as flames reached into the sky: where he expected the Blighted Woods to be.

"Dag!" he called. "Where are we?" But he knew where they were.

"I need to see her!" Dag replied, without turning to face him.

Calder grabbed the sail and pulled it hard to port, pushing the tiller almost flat against the stern. The sail flapped as it lost the wind but it filled again when a gust caught it on the other side.

"No!" Dag crawled over to him. "Don't turn around. I need to see Inger."

"You can't help her," Calder replied. He half stood, in case she tried to reposition the sail and send them in the wrong direction. "And we'll be caught." He glanced behind him at the port of Lavais. All four ships in the harbour were ablaze, and fire engulfed some of the buildings that lined the docks.

The flames were between their little boat and the town, so he couldn't see if anyone was trying to put out the fire. And then he had a terrible thought: what if there was no one left to put out the fire? What if the pirates had killed everyone before they set the fires? Or had they been able to escape? He hoped they'd taken whatever small craft they had and left.

Then he saw it sail out from behind the burning ships.

Ghost ship, Solvig had called it, and it did look ghostly. They'd whitewashed all of the wood except for the name: Diamanto. It was the *Bright Breeze* though; he'd sailed on that ship and would know it anywhere.

"Inger," Dag breathed.

Calder clamped a hand on her shoulder to keep her seated in case she was going to stand up. He followed her gaze. A figure stood at the prow of the ghost ship; loose blonde hair and white shirt fluttering in the wind. And even though he knew they were there, knew that Pilalians were working on the deck and suspended in the rigging, his eyes were drawn to Inger Lund.

"We can't help her," he said when Dag tried to shrug off his hand. "Look at me." Finally, she turned to face him. "We can't help her. Not today."

They were sailing away from the ghost ship, and Inger, but the *Bright Breeze* was faster than their little sailboat. If they were spotted, and if the pirates had done all the damage here that they'd intended, they would quickly be overtaken.

Calder adjusted the tiller and set them on a course that took them directly south and away from Lavais, towards the shore he knew was less than half an hour away. At any moment, he expected to hear a shout from the ship behind them signalling that they'd been discovered. Their only hope was to slip away in the dark and make it to the shore of the Blighted Woods, a place far too dangerous for a ship like the *Bright Breeze* to sail close to.

"Dag!" he called. "I need you to navigate. Now!" He didn't think she'd even heard him, and he was worried that she'd do what she'd done once before: jump from their small boat and go to her sister.

But she didn't. Instead, she closed her eyes and wiped tears away before turning and crawling back to the bow.

For the next half hour, Calder kept looking over his shoulder, expecting to see the pale ship following them. He didn't relax until the broken shoreline of the Blighted Woods was in his sights.

"Can you find us somewhere where we can tie up?" Calder asked, hoping that Dag's Trait would find what he couldn't: a safe place for him to rest. They'd been sailing most of the night, and the last time he'd been in a bed—he kept his eyes away from Dag and on the cliffs and scraggly trees that shrouded the shore—hadn't included much sleep.

"There."

He followed Dag's pointing finger to what looked like a small cove. A fallen tree that had been scoured of its bark and branches had sunk into the mud a few yards from shore. The silvery wood gleamed white in the faint light of dawn.

"That looks good." Calder pulled the sail in, rolling it and tying it to the boom. He grabbed an oar from the bottom of the boat and, with the blade squared, pulled it through the water, bringing them closer to the log. The boat bumped into the silvered wood, and Calder looped the painter around what was left of a branch.

The rope went taut, and the boat floated a few feet from the log. After a moment, Calder sighed: it seemed secure.

"That should hold us," he said. "Wake me if it doesn't. I need some sleep." He grabbed a waterskin and took a sip before handing it to Dag. He ignored the look she sent him, turned his back to her, leaned against the mast, and closed his eyes.

HE DIDN'T EXPECT to fall asleep quickly, not when Dag had betrayed his trust and put them both in danger. So he was surprised when he woke up to hot sun and biting insects and realized that he'd slept into the early afternoon.

He turned to find Dag seated in the bow, her back to him, staring out across the narrow strip of water to the edge of the woods. Half-dead trees leaned precariously over the shoreline, and behind them a wall of greenery was so dense that he couldn't see past it.

"Do you see anything dangerous over there?" he asked.

Dag swivelled to him and shook her head. "No, nothing but bugs. I didn't even see any birds. How can you have a forest without birds?"

He shrugged. He had no idea what to expect to find in the Blighted Woods: his time had been spent mostly at sea and in foreign lands.

"I need to apologize," Dag said.

Calder closed his eyes, not sure he really wanted to hear it; not sure he would believe anything she said. He'd always known that she would choose her twin over him, hadn't he?

"I mean it," Dag continued. She paused. "Please look at me. Please."

He opened his eyes and met her anguished gaze but stayed silent.

"I didn't mean to lead us there," Dag said. "To Inger . . . but when I started navigating, I just. I don't know . . . I just took us there. It wasn't on purpose." She looked away for a moment. "I didn't even realize that I was doing it until we were almost there. I am sorry."

"It could have been our deaths," Calder said finally. "*My* death." She bowed her head, and he sighed. "Tell me how I can trust you again," he said softly. "There is so much against us right now, and we need to be able to trust each other. So tell me how I can trust you?" Dag, her head still bowed, shook her head, and he sighed again.

"We'll talk about this later," he continued. "Right now, we are still in danger." He clambered over to the painter that tethered them to the log and pulled them close enough to untie the knot. He tossed the rope into the boat and picked up an oar and pushed them away from the log and back out to sea. A few minutes later, the sail filled with wind, and he steered them east along the coast.

DAG HUDDLED IN the bow of the boat, feeling miserable. She'd ruined things with Calder: there was no way he could trust her now, not after what she'd done. And she didn't even have a reasonable explanation for doing it. She'd risked both of their lives for what?

She knew she wouldn't be able to rescue Inger from the ghost ship: she *knew* that, so why had she taken them there? So she could see it? So she could understand what Inger's choice had led to? Or had she just needed to make sure her sister was alive?

She blew out a breath as she stared ahead, looking for any obstacles or dangers. Her allegiance as an Intelligencer was to the Fair Seas Treaty Alliance and her conscious choice, the choice she'd assured Calder that she'd made, had been to that cause. But her unconscious choice had been to see Inger. Why?

And even more importantly, how could she guarantee that she didn't make a potentially deadly, unconscious choice in the future? If she couldn't trust herself, then there was no way she could expect Calder to trust her.

And that: her not being trustworthy? That could put the whole region in even more jeopardy than it already was. Because only she and Calder knew that Joosep was being held by Tarmo Holt. Only she and Calder knew that the pirates were working with Holt for some undiscovered reason. And as far as they knew, only she and Calder were prepared and able to find out those reasons and try to stop Holt and the pirates.

"Left," she called out, and Calder steered around a submerged log. At least she could help them get to Tarklee.

The rest of the day was spent in silence only broken by her sporadic calls to go left or right around rocks and trees that lurked just below the surface of the water. Clouds covered the sky, making the heat just slightly bearable and, she hoped, saving her from a terrible sunburn.

"We need to find a place to land," Calder said, the first words he'd spoken since their conversation earlier.

"Are we sleeping on land?" she asked. She shivered as she stared out at the Blighted Woods. Nothing moved, there were no sounds of birds or any other animals, but something lived there, didn't it? And if not, then was it even safe for them for the night?

"No," Calder replied. "But if I can catch some fish, we can cook them. And I—," he paused and looked away from her, "can empty my bladder at sea, but you might not want to."

"Yes, of course." Dag hadn't had the need, but that was probably because she hadn't been drinking enough water. She grabbed a waterskin and took a drink. It was only half full. She picked up the other one: thankfully, it was full.

"We need to ration out water." Dag looked at the woods that lined the shore. "I don't think I'd trust a stream that's come out of these woods."

"Me neither," Calder said. "But we should be safe enough to land for a few minutes. A beach would work for what we need. It doesn't need to be big."

"I'll let you know when I see one," Dag replied. She hadn't seen a beach yet, but that didn't mean one didn't exist. Maybe Calder's Luck would supply one.

The boat rocked, and she looked back to see that Calder had tossed a fishing net into the water. It trailed the boat on the side away from the shore. Would fish this close to the Blighted Woods be safe to eat? She'd have to trust Calder on that.

The door opened, and Joosep shaded his eyes with his hand. He'd already been given his one cup of water today, so it wasn't his jailer bringing him that.

"I know who it is."

Joosep looked up at the shadow that was Tarmo Holt.

"Your Intelligencer," Holt continued. "The one the note was from. His name is Rahm and he's Pilalian." Holt walked a few steps to the left, and the light hit Joosep's eyes again, making them water.

"I'll have his family soon," Holt said. "There can't be that many Pilalians who come from the Three. Once I have his family, I'll have him." Holt's black boot nudged Joosep's leg. "What do you say to that, Master Intelligencer?"

"How?" Joosep croaked. If Holt looked for a Pilalian in Nordmere by the name of Rahm, he'd find Calder's father. But he'd have to go all the way to Pilalia to talk to the man.

"My privateer friends told me," Holt replied. "They say he's a sailor. Which explains how you always had such accurate information about events happening beyond the Pale Sea. It's too bad this Rahm can't be put to use by me, but my friends tell me he can't be trusted." Holt leaned down to look at Joosep. "He's with the Lund girl, so I expect he'll be easy enough to find."

Joosep's laugh sounded more like a cough. Holt must have thought so too, at first. Then his boot slammed into Joosep's thigh, and he winced in pain and fell onto his side. It didn't erase his smile though. Tarmo Holt thinking that Dagrun Lund would be easy to find was the most amusing thing he'd heard in weeks. Holt kicked him again before he stomped out of the cell.

He heard the door lock, and Joosep wondered what else angering Tarmo Holt would cost him. He was prepared to die, he'd always been prepared to die, but it was good to have something to laugh about.

Dagrun Lund, the strongest Unseen Trait he'd ever come across, would *not* be easy to find. And now that she was with Calder Rahmson, whose Luck was just as strong, he doubted they would ever be found. Unless they wanted to be, or Calder's Luck turned it into an opportunity for them. Joosep lay on his side, clutching his leg. A smile on his face.

A BIT OF beach, that's what he'd told her they needed. And that's all she found. At least it was clear of dead trees; unfortunately, once Calder pulled the boat up onto the beach, insects swarmed him. He looked over at Dag, who was fanning the air in front of her face, trying to keep the bugs away.

"I'll start a fire," Calder said. "You take care of . . ." he trailed off and turned his back on her. The beach allowed for very little privacy without heading into the woods. He didn't think Dag would want to get very far underneath the dark canopy.

He found some weathered branches along the edge of the

beach and dragged them closer to the surf. The driftwood would burn fast, but that's what he wanted. A quick fire to cook the two small bass he'd caught, then they could get back in the boat.

He had the fire lit and was holding the fish, fileted and skewered on branches, over it when Dag joined him. She rinsed her hands in the sea and accepted the branch he handed to her.

"Thanks."

He grunted his reply and bit into his fish. It was hot and tasted like bass. He'd been a little worried before he'd caught them, but they'd looked healthy and normal, and he'd reasoned that at this size they only ate insects. As long as the Blighted Woods didn't corrupt the insects, he and Dag should be fine. And cooking would kill most anything dangerous anyway. He hoped.

He finished eating and tossed the skewer onto the fire. The flames were already dying out, so he pushed sand onto them, smothering the embers. An out of control fire in the Blighted Woods might actually be an improvement, but it would also chase whatever lived there out into the open. He shivered. He didn't think it wise to unleash things that could survive in the Woods onto the rest of the world.

"I'll be back." He headed up the beach in the direction opposite to the one Dag had taken, stepped under a tree and emptied his bladder, trying not to look too deeply into the gloom in front of him.

"Let's go," he said to Dag, when he rejoined her at the fire. After one last check to make sure the fire was out, he picked up the fishing net and waded out to the boat.

Dag climbed in while he was raising the sail. She edged past him and settled in the bow, and he sat down at the tiller and steered them away from shore. He sighed at the absence of insects and the feeling of safety he felt on the open water.

Although they weren't safe, not yet, and maybe wouldn't be for a very long time. He sighed again. He and Dag had to talk: they had to decide what they were going to do next.

An hour after they'd left the little beach, the sun set.

"We should find a place to tie up for the night," he said to Dag.

"I'm fine to keep going," she said without turning to face him. "We should make as much time as we can."

"You need to rest," he replied. "I need to rest." He stared up at the waning moon and the few stars that were now visible. "By my estimate, we're as far away from any sensible route a ship would take to get to Tarklee as we can be. Another few hours heading east, and we might find ourselves off shore from a Swyford logging camp. It's safer to stop here than anywhere else."

"All right," Dag said. "I'll look for a good place to stop."

Calder frowned but didn't reply. It had barely been two days since they'd shared a bed, and now she wouldn't even look at him. And he was the one who should be angry; he was the one she'd deceived when she'd directed them to Lavais Port.

He paused. And the heart of the Lavais ship building industry; which he'd personally seen destroyed by fire. Had their destination been less about Dag wanting to save Inger and more about . . .

"I don't think it was your fault," he blurted out. "Going to Lavais Port."

"What do you mean?" This time she did turn to stare at him, and her eyes looked haunted.

"I think it might have been Luck: *my* Trait." She frowned at him, and he shook his head. As usual, when trying to describe how his Trait worked, he wasn't doing a very good job.

"If you hadn't directed us to the ghost ship, we wouldn't have seen what they did: the pirates," he said.

"What they did?" Dag repeated.

"Yes," he replied. "They burned everything. Ships in the harbour, warehouses along the waterfront, and the docks." He closed his eyes, trying to remember how he'd felt. He'd been so shocked when he'd realized they were in Lavais Port, that he hadn't paid attention to his Trait, but now, remembering, he thought that it had been triggered; his focus had narrowed on the fire. But at the time he'd felt too betrayed by Dag to notice.

"And the shipyards," he continued. "They were burning too. I think they might have been the main reason why the fire had been set." Now, while he was remembering, his focus narrowed to the dry docks and the shipyards. And the flames that trailed from the buildings and dry docks of the shipyards to the rest of the docks. Everything else on shore had burned as result of the shipyard being set on fire.

"So? I still took us directly into danger with no warning and no real reason." This time he heard the contempt in her voice for herself.

"No. It happened for *this* reason," he said. "So that we could learn that the shipyards of Lavais were specifically targeted by the pirates." He grinned. He felt lighter than he had since they'd sailed into the fiery Lavais Port. "My Trait made you do what you did."

"Your Trait? You're saying that Luck made me guide us into danger?"

"Yes. That's how my Trait works. I end up where I need to be so I can learn what I need to know." He paused. "I really believe that this was not your fault."

She stared at him, and he nodded, but she didn't nod back.

"I'll find us a place to tie up for the night," Dag said and faced forward again.

He nodded again even though she couldn't see him. It would take her a while to believe that his Trait was responsible, but she would eventually, wouldn't she?

Now that he realized that her actions were in response to his Trait, he knew he could trust her. But was it his turn to worry that Dag wouldn't be able to trust him? That she wouldn't be able to rely on his Trait? Which was the same thing in the end.

NOT HER FAULT. That's what Calder had said, but how could it not be her fault? She was the one who had navigated them right into the middle of danger. Could it really be his Trait? How could his Trait take away her choice? And if it had, she hadn't known that it was happening, so how could she safeguard against it in the future?

From her place in the prow, she stared out at the darkening waters ahead of them. If she was subject to the whims of Luck, would Calder's Trait save *her* if it took them both into danger?

"Right," she called and pointed towards a clump of trees that stretched out into the water. "There's a cove or something behind those trees." She couldn't see it but somehow, because of her Trait, she knew the cove was there. Calder steered the boat around the trees, and sure enough, there was a small inlet and a shoreline that wasn't a beach exactly, since there was no sand, but shallow water lapped against rocks smoothed by years of waves. The trees felt less ominous than the ones that had lined the beach they'd stopped at earlier.

"Perfect," Calder said from the stern. The boat rocked as he stood and lowered the sail.

She half-turned to watch Calder roll up the sail before she grabbed an oar. She did her best to copy him as they paddled to a large, jagged rock, and Calder tied the boat to it.

He hadn't even wondered if the cove existed: he'd steered them into it by simply trusting both her and her Trait that it was there. She supposed she should try to do the same and trust him and his Trait.

Once the rope was taut and Calder seemed happy with how the boat was positioned, he tossed her one of the waterskins. She took a drink of warm water and replaced the stopper.

"This one is less than half full," she said. "Will we be past the Blighted Woods tomorrow?"

"We should be," Calder replied. The boat shifted when he moved to sit closer to the mast. "I haven't spent time in this part of the Pale Sea so I'm not completely certain what we'll find along this coast. I do know that there are logging camps on this shore, along with a couple of rivers. I would guess that there are smaller streams too."

She stared at his profile for a moment.

"Why would seeing the fire at Lavais Port be important?" she asked.

"I'm not sure, yet," he replied. "But we know that shipbuilding in the Fair Seas Treaty Alliance will be non-existent for at least a season. Maybe longer depending on whether either of the Master Shipbuilders survived."

"If they . . ." Of course people might have died in that attack. Which meant that Inger would have helped the pirates commit murder. "Why would pirates want to do that?" She itched between her shoulder blades as her Trait activated. "It's Holt; he's behind it. Does he own the only other shipbuilding facilities in the region?"

"There aren't any others," Calder said, and then he frowned. "At least not on the Pale Sea. Ships are built along the coast of the Sapphire Sea, but we only see their larger ships, the ones that are built to travel long distances. Anything smaller like this sailboat, river barges, fishing boats, and the ships that haul logs can't make those long journeys and must be built here, on the Pale Sea."

"But Holt has business that includes shipping," Dag said. "He must own ships. Do you know how many?"

"No, I don't," Calder replied, "but ships are expensive: to build, to rig, to hire a crew for. And very expensive if the ship, the crew, or the cargo is lost at sea. You'd need to be very wealthy to own more than three or four ships. I'm not sure any Freeholder in the Three has that kind of coin."

Dag reached a hand back to scratch between her shoulder blades. There was something there; something still hidden that would explain why the shipbuilding facilities at Lavais Port had been destroyed, but she didn't have enough information to uncover it. Perhaps Calder's Luck would provide more. She laughed and shook her head.

"Is something funny?"

"I was just wondering if your Luck will help us uncover more information," she replied. "Which means I believe that it's responsible for us learning this much."

"I told you," he said.

"So you did." She stared up at the stars that dotted the sky. A bird screeched nearby. "That's the first bird I've heard since we left Lavais," she said. "I'll take it as proof that we are near the end of the Woods." She'd be grateful to leave the Blighted Woods behind; the fact that no birds lived there was unsettling.

"And back near civilization," Calder agreed.

"Yes. We need a plan. Although . . ." That wasn't how his Trait worked. Should she abandon how hers worked and rely on Calder's? "I usually have a plan," she finished.

"And I don't. But I do usually have a goal," Calder said. He was quiet for a moment. "I don't think either of us should change how we use our Traits."

"Neither do I," Dag agreed, relieved. She didn't like the idea of waiting around for something to happen; that wasn't how she used her Trait, nor was it how she'd been trained. "Joosep has a harder job than I thought. Finding those of us with Traits and determining what the Traits do is something I can do. But training everyone how to work with their Traits, as well as how to enhance their non-Trait abilities seems so much more difficult to me. And none of us have the same Trait."

"You know that for sure?" Calder asked. "That there are no duplicate Traits?"

"Yes," she replied. "Except that Joosep himself has a weak Unseen Trait. And that should be our goal, don't you think? Joosep?"

"Finding him?"

"I was thinking more along the lines of making sure that we can trust him," Dag said. "And if we think we can, *then* we find him."

"All right." The boat shifted and when she looked over, Calder had stretched out in the bottom of it. "I can work with that as a goal."

Dag lay down too but continued to stare at the sky, grateful that Calder had agreed with her.

Chapter 2

THE SOUND OF a door closing echoed down the hallway, and Gustav smoothed his shirt and stepped out of the empty room he'd been waiting in since just after supper.

He blew out a breath as he headed towards Joosep's office, concentrating on keeping his strides loose and his shoulders relaxed.

Joosep hadn't been seen in days, and his assistant Arnor was also missing. Gustav hadn't spoken to anyone about it: he'd stopped attending his classes once he'd realized that something was wrong, so he had no idea if there was some legitimate reason for the Master Intelligencer and his assistant to be away. But it didn't feel right.

Footsteps headed his way, and he looked up.

"Gustav?"

"Heya Vilis," Gustav said, stopping to face him. Vilis was one of his training partners. The two of them and Kaja were all around the same age.

"Gustav," Vilis said. "Where have you been?"

"I think I ate something that didn't agree with me," Gustav said. "Again." Vilis knew he'd been ill before, but Gustav was pretty sure he didn't know he'd been poisoned while working on a real Intelligencer assignment. "I was wondering what to do about my missed lessons."

"If you were planning on seeing Joosep, I'll save you the

trouble," Vilis replied. He smiled at him, or as Gustav thought of it, he smiled in response to his Trait. "He's not in his office." He held up a sheaf of papers. "He gave me these to study the day before yesterday, and I wanted to return them."

"Oh. I guess I'm off the hook for now," Gustav said. Vilis seemed to believe his story, but he didn't believe Vilis. He *knew* that Joosep had been missing more than two days. What was Vilis up to? "I guess I'll check to see if he's in later." He turned and settled in beside Vilis, and they walked down the corridor towards the more populated areas of the Hall. "What is that? An assignment?"

"Yes," Vilis replied quickly. "Joosep is testing me himself. Apparently, he does that for some students."

"Am I next?" Gustav asked.

"Maybe, if you're lucky," Vilis replied and beamed a smile in his direction.

Gustav smiled back: because of his Trait he was used to people being happy around him, and he usually mirrored their behaviour back to them. He was pretty sure that was part of the reason why people often told him things he thought they didn't mean to.

"I have to go," Vilis said. "See you." He headed down an intersecting hallway.

"Sure," Gustav muttered, as he stared after him. He didn't think Joosep personally tested students: he hadn't tested *him*, and he'd been assigned an actual Intelligencer mission. So, what had Vilis taken from Joosep's unattended office?

He headed in the direction opposite to the one Vilis had taken. He wished he knew who to trust. He paused in front of the door to his room. Maybe that meant he shouldn't trust *anyone*.

His decision made, he unlocked the door and entered his room. After making sure that no one was inside waiting for him, he grabbed a pack from a peg near the door and started piling clothing into it. Not too much, since he didn't want anyone to realize that he'd left: just a second set of clothes and a warm coat. He did make sure he had his patch. It wasn't the patch of a fully trained Intelligencer, but it marked him as a member of the Fair Seas Treaty Alliance, so it should buy him help, if he needed it.

The last thing he did was pull the small bag of coins from its hiding place under the desk. It wasn't much, but hopefully he could either trade or use Charisma to get anything else he might need.

Because if he couldn't trust anyone, then it was up to him to find out what was going on. And he was certain that it had to do with what Joosep had tasked him with: finding out what Tarmo Holt was up to. Who else would dare interfere with the Master Intelligencer?

CALDER WOKE TO the twittering of birds and rolled over and yawned. His shoulder ached from where a boat rib dug into it, and he shifted to try to get more comfortable. It was just barely dawn, and the forest nearby seemed filled with chirping birds. He slapped at his face, but the insects fed on. Giving up on sleep, he opened his eyes and rose on one elbow.

Dag was still asleep in the bow, her blonde head wedged into the tip and her knees tucked up almost to her chin.

The boat rolled in the gentle surf, the painter securing the bow to the rock. He shaded his eyes against the early sun, trying to see if it looked like a fair day for sailing.

Satisfied that a storm wasn't imminent, he unfolded the fishing net and dropped it into the shallow water. It was early enough to fish, but he was less certain that he would catch anything in this little cove.

While he waited to see if the fish would prove him wrong, he stared at the woods. Although they still had a little of the look of them, he wasn't certain these trees would be considered part of the Blighted Woods. But even so, he doubted this forest would attract loggers. His mother's family came from woodsmen and loggers. They prized large pine and spruce trees: straight trees that were easily cut into long planks, not these thin beech trees and scraggly hemlocks.

But there were birds here, so this forest was different from what they'd passed yesterday. As Dag had noted, the twisted forest they'd travelled beside for the past day had been empty of birds. He took a sip from a waterskin. It was almost empty; they had to find a safe stream soon.

When he judged enough time had passed, he pulled the net up. It was empty; should he give up or toss it back in and try his

Luck again?

"I guess that means no breakfast," Dag said from behind him.

"It's a safe place for us, but not a great spot for fish," Calder said, turning to her. She'd resumed her perch at the bow and was staring forward.

"Did you come up with a plan?" he asked.

"I don't think I should tell you," Dag replied. "In case your Luck interferes with it."

"I guess that could happen."

"It did happen," she said. "That's how we ended up at Lavais Port." She shook her head. "What if your Trait always interferes with mine? How can I trust my Trait again?"

"Both of our Traits worked on Strongrock," Calder said, but her comment made him wonder if his Trait hadn't functioned the way it usually did. The way he let Luck find him, he wouldn't know if his Trait had worked differently. "Should we split up?" he asked. "When we have a chance?"

Dag looked back at him and shrugged. "I don't think even Joosep would have an answer to that question."

"Unless it's why he's never paired Intelligencers up," Calder said.

Dag shrugged again and turned to look at the path ahead, leaving Calder to wonder how they could ever be certain that their Traits were either working with or against each other.

Dag relaxed. The Blighted Woods were finally behind them, and the coastline they were passing now was lined with the tall, evergreen trees of the Clearwood Forest. Seagulls shrieked overhead, and every now and then one would dive into the sea. If a fish was caught, the rest of the flock would give chase, screeching at the successful fisher until it either ate or dropped its catch.

She pushed her hair off her face to get a better look at the land.

"There," she called out to Calder. "A stream, I think." The boat headed towards the shore, and she nodded to herself. Water trickled over a small rocky ledge down to a sandy strip of beach. Above, thick bushes grew a few feet on either side of the stream. "And berries." Calder had been able to catch a couple of fish and had secured them in the net that trailed behind the boat, but fruit would be a welcome addition to their fish-only diet.

"And a good place to land," Calder said. The boat rocked as he pulled down the sail and grabbed an oar. In a few moments, he'd maneuvered them in close to the shore.

The bottom of the boat hissed across sand, and Calder pushed them along with the oar until they were closer to shore. He grabbed the rope from the bow and jumped into the surf, climbed up past the beach, and tied the boat to a thin tree.

"I'll get a fire started," he said and headed up into the trees that lined the edge of the beach.

"I'll fill the waterskins," Dag replied even though she was certain Calder was too far away to hear her. She grabbed the two skins and waded through ankle-deep water. It was much warmer than she'd expected, and she wondered if it really was or if it just felt warmer because the forest here looked serene. And safe.

She had to go a few yards upstream before the stream was deep enough to fill the waterskins. She took a tentative sip: it was cold and tasted fresh. She pushed the two waterskins into the shallow water until they were full. Once they were stoppered, she headed back to the beach. Calder was hunched over a small pile of dried wood, trying to start a fire with a rock and a piece of flint. She dropped the waterskins to the ground near him.

"The water tastes fine, but before you drink, you should wait to see how I fare." They couldn't afford to have them both stricken by any stream-borne illness, and it was better if she was the one who was incapacitated. Calder would still be able to sail them to safety.

She headed back towards the stream and the windswept seaberry bushes. She really should learn how to sail.

With a couple of handfuls of orange seaberries cradled in the bottom of her shirt, she rejoined Calder by the fire. The fish were already gutted and halved and Calder had laid them on some flat rocks.

"I'll take those," Calder said. "Unless you want to eat them plain."

"Not unless I have to," Dag replied. Seaberries were edible

but very sour. "If you have a better idea, then go ahead." She stretched her shirt to make it easier for him to grab the berries from it.

One of Calder's hands skimmed the bare skin of her midriff when he scooped the berries from her shirt. Ignoring his touch, Dag smoothed her shirt back down, brushing away a few berry bush leaves.

Calder crushed the berries between his hands and smeared the juice on the four pieces of fish. He dipped a stick in the sea to wet it and used it to push the rocks into the middle of the fire.

"It should only take a few minutes," he said, sitting down a few paces from the flames.

Dag sat beside him. "Do you think we should sail right into Tarklee?"

"I thought you didn't want to tell me your plan?" Calder said. He poked at a piece of fish with the stick.

"That might be impossible," she replied. "Since we're in the same boat." She sighed. "I think we should enter South Tarklee on foot. Or at least I should."

"You do want to split up."

"No." And she didn't. She thought that no matter what concerns they had about how their Traits might affect each other, staying together was the best, and maybe the only, way they would find out what they needed to know and make it safely to Tarklee. "I want—*need*—us to stay together. But I don't want to make any decisions for you."

"In case my Trait has other plans for me, you mean?"

"Yes," she lied. What she really meant was that she was afraid that if they parted, neither one of them had a chance of finding out what Tarmo Holt had done with Joosep. Or whether Joosep could be trusted.

"All right," Calder said. He poked at the fish again before dragging the stones out of the fire. "We'll follow your plan unless my Trait shows us another way."

"Thank you." Dag closed her eyes in relief. It hadn't been her Trait that wanted her and Calder working together, but it had been a strong feeling just the same.

"Give it a minute to cool off and then dig in," Calder said as he pushed a stone with fish in front of her.

She leaned over and sniffed. "This smells great, thank you."

"Ahh, I see," Calder said, and she could hear the smile in his voice. "You want to keep travelling together because you'd miss my cooking skills." He scooped up a piece of fish with his hand and popped it into his mouth.

"Maybe," Dag said. She copied him, picking up a berry juice-covered piece of fish. The sourness of the seaberries contrasted nicely with the sweetness of the fresh fish, and she sighed. "Definitely. This is delicious." Sadly, her share was gone in a few more bites. She wiped her hands on her trousers and sat back.

"I like to eat well," Calder said. He shoved the stick back into the fire, this time scattering the glowing ashes. Then he pushed sand on top of everything, smothering any remaining embers. "I think it should be all right for me to drink some water now."

Dag concentrated for a moment. She didn't feel any ill effects from the stream water. "Yes," she replied.

Calder got up, walked into the sea and bent down to scrub his hands before picking up a waterskin and taking a drink.

"We should go," he said, staring up at the sky. "My guess is that we'll reach a settlement soon." He gestured to the stream. "That's not enough water to supply a logging camp, but the next stream might be."

Dag cleaned her hands in the sea as she made her way to the boat. In a few moments, Calder had them headed away from the beach. Once the sails were up, she settled back into the prow, scanning the shore and the route ahead.

JOOSEP DIDN'T EVEN raise his head until whoever had entered his cell had left. Then it was all he could do to lift his head to look for the cup of water. It was there, along with a bowl. He crawled over to it. Porridge: were they trying to keep him alive but just on the edge of starvation? Did it matter? He knew he would eat it, just as he knew that he'd do whatever he could to stay alive. Except tell them what they wanted to know.

They weren't foolish enough to leave him an eating utensil that could be turned into a weapon, so he dipped his hand into the bowl and scooped the mushy grains into his mouth. They didn't taste like much of anything, which he assumed meant that they hadn't added poison. And if they had and he died, it would end this almost unbearable captivity.

He picked up the bowl and licked the last morsel from it

before turning to the water.

He had just taken his last sip when the door opened. He averted his eyes from the light and edged away from the bowl and mug, thinking that the woman who was his jailer had come to take the dishes away. He assumed they understood that he could make a weapon from broken crockery if they left anything in here with him.

"I know who the instructors are."

Joosep looked up to find Tarmo Holt staring at him, a sheaf of papers in his hand.

"This is the list from your office," Holt said. "I am surprised it was so easy to find."

"From my locked office." Joosep's voice came out in a croak, although Holt seemed to understand his words.

"Locked, unlocked, who's to say since your assistant seems to have disappeared?" Holt paced in front of him. "Three names on the payroll of the Master Intelligencer along with three students. Where are the rest? There are more than three instructors and three students."

"I keep separate lists," Joosep said. "Have you spoken to the instructors? Discovered what it was they were teaching?" Which list had Holt found? And how had whoever found it recognized it as a list of instructors? His thoughts were becoming clearer, no doubt due to the food and water, and he could almost sense what Holt was trying to hide.

"I have a source that confirms these six people," Holt said. "A lot of history lessons were taught, so I'm told."

"History is important," Joosep replied. Holt must have spoken to one of the early stage students. Just after the halfway mark, they graduated to more specialized studies, including weapons and interrogation.

"But who are the rest?" Holt asked. "If you tell me, I will spare these instructors." He slapped the papers against his thigh. "Along with these three students."

Joosep closed his eyes, thankful that even the early year students were kept in small groups of three or four. It meant that only one group had been compromised.

"It was clever of you to have young Gustav Gunnarson attach himself to my daughter. Very clever, but it's all for nothing now that I know he's one of yours."

So, Gustav, Kaja, and Vilis were all compromised, and one of them had either been tricked by Holt or had betrayed the others to him. But not Gustav: if it had been, Tarmo Holt would have taken great pleasure in telling him that.

"He's untrained," Joosep said. "Whatever friendship Gustav has with your daughter, it has nothing to do with me."

"Do you take me for a fool? You sent him to spy on me. And you used my daughter!" He threw the pages at him. "If the boy could be found, I'd try him for treason! Spying on the Grand Freehold—give me that."

Joosep had picked up one of the scattered pages, and now Holt ripped it from his hands. He straightened and kicked Joosep in the ribs so hard that he fell backward against the wall. Holt scrambled to pick up the papers he'd thrown just a moment ago.

But there had been just enough time for Joosep's Trait to find an answer. He recognized the writing at the top of the page: Vilis had betrayed them. He smiled. And Gustav had run before he could be captured. For the first time in days, he felt as though there was hope: Gustav knew almost as much about Tarmo Holt's activities as he did. Even if Joosep himself was lost, Holt might not win.

He smiled, and Tarmo Holt bent down and glared at him.

"What is it? Tell me!"

Another boot hit his ribs, and Joosep sucked in a breath. And smiled again. Tarmo Holt could kick him to death; it wouldn't change the fact that someone Holt had no control over knew about him.

Furious, Holt kicked him one last time before swearing and leaving the cell. The door slammed shut and the lock turned and then it was quiet.

Joosep crawled to the cup and swiped a finger around the rim, hoping for one last drop of moisture in case it was the last water he was given. Then he noticed that they'd also left the bowl. He grabbed it and tucked it under his shirt between his ribs and his arm. He lay on his side, ignoring the pain where the bowl dug into his bruised ribs.

"STOP."

Calder looked past the sail to Dag, who had raised a hand in the air as she peered ahead. It was dusk, and the shoreline was little more than a shadow. Insects swarmed around him, and he waved a hand in front of his face to clear them away for a second.

"I think there's a pier up ahead," Dag whispered.

Calder rose to a crouch and quickly lowered the sail. They didn't want to be seen, not until they knew what they were dealing with. He wrapped the sheet around the sail, tying it to the boom and then securing the boom to the port gunnel. After securing the tiller, he picked up both oars from the bottom of the boat.

"Are there any boats near the pier?" he asked.

"Not that I can see," Dag replied. She turned to him. "Maybe it's not a pier, maybe it's something else."

"We'll go in slow, just in case." The wind was still brisk, and the resulting waves were pushing them slightly forward, as well as toward shore. He fit both of the oars into the oarlocks and sat down, facing the stern.

"I still don't see any boats," Dag called softly. "But it is a pier."

Calder had to fight the wind and waves to keep their little boat away from the shoreline. He leaned over and pulled hard on the oars as the boat dipped into the trough of a wave. A few more strokes and he had them far enough out from shore that the waves were gentle swells.

"Let me know if you see anything," he called over his shoulder.

"Nothing yet," Dag replied. "No lights, no movement. Shouldn't there be someone here?"

"I'm not sure," Calder replied. He wished he knew more about the settlements in this part of Swyford. He knew that logging took place here, so there would be logging camps, but were they permanent settlements or camps that were inhabited just for the summer harvest season? In the north, small villages dotted the coast, but loggers often stayed inland during the short summers, coming back out of the forest to take their harvest to ships at the end of the season, before the weather turned cold.

After a dozen more strokes, he looked over his shoulder. Dusk had turned into evening, and he couldn't see a single light on shore ahead of them.

"We're almost there," Dag said. "I see a place where we can go ashore before we reach the pier."

"Good idea." He followed Dag's directions until sand scraped the bottom of the boat. He lifted the oars from the oarlocks and set them in the bottom of the boat before jumping into the surf.

The beach was small and exposed if the pirates happened to sail past, but it was free of rocks that might damage the bottom of the boat. Dag jumped out and helped him pull the boat up onto the beach.

"Should one of us watch the boat?" Dag asked.

"No. I think it's better if we stay together." Calder reached in and grabbed the two waterskins. "We'd miss these more than the boat at this point in time." He handed one to her and tucked the other one under his shirt. "Come on, let's see what's happening near that pier."

Dag led the way. She kept them as close to the shore as possible, and he was grateful for the breeze that blew in from the sea. When they were forced to push through the bushes and thin trees that lined the coast, insects swarmed them, making even breathing a challenge. Calder took to walking with his hand over his mouth and nose to try to keep from sucking in bugs with each breath.

Dag reached a hand back to him. "We're here."

He crept closer to her and peered past her shoulder at a clearing. Weak moonlight illuminated a huddle of wooden buildings. The ones closest to them were smaller than the others; workshops maybe, or storage for tools.

"There should be people," he whispered in Dag's ear. "This is a permanent camp."

"How do you know?"

"All the structures are wooden. You don't build that for a single season." At least they didn't in the north: canvas tents were set up and taken down each summer, but the main settlements by the sea were built of wood and stone. If this was a main settlement for loggers, there should be year-round inhabitants.

"I'll go first," Calder said. "There's enough light for me to see. You wait here."

"But—"

He silenced Dag by stepping in front of her and meeting her gaze.

"My Luck should give me an advantage over whoever or whatever is here," he said. "And if it's not enough, then I'm counting on you to come to the rescue."

"All right," Dag said. "I'll watch for your signal and join you then." She swatted at her cheek. "If there's anything left of me with all these bugs."

Calder had to suppress a grin. He was actually grateful to be leaving the trees and the insects behind. He stepped out into the clearing, feeling exposed. In this case Dag's Trait might have been better; it would have kept her Unseen and she would have uncovered whatever secrets were here, but his brother lived in a settlement with much the same purpose as this one: he knew what he was looking at. That and his Luck made him believe he was the better choice to scout.

He frowned as he made his way toward a neat, wooden building. That might be yet another reason why Joosep had never paired up Intelligencers. It was difficult to determine which person's Trait would be best in each situation. He'd ask him, when he had the chance.

Up close, he could see that the building was well kept. Wild flowers grew next to the wall, and the taller blooms beneath a small window had been trimmed. This building hadn't been abandoned for very long. He tried to look in the window, but any view inside was blocked by interior shutters.

He peered around the corner at the front of the building, where a step led up to a closed door. Expecting the door to be locked, he used too much force when he pushed it open, and a gust of wind snatched the door from his hand. Before he could grab it, the door banged against the interior wall.

Still outside, Calder froze and flattened himself against one wall wondering if he'd be better off inside. No lights went on either in the building he was outside of or in any of the other structures he could see. No lights, no movement, no calls of alarms.

He stepped inside. Very little moonlight streamed in through the open door but it was enough for him to recognize that it was a toolshed. Saws of every length and type hung along one wall and a large worktable held coils of rope and a couple of adzes.

He crossed to the window, lifted the latch on the shutters, and opened them to look out on the clearing.

He saw no sign of Dag or anyone else. He headed back to the door and stared out it for a few moments before stepping outside.

The next three buildings were much the same: well-kept structures used to store and repair tools of the logging trade. A larger building seemed likely to house more than just tools.

The wind shifted and he paused at the sound of running water. It would be the source of water for this settlement and it sounded substantial. It was coming from just past the next building.

He took the time to make sure this last building, someone's home, was empty before he headed towards what he assumed was a stream.

It was wider than he'd expected: could it be the Elorelle? Had they come that far? A bridge arced across the river, and a few dozen more buildings sat on the opposite side.

If this was the Elorelle, then he was in the village of Setberg. They were less than half a day's sail from Nurmi, an even larger village along the coast between the Blighted Woods and Tarklee.

But Setberg should be bustling. If he remembered correctly, around fifty people called this village home year-round. During logging season, like now, it would easily double in size.

He stopped in the middle of the bridge and looked upstream and then down to where the river spilled into the sea. No one was upstream, and there were no ships or boats tied up at the pier that sat near the mouth of the river.

A gust of wind brought the smell of smoke, and he stared across the river at the houses and outbuildings that huddled along the pier. There. Some of the buildings closest to the sea looked like they had been damaged by fire.

What he didn't see was a light or movement or the sound of people; not one solitary sign of life. He shivered. It was time to get Dag: he thought her Trait would be needed if they were to find some answers.

CHAPTER 3

WHEN SHE SAW Calder wave, Dag stepped out from under the trees at the edge of the clearing. She waved back before breaking into a jog. He paced alongside a building for the few minutes it took for her to reach him.

"Did you find anyone?" she asked when she stopped at his side. She stared past a couple of buildings straining to see anything . . . was that . . . ? "What river is that?"

"I think it's the Elorelle," Calder said, his expression grim. "Which means this is the village of Setberg."

"But that's good! That means we're close to Tarklee." Dag paused when Calder shook his head. "Not good?"

"It's good that we know where we are," he conceded, "but not good in that there should be over a hundred people here. So far I've seen no signs of anyone and some of the buildings along the pier on the other side of the river have burned."

"Burned?" He nodded and Dag shivered. "And potentially one hundred people missing? First a ghost ship and now a ghost town." She felt the tell-tale itch between her shoulder blades. "It's all related: this village being abandoned, pirates attacking Lavais Port, and Tarmo Holt."

"Do you know how?"

Dag closed her eyes and concentrated on this town, the ship Inger was on, and Holt, but no direct connection jumped out at her. She shook her head and opened her eyes, staring at the dark shadows of the buildings. "Not yet." Would she figure it out in time? She turned to Calder. "Let's take a closer look at the village in case my Trait finds something. Besides, we should make sure there aren't any survivors here before we head along the coast to the next village."

"Nurmi is next, I think," Calder said. "Unless there's a temporary logging camp, Nurmi is the next settlement between here and Tarklee."

"Nurmi," Dag said. "That's where my first assignment was. *Skit!*" Why hadn't she made this connection before?

"What?" Calder asked.

Dag sighed. "My one and only Intelligencer assignment was in the household of Swyford Clan Freeholder Tavet Timonis. Whose territory includes Lavais Island." She paused. "And who everyone expects will be the next Grand Freeholder of the Fair Seas Treaty Alliance."

"Replacing Tarmo Holt." Calder nodded. "So we know why Lavais was destroyed."

The spot between Dag's shoulders itched. "That's part of it, but not all of it." She sighed. "I'll let you know if I figure out anything else. In the meantime, we need to find out if anyone is left here."

"Lead the way," Calder said.

Dag crossed the bridge and paused in the village square.

"Hello?" she called and paused, but there was no response.

They opened the doors to a couple of dozen homes and workshops as they passed through the village, but no one answered their calls.

Three structures closest to the pier were damaged: two had their roofs burned away and the third, what looked like a warehouse, had been reduced to charred timbers. The pier itself still stretched out into the sea, although much of the decking was missing.

"I don't think anyone is here," she said, scanning the village they'd just passed through. "No one is hiding. At least my Trait isn't telling me anyone is."

"I don't smell death," Calder replied. "Let's hope everyone escaped."

"If they did, they most likely went to Nurmi," Dag replied. "So should we."

She turned and Calder followed her as she headed back through the village, across the bridge, through the clearing and the forest to the sailboat.

GUSTAV WAS BEGINNING to worry that the hat he'd traded for had fleas. Maybe there was another reason why it was so itchy. He hoped.

He pushed the cart through the narrow street towards a wider boulevard.

As soon as he'd left the Hall, he'd realized that his current clothes were not going to allow him to blend in unnoticed; not in the poorer area of the city that would be the best place to hide in.

So, he'd used his Trait to convince the tinker to trade his cart and a set of threadbare clothing for his two sets of good clothing, a warm coat, and just a few coins. It had been easy. Not that he'd expected it to be difficult; most people couldn't do enough for him.

That had been hours ago, and he'd been keeping his head down, trying to blend in, ever since.

He shuffled past the lane that led to the Hall and sighed. It was his second time going past it, mostly because he wasn't sure what else to do. He kept hoping to see Joosep; that somehow the Master Intelligencer would show up, explain that he and his assistant had left to deal with urgent business elsewhere, and that now everything could get back to normal.

But Gustav knew that wasn't going to happen because Joosep was in trouble. And Vilis knew something about it. Why else had he lied to him about seeing Joosep and getting an extra assignment?

Someone was hurrying down the lane towards him. Gustav tucked his chin to his chest so the brim of the hat hid his face. It was Vilis! Where was he going? Did this early morning trip have anything to do with Joosep?

His training mate swept past him, and Gustav slowly turned his cart around. He didn't have a better plan, so he'd do his best to follow Vilis. Unfortunately, it wasn't quite dawn, and few people were out. He had to move slowly in order to not attract attention, and he lost sight of Vilis before he'd tracked him through more than a few streets.

Gustav pushed his cart past a corner and looked down a street, trying to determine where Vilis had gone, but he didn't see him. The New Bridge was just ahead, spanning the Dareveth River from North Tarklee to South Tarklee.

Had Vilis gone to South Tarklee? He was Swyfordian, like Gustav, but he was from a small village along the coast. He didn't think his training mate was leaving the Hall and returning home, not by foot, not when he hadn't taken a pack full of supplies with him.

Gustav parked the cart next to a building and sat down beside it. Vilis was coming back, he was certain of it, so he'd wait here until he returned. And if he didn't return? Gustav would have to figure out what else he could do to find Joosep.

DAG KNEW BEFORE she saw Nurmi that people were in the town.

She and Calder had beached the boat in a small inlet she'd spotted. From the sea, it looked like nothing more than a stand of trees on a small rocky outcrop, but once they'd rowed past the trees, they found a beach with fine sand and a gentle surf. They'd pulled the boat as far up the beach as possible, trying to camouflage the mast among the trees. Calder had insisted they take the time to dry the sails and store them properly. He wanted to make sure that the boat was ready whenever they needed it.

Dag's plan was to head into the village and find out as much information as they could. She wanted to know if Setbergers had fled here, and if the pirates had driven them from their homes. Calder said that he was fine with her plan, unless and until his Luck intervened.

Once they found out what had happened in Setberg, they would head to Tarklee.

Calder tied the sail between two trees and caught a couple of fish while Dag gathered enough wood for a small fire.

The sun was high overhead by the time they'd eaten, and Calder had folded and packed the sails in the bow of the boat.

Now, half an hour later, Dag held her hand up to signal Calder to stop. She crouched low and peered through the trees. According to Calder the forest here was mostly young hemlock: terrible for both boatbuilding and fires, which was why the trees were still standing so close to a settlement based on logging.

A log fence ran along the edge of the forest and a small house sat on the other side of the field. No smoke issued from the chimney, but on a warm day like this, that didn't mean no one was home.

Suddenly, a door opened, and she sat back, bumping into Calder, who had been peering over her shoulder. A man stepped out of the house and went around it and out of sight.

"At least someone is still in Nurmi," Calder whispered into her ear.

"I think everyone is," she replied. "That man didn't seem to be in a hurry for anything." She stood up and brushed her hands over the knees of her trousers. "I spent most of my time here at the Freeholder's estate. I doubt anyone would recognize me. Should we just show ourselves?"

"I'd rather not," Calder said. "People tend to remember a Pilalian. I think it best if we're not noticed."

"Oh, right." People from the Sapphire Sea had been settling in the Three for decades, but mostly in Tarklee. In a smaller town like Nurmi, Calder's dark skin would make him memorable. "Then we should circle the village; there's a road that has only a few houses on it. Come on."

She led them along the row of hemlock, away from the house, until they reached a separately fenced field. Dag climbed over the fence and waited for Calder to join her.

"The Clan Freeholder raises horses around here," she said softly. "Some are for riding, but mostly he breeds them to pull the logging wagons and sleds to and from the camps deep in the forest."

"Horses hate me," Calder said, and Dag snorted. "They do. I've been bitten, almost trampled, and thrown. Even Joosep agreed to allow me to give up on them."

"Your Trait doesn't work on them?" Dag had to stifle a laugh. She couldn't imagine Calder, a man who seemed so skilled and competent, being thrown by a horse. "I get along quite well with them." She'd loved the riding lessons she'd had at the Hall and had been sad when she was declared proficient enough that she no longer needed them.

"Then you can save me from any we come across. My Trait seems to make me some sort of target; they find me, but they don't like me when they do."

"I'll do my best to keep you safe from horses," Dag said. "This way." She headed straight across the field towards the road she knew was somewhere on the far side. When disguised as a maid, she hadn't spent much time on the road, but she'd studied maps of the area before her assignment and knew its location.

The road wasn't much more than a grassy path, and Dag didn't think it was travelled very often; at least not by wagons. Rather than stay on the road, they decided to walk on the other side of the fence. It would allow them some cover and a way to escape in case someone came their way. They'd only seen the one house, but the road was built all the way out here for a reason.

They crossed a number of empty fields, climbing the fences that separated them, until they reached a field with an occupant.

Dag was balanced on the fence, about to drop to the ground, when she heard the sound of hooves bearing down on her. A horsed pranced to a stop a few feet from her and snorted, tossing its head.

"Heya," Dag called softly. "Come to see who is trespassing?" The horse walked over to her and snuffled at her outstretched hand before backing up again.

Dag slowly climbed down from the fence and faced the horse, which backed up another step. Suddenly, the horse's ears pricked and swivelled away from Dag. With a whinny, the animal pivoted and galloped away, paralleling the road.

"I think someone's up ahead," Dag said, turning towards Calder. He stood in the other field, just far enough from the fence that the horse couldn't reach him.

"We should move back to the trees," he said, "and then wait until it's dark."

"All right," Dag agreed. She climbed back over the fence to join Calder and followed him to the forest that lined the opposite end of the field.

They were barely a few miles away from the coast, but the forest was so much thicker and wilder here. Birds chirped and wind tugged at the ends of branches. More hemlock, from what she could tell. She peered up at the sky.

"We'll have a few hours," Calder said. "And I wish I'd brought the sail to keep the insects off."

In the end, the clouds of swarming insects forced them out from under the trees and into the narrow strip of tall grass that grew between the forest and the fence. Dag spent a few minutes stomping the grass flat before she lay down. She rolled onto her side and fell asleep before Calder had time to join her.

THE BOWL DUG into his bruised ribs, but Joosep ignored the discomfort. He'd found that it was possible to get used to almost anything if he tried. And this pain was caused by something that could be the difference between him surviving or not, so he was determined to get used to it.

His jailer had never come to retrieve the bowl. She'd grabbed the mug a few minutes after Holt had left, but by that time, Joosep had already hidden the bowl under him. He hadn't had to pretend to be in pain, and the woman had ignored him.

She'd been back in once with water, but she'd left without watching him drink it. As soon as she left, he'd dragged himself to the water and drank every drop.

A few days, that's all he needed. A few days and then he'd be strong enough. But in the meantime, he wanted everyone to believe him more seriously injured than he was. So he could surprise them.

He lay back down, making sure the bowl was completely hidden beneath him. Now all he had to do was figure out a plan for after he escaped. Who to trust? Who to turn to? And how to find any of them?

CALDER WOKE WITH a start. A bird called from close by and he rose to one elbow. Dag was stretched out beside him, still sleeping, her chest rising and falling with each breath.

A high-pitched whinny sounded, and he relaxed. That was what had woken him. He got up and made his way to the fence. It was dark, but he could see that in the next field, a few dozen yards away, the horse they'd seen earlier was staring at him. It snorted, and Calder shook his head. He hadn't been joking earlier: horses seemed to gravitate to him, but once they got close, they didn't like him.

"Do horses actually seek you out and then try to hurt you?"

He turned to find Dag staring at him, a smile on her lips. His heart stuttered; they'd been too busy with their immediate safety to talk about what they'd shared in Solvig Madsen's home, but it was there, under the surface. At least he felt it; he was less sure that Dag did.

"Yeah." He shrugged. "It's not a problem since I'm usually at sea, but I've travelled to half a dozen countries, and everywhere it's the same. Horses find me and then try to hurt me. They won't let me ride them, and even being in a wagon is a challenge." He turned back to stare at the horse. They were useful animals, but not to him. "We should be safe enough to travel now," he said.

"Yes," Dag replied. "At this time of night, we can probably walk on the road." She climbed the fence, and he followed.

"Let's hope so," he said. He didn't want to chance climbing into dark fields to have horses find and attack him.

She led them through the field and back down to the road. The horse trotted alongside them on its own side of the fence, following them to the end of its field.

The road crested a hill, and Calder paused. The harbour was spread out below them, lights flickering. A pier jutted out into the sea, and a couple of the small timber haulers were anchored nearby. Clouds obscured the moon, and he turned to catch up to Dag. When the clouds cleared, weak moonlight illuminated the small harbour.

"What in Nyorden . . . ?" he trailed off. He knew what it was. "Dag," he called.

"What?" She was a few paces ahead of him on the road. By the time she reached him, he could already hear the sound of gunfire.

"The ghost ship!" Dag said, staring at the scene.

"Yes." The boom of a cannon echoed across the small bay, and he briefly closed his eyes. When they'd disguised the *Bright Breeze* as the *Diamanto*, they must have put the wrecked ship's cannon on board. Screams and the sounds of wood splintering filtered up to him. "Come on," he said to Dag. "No one will care about a Pilalian in the madness this brings."

The road should take them to the harbour, so he set out at a jog. They would arrive too late to change the result of this fight, but they could help in the aftermath. At the very least, they could witness this attack and let the Fair Seas Treaty Alliance know what had happened. And who was behind it.

"Calder," Dag called to him. "Calder."

He stopped and waited for her to catch up to him. There was no view from where they were, but he could still hear the sounds of gunfire. A second cannon blast shattered the air, followed by screams and shouts.

"We need a plan," Dag said. She grabbed his arm and made him face her. "We can't just run into whatever is happening. We need a plan."

"I know what's happening," he said with a shudder. He'd been in enough battles to know that each time a gun was fired, someone's flesh might have been ripped into, and that a cannon ball smashing into wood sent projectiles of shards and splinters in all directions, shredding anyone in its path.

"But you're right, we need to decide what to do." He nodded and felt Dag relax. Alone, he'd hurtle head-on into danger, trusting his Luck to keep him in one piece. But he wouldn't blindly lead Dag into it, not when it might be her flesh that was shredded, her life that was lost.

"We need to get a look from somewhere high up," Dag said. "To see if the pirates are landing or if they're just attacking by sea." She looked around. "And we should get off this road. The estates will send out men on horses to try to stop this. Come on." She pulled him with her into the trees that lined the road on the harbour side.

Hemlock branches whipped across his face as he trailed Dag through the trees. She stopped and stared up, and he paused behind her, swatting at a swarm of insects before following her gaze. The mature pine tree, out of place amongst the thinner hemlocks, rose above them.

"Give me a boost," Dag said. She stood in front of the trunk, and he bent down with his hands laced together. She stepped into them, and he lifted her up high enough to grab a tree limb.

He quickly lost sight of her as she scrambled higher amongst the branches. He jumped, grabbed onto a branch, and pulled himself up after her. His years spent in rigging made the climb up easy. Dag had perched on a branch, and he settled on one just below her and peered out towards the harbour.

They were close enough to smell the fire now, and he saw flames reaching up into the sky. The three ships and the pier were ablaze; as he watched, flames stretched towards a row of buildings near the pier.

"Do you see any cannon damage?" he asked. "There should be holes in the roofs of buildings." *And bodies littering every surface*, he thought, but he didn't say.

"I see the ghost ship," Dag said. "And the fires, but no other damage." She paused. "There's a crowd gathering in the town square."

"We need to be there," Calder said. Without waiting for Dag's reply, he started climbing down the tree. He dropped to the ground and stepped away. Branches shifted above as Dag made her way down. When she landed beside him, she wiped her hands on her trousers.

"I'll lead," was all she said.

A LOW MURMUR from up ahead was the first sign Calder had that Dag had led them to the edge of the town square. He leaned over her shoulder and looked over a hedge. Torchlight revealed people milling about, many in their nightclothes: evidence that they'd been surprised in the night. A baby cried, and a child called for its mother. A half a dozen men, dressed and leading horses, made their way through the crowd to a set of stairs. Two of the men dropped the reins and strode to the top of the stair.

"That's Clan Freeholder Timonis," Dag said over her shoulder.

The Clan Freeholder, a short man with a stocky build and close-cropped grey hair, raised his hands. The men who had come with him started clapping. Others in the crowd joined in until everyone stopped talking. The clapping ended suddenly, on cue to some signal Calder didn't see, and the Clan Freeholder lowered his arms.

"We have been attacked!" Timonis called out. "By a ghostly ship that fires real guns and cannons. Exactly what we all heard was done to Setberg. Their warehouses were destroyed and they fled their village thinking to find safety in Nurmi, only to have the same thing happen here." He paused and looked around. "Our warehouses and the ships in our harbour were set on fire, but not by ghosts. Live people are behind this, and I for one will not let them chase me out of my home. I say we fight to save our town! Let's get this fire out."

"Come on." Calder put a hand on Dag's shoulder. "Let's take

a closer look at the damage."

This time Dag followed his lead. Most harbour towns had similar layouts, and it was simple to find an alley that led from the square to a street near the sea lined by warehouses. Although all that was left of the warehouses were smouldering shells. He didn't see any dead or injured: just exhausted, soot-covered people. One man looked up when they arrived and beckoned them over.

"Take this." He raised a wooden bucket. "I can't lift another pail of water from the sea. Too tired." He pushed the bucket at Calder's chest and left.

"We heard shots," Calder said. "And a cannon. Are there injuries?"

"Didn't see any," the man replied. "Just the fire. It's still burning, and we need everyone to help put it out and make sure it doesn't spread."

"Here," Dag grabbed the bucket from Calder. "You find another one."

"Are you sure?" He was still confused. The ghost ship had been close enough that the dock was in range of their guns, not to mention the cannon. Why was no one hurt?

"I'm beginning to understand how your Luck works," Dag replied. "And this is as good a way of finding out what's happened as any." She turned and headed along the alley to where a group of people were still battling the remnants of a smoky blaze.

Calder headed in the opposite direction. He'd look for casualties, but he had a feeling that he wouldn't find many, just like they hadn't found any in Setberg. The pirates were attacking with guns and cannon, but they weren't hitting anything other than structures: warehouses and the piers and ships used to fill them.

He wanted to know who owned these warehouses and what exactly had they stored; that was what the pirates had targeted.

DAG PULLED YET another bucket of water up from the sea and handed it off to the man next to her. In turn, he passed it to a woman who then gave it to group who seemed to be directing the firefighting effort.

She wiped her sleeve across her forehead and it came away

covered with soot. She was well and truly disguised now; he doubted anyone she had worked with in the Timonis household would recognize her.

This was the last warehouse still burning; the frame still stood, and instead of flames, there were smoking piles of goods that she imagined at one time were in neat stacks.

"That's it, folks," someone called, and she recognized Clan Freeholder Timonis. "Thank you for your efforts," he said. Dag ducked her head as he walked along the line of volunteers. "We've reports of only minor injuries, and we saved the village." He glanced at her as he went past, and there was no sign that he recognized her as a servant who had worked in his household for less than a month.

"Only minor injuries."

She spun to find Calder beside her, leaning in to whisper in her ear. He too was covered in soot; although it was less of a contrast on his darker skin.

"The Clan Freeholder confirmed what I've noticed," he said. "There's a lot of very specific property damage, but most of the injuries aren't from gun or cannon fire, they're from fighting the fire."

"Is that important?" Dag asked, but her Trait had already activated, so she answered herself. "That's important, but I'm not sure why." At least Inger wasn't complicit in causing any deaths here. She wiped her sleeve across her forehead again. She needed to clean up. She eyed the sea. Even saltwater would be better than this and safer than trying to find a proper bath.

"Come on," Calder said to her. "They've set up a table for food and drink. I think we've earned that much, don't you?"

It took Dag three mugs of water before she'd drunk her fill. Someone handed her a bowl of porridge, and she grabbed a slice of bread topped with pickled fish before wearily sitting down beside Calder. The other three people sharing their small table were also soot-smudged. Only one of them, a woman, glanced at her before concentrating on the food in front of her.

Dag scooped up porridge with her hand, ignoring the dirt and soot that covered it. She'd been breathing in worse all night; ingesting a little more wouldn't make much difference now, and she didn't have the energy to find a place to wash her hands. At least, not until she'd eaten.

In a few minutes, her porridge was gone, and she felt sated enough to look beyond her bowl.

Calder had finished his meal and was staring past their table companions to the pier. The sky was lightening, and the extent of the destruction was becoming visible.

"Only the warehouses and the ships in the harbour were completely destroyed," Calder said to her. "It was very well executed."

"You don't think it's lucky that nothing else burned." She'd thought the town had been spared because of the hard work that was put in to save it, but she could see that anyone planning this would expect that.

"I'm better acquainted with Luck than anyone I've ever met," Calder replied. "This does not feel like Luck to me. What do you think?"

"I think you're right." She sighed. "The pirates would have expected the whole village to rally and put out the fire. They might have been fine if all of Nurmi burned, but they had a goal: there was a minimum that they needed to accomplish. I think the lack of casualties is part of it."

"You might be right. Deaths would make it far more likely that the Three would need to try to retaliate," he said. "Neither Holt nor the pirates would want that. Holt probably tells the pirates which targets to damage. So far it looks like ships, piers, and warehouses."

"But why?" Dag asked. "I'm too tired and hungry to work that out right now." She picked up the slice of bread and bit into it. It tasted of smoke and soot, most everything she ate for a while might taste like that, but she ate it anyway. She could already feel some energy returning after the porridge: the bread and fish would help her sustain it. Once done, she wiped her hands on her filthy trousers.

"I need to clean up," she said to Calder. "I think a swim is in order." She stood up, picked up her bowl, and headed for the stack of dirty dishes. Calder put his bowl beside hers.

"Come on," she said to him. "I know the perfect spot."

NO ONE WAS at the tiny beach when they arrived, and she was grateful for the privacy. She'd noticed this protected beach when she'd completed her mission and had boarded a ship back to

North Tarklee. Nestled in a cove that was almost hidden from the sea, it had been deserted even when the rest of the harbour had been busy.

She stepped out of the trees onto the sand, and without bothering to remove any of her clothes, simply walked into the surf and lay down in the water with her face to the sky.

Gentle waves cooled her, and she sighed as she stared up at the brightening sky. After a moment, she sank under the waves, grabbed some sand from the bottom, and scrubbed her face. Spluttering, she stood up.

Calder was a few feet away from her, floating on his back. He'd stripped off his shirt, and it floated near him. A wave pushed them both towards the shore.

Dag dove into the next wave and then stood up. She pushed her hair out of her eyes and turned back to the beach. She was exhausted. It was hard work hauling water, and she needed to rest. Calder had already flopped down on the beach, his shirt spread out beside him to dry.

"I think it will be days before my hair no longer smells of smoke." She dragged a wet hank up to her nose, sniffed, and made a face. She stopped in front of Calder. Water glistened along the contours of his muscled chest. Another time she might have been able to appreciate him, but not right now. "I'm going to try to get some sleep," she gestured up towards the tree line. "I don't even think the insects can keep me awake."

She plodded up the beach, and after a glance overhead to try to judge where the shade would be in a couple of hours, she lay down.

CHAPTER 4

SOMETHING BUZZED IN her ear, and she swatted at it and rolled over. Sand brushed onto her lip, and she sat up, wiping it away. The sun was high overhead, but she was lying in a small patch of shade. Calder was propped up against a rock a few feet away, asleep.

Wondering if it had only been insects that had woken her, Dag looked into the trees. Was something—? There! She crawled under the trees, trying to find a better viewpoint.

Past the trees she could see the blue of the sea. And there, just out of view of the village, was a ship, a whitewashed ship. The ghost ship.

Dag scrambled to where Calder slept. She gently shook his shoulder, and when his eyes opened, she signalled for him to be quiet. He nodded, and she retraced her path into the trees and lay flat, watching the ghost ship where it was anchored a few dozen yards away.

"They're not done with Nurmi," Calder whispered to her, and she nodded. "This might mean the pirates haven't yet accomplished their goal," he continued, "whatever that is."

"It could be they want what happened in Setberg," Dag replied. "Maybe they want everyone to leave."

"But why?"

Dag looked at him and shrugged. She didn't have enough information to find the hidden truth. Movement on the ship caught her eye, and she frowned. It was Captain Margit Ansdottir: she'd recognize her anywhere. But what was she doing on this ship?

"I thought your friend was going to captain this ship—Inger!" Her sister had joined Ansdottir, and the two of them stood side by side, staring out at the sea. When Ansdottir's gaze swivelled to where she and Calder were hiding, she sank lower. Inger wouldn't see her, but Ansdottir had a touch of the Unseen Trait.

"We need to leave," Dag said, inching backwards towards the beach. She needed to go, and not just because they could be caught. Seeing Inger, her twin, so comfortable with the captain of the pirates made her sad and angry and afraid all at the same time.

She and Inger were on opposite sides in this fight, and it *was* a fight. She wasn't sure what either one of them would do if they crossed paths right now.

CALDER REMAINED SILENT as he and Dag took a few moments to erase any sign of their presence on the small beach. He'd seen Inger with Ansdottir on the *Bright Breeze*. But did that mean Inger was a willing participant in whatever the pirates were doing? So far it seemed that they were scaring people and destroying property, but he'd been at sea long enough to know that it didn't usually stop there. And no matter what Inger's motive might be, based on her actions, she would be considered an enemy of the Fair Seas Treaty Alliance. Her part in what had been done so far would land her in prison or worse. Would Dag be able to deliver her sister—her twin—to justice when it might result in her death?

The village was quiet when they walked through it. The warehouses were still being monitored in case flames reignited, but most townspeople seemed to have headed to their homes.

"I have grain if you be needing it," a vendor said from behind a table. "In a small storehouse that wasn't set ablaze. It might be the last we see until spring."

Calder stopped and put a hand on Dag's arm when she would have walked past.

"What do you mean the last until spring?" he asked the vendor. "Won't more be shipped in before then?"

"The ships that could bring it were lost to fire too," was the reply. "And even if we hire other ships, there's nowhere left to store it in any great amounts." The vendor shrugged.

"What about the road?" Dag asked. "Grain can be brought in on wagons, can't it?"

The vendor shrugged. "It's possible, but we need to be able to buy more grain in order to do that, don't we? Harvests have all been spoken for all along the coast. What was here," he gestured towards the remains of the warehouses, "can't be replaced. Except at a much higher cost. And if it is replaced then we takes from somewheres else."

"Did the warehouses only store grain?" Calder asked. "This is a logging camp."

"Timber don't get stored with food," the vendor said. "And the warehouses stored more than grain. But the grain will be missed come winter, that I know."

"Who owns these warehouses?" Dag asked. "Who would be able to buy more grain?"

"Freeholders own them," was the answer. "Freeholders own pretty much everything, don't they? Two of them even belong to Clan Freeholder Timonis. Him's that got everyone to help put the fires out." The vendor spat to the side of his table. "And who made folks think he did it to save the town."

"He did rally everyone to save the town," Calder said.

"Sure, because he was trying to save his own property. Put people at risk, is what I heard. And some of them are none too happy about that." He turned away from them when a customer approached his table. "Grain to sell, sure," he said to the woman.

Calder walked away, deep in thought. The Clan Freeholder had made himself out to be a hero during the fire: he'd urged people to fight the fire. Even he and Dag had been asked to join the bucket line. But if he'd also decided where and how to fight the fire . . . He stopped and turned to stare at what had burned: the three ships, the pier, and the four warehouses.

"What do you see?" Dag asked.

"I'm not sure." Until last night, the only fires he'd helped fight had been aboard a ship, and on board even the tiniest fire had such potential for disaster that it was all hands on deck to get the fire out. And no cost, including lives, was too great a price to pay. "Would there have been a safer way to fight last night's fire?"

Dag looked from him to the charred remains of the warehouses. "Sure, probably," she said. Then she stopped and squinted. "I see what you mean. They could have let the warehouses burn by creating a line up here," she pointed to the road. "I'm not sure it would have made it safer for the village, but it would have been safer for those of us fighting the fire. You think Timonis really did put people in harm's way for his own gain?"

"Maybe," Calder said. He glanced over his shoulder at the grain vendor. "Some people seem to think so which makes me think Timonis is not well thought of. But it could also be that what was in the warehouse was worth trying to save: it was worth risking lives over."

"It was the grain," Dag said. She looked at him. "My Trait is telling me that it was the grain. That was what the pirates wanted to destroy."

"Why?"

"Timonis is slated to be the next Grand Freeholder," Dag said. "Holt doesn't want that to happen. Maybe he's trying to keep Timonis busy with problems close to home so he doesn't push too hard to become Grand Freeholder. Maybe he'll even pass it up to concentrate on helping his people."

"Timonis has to have been positioning himself to become Grand Freeholder for most of his life," Calder replied. "People who do that don't just give up. Not in my experience." He looked past Dag towards the square, where it looked like a crowd was gathering. His focus narrowed on a man with a wagon. "Come on," he said to Dag. "My Trait just activated." He pushed through the gathering crowd, Dag at his back, until he was right beside the wagon.

Clan Freeholder Timonis was once again standing in front of the crowd. Calder didn't hear what he said, but the crowd roared its approval.

"Fools, all of them," the man with the cart muttered. He turned and bumped Calder, who smiled.

"I confess, at times I am a fool," Calder said. He pulled Dag into his embrace. "My better half here would no doubt agree with that."

The other man looked Calder up and down before his gaze

settled on Dag. "What are you doing with a foreigner?"

"He's a very good cook," Dag said. She paused and smiled up at Calder. "He's very good at quite a few things."

The man laughed. "Now that makes more sense than anything this *Freeholder* has to say." He almost spat the word Freeholder and Calder had to suppress a grin. His friend with the wagon hated authority.

"And I am not a foreigner," Calder said. "Although my father was. I am Cutterstown born and bred. My mother still lives there."

"You're a Byholter," the man said. "That's pretty much foreign to me." He laughed again. "Help me get my wagon free of this crowd and on the road to South Tarklee, and I'll let you cook for me. Using my food." He winked at Dag. "That ways I can judge whether he might be good at other things."

"Sure," Calder replied. "I warn you that your horse will not like me."

"I don't like my horse," the man replied. "So his judge of character won't make a difference to me."

Calder met Dag at the back of the cart while the man grabbed his horse's lead.

"Should we leave the sailboat?" she asked.

"This is my Trait working," he replied. "I take it where it leads. Is that all right with you?" He had assumed their only option was to sail into Tarklee harbour, but Luck was directing him to the road. "Besides, you said you thought we should enter Tarklee on foot."

"I did," she replied. "I do. And while I can't sail the boat so I don't have a choice, I think this will be best. I was worried about the time it will take to get there by road, but the wagon will be faster than walking."

"Good." He clasped her hand for a moment, then dropped it and gestured to the front of the wagon. "Then let's help get this wagon on the road to South Tarklee."

It took time, but they finally got the wagon out of the crowded square and onto the road that led north, towards Tarklee. The wagon owner had laughed when Calder had stepped in front of the horse. One sniff and the horse had followed Calder out through the crowd, forcing people to scramble out of the way of the single-minded animal.

"I think my horse likes you," their companion said. They were in a small clearing by the side of the road. "I'm Pavil. Pavil Barda." He tugged the horse over to a tree and tied the lead to a thick branch.

"Well, Pavil Barda," Calder said. "You'll think differently if your horse ever catches me." He kept a few paces away from the animal: its ears were flat as it stretched the rope and tried to reach Calder. "I'm Rahm and—" the horse's teeth snapped at air, and Calder edged another step away from it. Pavil laughed.

"I'm Sigrun," Dag said as she came up behind him. "We really appreciate the offer of a meal. We spent last night helping put out the fires and today, well, it looks like our kit either went up in flames or someone thought it had been abandoned."

"So Nurmi's now full of thieves as well as fools." Pavil shook his head. "Don't recognize my own village no more." He leaned into the wagon just behind the seat and grabbed a basket. "Here's all the fixin's I have." He handed the basket to Calder. "Let's see what you can do with them."

Calder took the basket behind the wagon hoping that if he was out of sight of the horse, it would forget he was there. He gathered wood and started a fire even before opening the basket. Besides a couple of cooking pots there were onions, potatoes, a chunk of cheese, and a small crock of butter. It was a pretty small store of food, and the spice collection was even more meagre. He sighed, resigned to another bland meal, and got to work.

He could hear Dag talking to Pavil in low tones, and he smiled. No doubt her Trait was at work, finding out all of their host's secrets.

He sliced two onions and set them to fry in a dollop of butter while he did his best to shred the potatoes. He added the potatoes, mixing them up with the onions and letting them cook for a few minutes. After another stir, he flattened everything into a pancake. He lifted an edge: it looked nicely browned, so he flipped it over.

"Smells good already," Pavil said, leaning over his shoulder. "Sigrun says you're heading to Tarklee. I'm heading down that road aways myself. If you do the cooking, I'll supply food and bedrolls for the two of you."

Calder slid the pancake from the pan to a plate and put the

second batch of potatoes into the pan. "That's a very generous offer," Calder replied. "You haven't even tasted one of my meals yet."

"Sigrun said you can do wonders with salt fish," Pavil replied. "Knowing a good way to prepare that skit is worth more than you two can eat in a few days. I just barely tolerate it, but it's a staple that gets me through winter. I hate waking up on a bleak winter day knowing there's nothing to eat but salt fish. I'd be grateful to have a way to make it taste better."

"You don't have any for me to prove my skills to you with," Calder said. He flipped the pancake and layered cheese on it before he topped it with the other pancake. "But I can give you instructions. You'll need to buy some spices, though."

"You tell me what I need to get," Pavil said. "When I stop for supplies after we eat."

"So, you'll have more than this? Good, I was worried that you'd expect miracles."

"Don't believe in them," Pavil said. "But you tell me how to make salt fish taste decent and I just might start."

"WHAT DID YOU find out?" Calder asked Dag. They were waiting a few steps away from the wagon while Pavil picked up supplies from a small shop that was set back from the road. Calder had given him a list of ingredients, and the man had promised to do his best.

"He's a trader," Dag said. "He has a cabin just past the halfway mark between Nurmi and Tarklee. There's a small spring there, and he keeps a couple of goats that he milks for cheese. He earns most of his living selling to people who take the road and then run short of supplies." She grinned. "It sounds like we're not the only people to travel without a kit." She paused. "I think that's another reason why he wants your recipe for salt fish. It's cheap and filling, and he can sell it for a good profit when supplies are low."

"As long as it tastes good," Calder finished. "You can keep a pot of it simmering for days so it's always ready whenever anyone happens by. It's a good plan."

"Yes. And thank you for your part in ours. That pancake you made was delicious."

"So Pavil kept saying," Calder replied. "But if he can get

everything on my list, supper will be much better." Calder didn't mind the work; he never minded cooking, and even he was getting excited about his meal plans for the next day or so.

GUSTAV PULLED THE scarf up to his eyes. He'd used his Charisma on a washerwoman who had traded him the moth-eaten woollen scarf in exchange for some trinkets from the cart. She would have given him a better quality one if he'd asked, but he preferred this one. It allowed him to blend in with the rest of the people who eked out meagre livings on the streets around the bridge.

Besides, once she was away from the influence of his Trait, the woman might have regretted making such a poor trade. He never wanted people to feel cheated: not only was it not fair to take too much from people with so little, but they might recognize him on the streets later. Dealing with angry people would not help him blend in.

He stood up, grabbed his hat, shuffled across the road, and sat down with his back against a different building.

The day after he'd seen Vilis cross back into North Tarklee on New Bridge, he'd tried to follow him again. He'd seen him leave the Hall, but Vilis had taken a convoluted route, and he'd lost him even before they reached the bridge.

Gustav was finally rewarded for the hours he'd waited when Vilis had used the same bridge on his return. Since this seemed to be the usual route Vilis used to cross the river, Gustav decided it would be better to watch for him on the far side of the bridge and start following him once he was in South Tarklee.

He almost missed him. Dusk had fallen, and Vilis was wearing a disguise. It was his walk: Gustav recognized it before he realized that the man in the drab clothing was his fellow student.

Vilis stepped off the bridge and onto a rutted dirt lane and headed south, following the river. Wrapping his scarf more tightly over his face, Gustav rose and followed.

They'd both had the same lessons on how to evade potential trackers, so he was prepared for the twists and turns Vilis took as he seemingly wandered through the streets.

Eventually, Vilis stopped in front of the weathered door of what looked like an old warehouse. He knocked three times before letting himself in. Turning his head in case Vilis looked his way, Gustav shuffled past and all the way to the far end of the warehouse. An attached stable that looked like it hadn't housed a horse in decades was set back into a narrow lane. He didn't pass any windows, so he crossed the street and returned to the door Vilis had disappeared through. Just past the door a small window was set into the wall, and he slowly crept towards it. The window was partially open, and after a glance around to make sure no one was watching him, Gustav crouched beneath it.

Very faint voices drifted his way. They weren't loud enough for him to decipher what was being said, but a man seemed to be doing most of the talking with a few comments made by a woman. A couple of times he thought he heard Vilis give one- or two-word answers to questions asked by the others. As soon as he realized that the conversation had ended, Gustav dashed around the corner. He sat down, leaned against the wall, and peered back at the door.

Vilis stepped out of the warehouse, looked around for a moment, and then headed towards the bridge.

Once Vilis was out of sight, Gustav crossed the narrow street and sat under a scraggly bush. He tucked his feet under him and wrapped the scarf around his arms, trying to disappear.

An hour later the door to the warehouse opened, and a familiar figure stepped out. He brushed something off his well-tailored coat, settled his hat on his head, and walked away.

Gustav returned to the bridge, wondering exactly what Vilis was doing with Tarmo Holt. He didn't think it a coincidence that Joosep had asked him to spy on Holt, and now Joosep was missing. And now another Intelligencer student was meeting with Tarmo Holt. What was Holt up to?

Joosep lifted his head and stared up at the dark ceiling. His Trait had activated even though nothing had changed in his prison. He wrapped his arms around himself, feeling the shard of the broken bowl dig into his skin.

No one had entered, nor had he heard any sounds from beyond the door to his cell. But something had happened, something hidden. But what? And how could he find out?

The lock turned, and the cell door opened. His jailer entered, carrying a cup of water in one hand and the key to the door in the other.

And she was smiling. Not a happy smile, no, this was more of a spiteful, I-know-what-terrible-thing-is-going-to-happen smile.

So Joosep decided to prove to her that she didn't know what was going to happen. At least not right this minute.

He reached under his shirt for the sharp piece of ceramic. He clutched it in his hand and rested it against his hip. As soon as the woman bent down to set the cup on the floor, Joosep pounced.

At least he tried to pounce. What he actually did was lunge towards her, crash into her legs, and topple her on top of him.

She started swearing as she punched and kicked at him, trying to roll off of him. But it was too late for her. Joosep had already wrapped one arm around her neck while the other struck her back with the shard of pottery. She screamed as he struck as hard and fast as he could, expecting someone to rush to her aid and kill him at any moment.

It was exhausting, but he kept pounding on her back as she writhed and shrieked in fear and anger and then pain, as the shard pierced her skin and battered against her ribcage.

She was finally able to twist off him, but it didn't help her. Joosep rolled on top of her and now his hand, still clutching the shard, hit her unprotected belly. She howled in pain, but he kept shoving the shard into her again and again and again.

At some point, her screaming ended, and the small cell was silent except for Joosep's laboured breathing. He stopped, and the shard slipped from his hand into a pool of blood.

He dragged himself off his jailer: she was dead, her blank eyes stared up towards the ceiling, and her mouth was open in silent agony.

Joosep eventually found the strength to crawl away from the body, leaving a trail of blood on the floor behind him. He made it outside the door of the cell before he collapsed, unable to go any further.

Just a few minutes, he told himself. He'd rest just a few minutes. The sounds of the fight must have been heard, someone must be coming, and he couldn't count on it being a friend.

He lay his head on the floor. *Just a few minutes.*

CHAPTER 5

THE WAGON LURCHED, and Dag grabbed the pot. Water sloshed over the lip and onto the barrel the pot rested on. Calder looked over his shoulder from his seat on the wagon's bench.

"That was close," Dag said to him. "But your precious salt fish is safe." He'd insisted on starting the soaking process yesterday, as soon as they'd helped Pavil load all of his supplies onto the wagon. Calder had changed the water twice since then, but it was Dag who ended up sitting in the back of the wagon, making sure the pot didn't tip over. Pavil's horse wouldn't move unless Calder was either on the bench with Pavil or not in the wagon at all.

"Pavil says we're almost there," Calder said. "Just another hour or so."

Dag nodded. She ached from sitting on a barrel while hunching over the pot of salt fish, one hand on it at all times. She tried to stretch without moving too much. The wagon swayed, and she gripped the pot more tightly.

At least the meals had made the trip bearable. Calder hadn't been exaggerating when he'd said he was a decent cook. She'd eaten his cooking before, but always when he'd made limited ingredients more than passable. But now that he had a full selection of food and spices? Her mouth watered just thinking of the dish he'd made last night: cabbage and potatoes fried with butter alongside roasted pork he'd rubbed with some spices. All cooked over a fire.

She eyed the salt fish. At least he wasn't planning on feeding them *that* tonight.

She watched the road behind them as the wagon continued its slow and steady trek. Every once in a while, she could see the sea through the trees. The road hugged the coast for the most part, Pavil had said. She tried to remember how it looked on the maps she'd had to study during her lessons at the Hall: a thin line that squiggled from the edge of South Tarklee to Nurmi, with only a few clearings in the woods that surrounded it.

The coast along here was rugged. With no natural harbours, and a very rocky shoreline, landing a ship was impossible. There were also only a few small streams; the larger rivers didn't feed directly into the Pale Sea from here and instead drained into the Dareveth River which divided North and South Tarklee before emptying into the sea.

The wagon slowed and hit a bump, and Dag had to grab the pot with both hands.

"We're here," Calder called to her. Trees brushed against one side of the wagon as it turned off the main road and rattled to a stop in front of a weathered house.

With her hands still on the pot, Dag rose to her feet. Calder hopped off the wagon, reached over the side, and picked up the pot.

Grateful to be relieved of her duties, Dag stretched. The horse neighed, the wagon jerked, and she almost lost her balance.

"Sorry," Calder yelled. Carrying the pot, he circled the horse which was straining at its lead trying to reach him.

"Never seen anything like it," Pavil said. He was standing beside the horse's head, shaking his own.

Dag climbed down from the wagon to stand beside him. "Let's leave Rahm to figure out what to feed us," she said. "I'll help you unload and store your goods."

It took just over an hour to haul everything into either a dry storage room or the root cellar. Calder poked his head out of the house once, but she waved him off. Pavil usually unpacked everything by himself; she didn't think it required three people.

Once the wagon was empty, Pavil unhitched his horse and led it down to a small fenced-in field. Dag grabbed a bucket and headed along a worn path. The stream ran cold and clear, and she drank her fill before filling the bucket and heading back to the house.

"I've a nice room that'll do for you and your man," Pavil said as he opened the door and led her inside. "And I haven't forgot about your lost kit. There's some spare clothes folk have left here over the years; you're welcome to take your pick."

"Thank you." Dag followed Pavil down a short hall to a kitchen. Calder already had the stove lit, and a kettle was boiling on top of it.

"I made myself at home," he said to Pavil. "I hope you don't mind." He lifted the kettle from the top of the stove and poured hot water into a pot.

"Said ye could," Pavil replied. "And if that's tea already made, now I really mean it."

Calder chuckled and poured steaming tea into three waiting mugs. He handed the first one to Dag, and she held it, enjoying the warmth against her palms.

"Supper will be ready in about an hour," Calder said, passing a mug to Pavil. "And afterwards I will give you a lesson on how to create a delicious salt fish soup."

"I'll settle for edible," Pavil said. He took a sip of tea and sighed. "You find everything you need?"

"Yes," Calder replied, stirring the pot Dag had tended to in the wagon.

She took her tea and sat down at a small table and looked around Pavil's home. This room was small, as was the window, which was typical of houses that had to deal with harsh winters. The furnishings were well worn, but they looked clean. Even the stove Calder stood beside was free of layers of grime.

"Do you have many guests?" she asked Pavil.

"Not really," Pavil said. "The road's not very well travelled. It was built by a few traders when the Fair Seas Treaty was first signed: folks wanting to avoid paying the tariffs the Treaty put on everything transported by sea."

"But now the tariffs apply to everything," Dag replied. "So there's little reason to travel by land."

"That's right," Pavil agreed. "Nowadays most people on the road have livestock that they're taking to or bringing from Tarklee." He drained his tea and set the mug down on the table.

"If you're ready, I'll show you your room and dig out the spare clothes I told you about."

"Thank you." With a nod to Calder, Dag followed Pavil to the front door and down a second hallway. The room was small, of course, and she felt her face get warm when she saw the narrow bed she was to share with Calder.

Last night they'd all bedded down in a clearing; the only issue being how far from the horse Calder could get and still be warmed by the fire. Their story that she and Calder were a couple hadn't meant any changes to their sleeping arrangements. Not so tonight.

Pavil left to find the cast-off clothing, and she stood in the doorway. A small window was set into the wall above the bed, which took up almost all of the floor space in the little room. She and Calder would have no choice but to share the bed; there wasn't even enough room for one of them to stretch out on the floor.

The last time they'd shared a bed had been at Solvig's warehouse. That had turned into something more: something she wasn't sure either of them wanted to repeat or pursue right now. Not when there was so much they didn't know about Tarmo Holt, Joosep, and Inger and the pirates.

"Take what you want," Pavil said when he returned with a basket. "Everything in here has been cleaned by me. There's a wash tub next to the kitchen for you or your clothes. It'll be cold water unless you want to wait for your man to heat some."

"Thank you," Dag said, but Pavil had already left. She dumped the contents of the basket onto the bed and started sorting through the pile.

There was more than she'd expected, and most was so threadbare that it likely wasn't missed by its owner, but she did find a pair of trousers for Calder and a skirt that would do for her, along with a couple of shirts that would suit either of them. She preferred to wear trousers—she felt inconvenienced in a skirt even though it was less restrictive. In a practical sense though, trousers never got tangled in anything, they never blew around when it was windy, and they allowed her to climb and run when needed. She'd had to do those things many times since leaving Strongrock and was certain she'd need to do them again before long.

But the skirt would do until her trousers were washed. She quickly changed out of her clothes. Once she was out of them, she realized how strongly they smelled of smoke. She lifted a hank of hair to her nose; just like her hair.

Leaving Calder's fresh set of clothes on the bed, she went in search of him.

"Can you heat some water?" she asked as she entered the kitchen. He looked up from a chopping board where he'd been cutting vegetables.

"For a bath? I'm already doing that." He gestured to a large pot that sat on the stove. "I used the bucket of water you brought in earlier. It should be hot enough soon."

"Thanks." She spied the bucket and picked it up. "I'll get more water to wash out my clothes. They stink."

"I'm sure I do too." Calder set the knife down and wiped his hands on a cloth. "I see you found something to your liking to wear in Pavil's supplies."

"Something that will do," she replied. "And I am grateful. I left a set for you on the bed." She turned and headed back down the hall to the main door. It was darker out now, but she'd already been down this path, so finding the spring again was simple. She headed back to the kitchen with another bucket of water.

The tub was in a small storage room that was really just an alcove off the kitchen. Dag started filling it with hot water before adding some of the cold water from the bucket to adjust the temperature.

"I'll warn you if Pavil comes in," Calder said. "He's taking care of his horse and checking on his goats." Calder was wearing the other set of clothes, and she almost laughed. The trousers only reached his ankles, and the shirt was stretched tight across his chest.

"Thanks." Deciding not to worry about Calder seeing her skin again, she stepped out of the skirt, pulled the shirt over her head, and settled into the tub.

It wasn't a huge tub, but it covered most of her. She grabbed a bar of soap from a nearby shelf and scrubbed at her skin. Once she was rinsed off, she climbed out, knelt over the tub, and awkwardly dipped her head and hair into the water. She lathered it with soap before dunking her head into the water again. Satisfied that she'd done all she could, she squeezed water from her hair, dried herself off with a cloth, and put her clothes back on. And even though she was aware that he was standing only a few feet away from her, not once did she look at Calder.

CALDER DELIBERATELY KEPT his eyes on the vegetables he was cutting and away from the corner where Dag was bathing. But he could hear the water run off her when she stepped out of the tub, and try as he might, he could not stop himself from imagining what that looked like.

"I'm finished if you want a bath," Dag said from behind him.

He turned. She ran a hand through her wet hair.

"You might need to add some more hot water."

"Uh, sure." He did need a bath, so he grabbed the pot of still-hot water and poured half of it into the tub. "That's all I get. The rest will be used for stew." He dumped the turnip and rutabaga into the pot, along with a chopped onion. "Can you stir this while I clean up?"

Dag nodded, and he went back to the tub. Feeling self-conscious, he stripped off his clothes and settled into the tub as fast as he could. He did a very quick scrub and wash before getting out, drying off, and putting his borrowed clothes back on.

"That makes me miss the shower on Strongrock," he said as he rejoined Dag at the stove. "And the ones in Pilalia that have heated water, even more."

"I'll wash our clothes," Dag said, moving out of his way, "when you give Pavil his lesson on how to cook salt fish."

"You don't think you need to know how to do that?"

"Not when you're around," she said. "And when you're not? I don't plan on eating salt fish."

"I swear that horse knows you're here and is trill trying to get to you," Pavil said as he entered the kitchen. He tossed his hat on the table and sat down. "I see you've managed to clean up some."

"Yes, thank you for the bath and the clothes," Calder said. He looked down at his too snug shirt. "It's nice to be clean."

"It's nice to have someone else cooking fer me," Pavil said. "And I appreciate the company."

Calder grabbed a gnarled root of ginger and cut off a piece, shaved the peel off, and then sliced it thin and added it to the pot. Then he crushed a few peppercorns and tossed them in as well.

"There should be enough stew for a few meals," Calder said. "As well as the salt fish that we'll fix later." He headed to the cold room and sliced a chunk off the slab of bacon that was hanging there. It was well-cured and salted, so all he needed to do was cut it up and add it to the stew.

He wiped his hands on a cloth and took a step away from the stove. Dag had gathered their dirty clothes and dumped them in the tub to soak.

"Ever see pirates along the road?" Calder asked Pavil. "Or privateers?" To him they were the same, but others who might have reason to trade with them might not think that way.

"Nope, it's too rough for ships around here. If it wasn't, this forest would have been logged long ago."

"Can't they cart the logs along the road?" Dag asked. She sat down at the table across from their host.

"They could," Pavil said. "But it's cheaper to move them by sea. You'd need dozens of carts, horses, and drivers to replace each ship. Besides, there are only a few springs along the route and you have to know where to look. Even then, they can dry up in the summer."

Calder stirred the stew once more, tasted it, and then added another crushed peppercorn. It didn't need salt since the bacon had more than enough.

"The stew is ready," he said.

It would taste better the second day, once the flavours blended, but both Dag and Pavil seemed to like it well enough. After their meal, Dag finished washing their clothes while he talked Pavil through a couple of ways to cook salt fish to make it taste good. By the time they were finished, Dag had disappeared.

He said goodnight to Pavil and made his way to the door of the room he was to share with Dag. He paused outside the room; he didn't hear any sounds from within, so he quietly pushed the door open.

Their wet clothes were laid out or strung up around the small room, and a single lamp on a table beside the bed was casting shadows. Dag's blonde hair peeked out from under a blanket on the side of the bed closest to the window. Calder stripped off his clothes, and as carefully as he could, he slipped under the covers. Dag smelled of soap with just a faint whiff of smoke. He sighed and blew out the lamp and settled in on his side of the bed.

And stared up at the ceiling until eventually, finally, he fell asleep.

CHAPTER 6

CALDER WAS AWARE of the exact moment when Dag woke and realized that she was tucked up beside him.

He'd been awake for a while: earlier, she'd mumbled something in her sleep and then rolled into him. He hadn't moved because he hadn't wanted to disturb her. And he liked the feel of her body pressing against him even if it was just against his back.

In order to avoid any awkwardness, he pretended to be asleep as she carefully eased out from under the covers, slid down to the end of the bed, and rose. Once she'd left the room, he sighed.

They had difficult days in front of them, and they couldn't afford any personal feelings to complicate their decisions or make them wary of each other, no matter how much he wished they could recapture what they'd shared on Lavais Island.

He lay in bed for a few more minutes before boredom and his empty stomach forced him up.

"Ah, Rahm, there you are." Pavil was at the stove, staring into the pot of salt fish. "Sigrun already made tea."

"Where is she?" He poured from a pot into a mug and sat down at the table. The small window showed a clear morning.

"Fetching more water," Pavil said. "For porridge." He made a face, and Calder suppressed a grin. "That what you planning on cooking?"

"Sorry, but yes, a simple millet porridge."

Pavil sighed. "I have plenty of millet."

"You're up," Dag came in, carrying a bucket. Her face was scrubbed, and she smelled of fresh air. "I looked in on your horse. I think it smelled Rahm on me." The minute she said that she blushed. "I mean, on my clothes." She was wearing the skirt and top from yesterday, just as he was wearing the clothes Pavil had offered.

"And you say every horse?" Pavil asked. Calder nodded, and the other man shook his head. "Don't seem reasonable."

"Thank you," Calder replied. "It doesn't to me either. But horses are notoriously hard to reason with." He drank his tea and stood up. "I'll make the porridge, and after that, we will be on our way."

After tasting the millet porridge, Pavil decided he needed to know how to make that as well. While Calder told him, basically add plenty of butter and a touch of soured cream, Dag rounded up their things and packed them into a small sack that Pavil gave them.

Another small sack contained food: millet and bacon along with some butter and half a wheel of goat cheese that Pavil said needed to be eaten. Once the waterskins were full, they were ready.

"Thank you," Dag said when they reached the door. "For all of your help."

"I got the best of it," Pavil said. "I'm gonna miss having someone else do all the chores. And the cooking."

"You know how to do it now," Calder said. He clasped the man's hand. "But thank you for everything. We're much better prepared than we would have been if we hadn't run into you."

"Well, it were lucky for both of us," Pavil said. "It shouldn't be a bad walk from here. You should get to Tarklee tomorrow. I'll let my horse know you're gone." He chuckled.

"Just make sure you don't let it off its lead for a day or so," Calder said. "It could come after me." He waved and joined Dag outside.

"Might it?" she asked as they walked away from Pavil's house. "The horse?"

"I think it's possible," he replied. He looked back: Pavil had gone inside, and the door was closed. "Usually when I leave horses behind it's because I'm heading to sea. The first ones I've walked away from were in the fenced in fields we passed when we landed at Nurmi. For all I know they're still trying to get out and find me."

Once they were past a bend in the road and Pavil's house was no longer visible, Dag turned to him.

"That's how it works, isn't it? Your Trait. I didn't completely understand until Pavil said that at the last . . ." she paused. "That meeting was lucky for both of you. He got cooking lessons that he considers valuable, and we were supplied with a ride, food, and clothing." She raised the bag she carried. "That was your Trait at work. All of that happened because of Luck."

"Yes," he replied. "I told you my Trait was activated when we were in the crowd. I followed that feeling and here we are, on our way to Tarklee on a path that would be the least expected—especially for a sailor like me. And to be honest, if we'd sailed that small boat into Tarklee Harbour, half of the city would hear about it within an hour. There would have been no way to slip in unnoticed, not even in the dead of night. And very often, that's how my Trait works."

"Luck," she said. "After what happened with Pavil, I can see that it would be hard to try to force it."

INSECTS BUZZED BESIDE his ear, and he opened his eyes. There was a faint light coming in through a window, which was not something he'd ever seen from inside his cell, where it had always been dark.

Joosep raised himself to his knees. His hands were sticky with dried blood, and flies, disturbed when he moved, swarmed around him. He glanced back into the cell. The woman's body lay where he'd left her, and there was a dark trail that led from it to him. All of it attracting clouds of flies.

He gripped the side of the door to his cell and struggled to his feet: it had taken so much effort to crawl such a short distance.

He was battered and bruised from the fight with his jailer, but he didn't think any bones were broken. He sucked in a breath: his ribs were sore, but nothing shifted when he breathed.

Letting go of the doorframe, he shuffled unsteadily across

the empty space towards the window. He recognized the interior as the warehouse he'd been investigating when he'd been caught; they hadn't even had to move him.

The door to the small office he'd been caught searching was open, and a low table next to it held a bucket. When he finally reached it, he almost stumbled in relief. Water. A mug sat beside the bucket, and with it he scooped up water, careful to keep his bloodied hands from getting wet and tainting the water.

It took all of his willpower to make himself sip slowly, but he did. Three mugs, then four, until his thirst subsided. He looked down at his hands. Blood covered them up past his wrists and had soaked through his shirt sleeves. He'd need to clean himself off if he hoped to escape notice on the streets. But not until he was certain he'd drunk enough water.

He opened the door to the office and slumped into the chair. He'd take another look while he was here, now that he knew for certain that Tarmo Holt used this warehouse. He didn't expect to find much: Holt would have moved anything important by now. But he also had different needs, and there might be something he could use when he left this building.

The few drawers were empty, but a cupboard yielded a shirt; it was well used and smelled of lamp oil, but at least it wasn't covered in blood. He placed it on the table beside the bucket.

A small basket was tucked onto a lower shelf of the table, and when he lifted the lid, his mouth watered. There was a chunk of bread and a wrapped wedge of cheese. He nibbled on the cheese and the bread, not wanting to eat too quickly after so many days of near starvation.

Once he'd eaten his jailer's meal and had downed another two mugs of water, he took off his shirt. Using the mug, he dribbled water on the back collar, which was relatively clean, and scrubbed away the blood on his hands and wrists

Once his hands were clean, he wiped his face with another part of his shirt. He had half a bucket of water, and because he'd been without for so long, he took one last drink before he upended the bucket over his head. Water sluiced down his head and ran across his chest, and suddenly chilled, he shivered.

The he stepped out of the puddle of water, pulled on the dry shirt, and much more steadily walked to the door.

It was still early when he cracked open the door and peeked out. He guessed it was just before dawn, and no one was around. He left the warehouse, closed the door tightly behind him, and slowly walked away from captivity.

His energy faltered when he was only a few streets away from the warehouse. Exhausted, he crawled under a hedge. He'd rest and then travel back towards North Tarklee when he had recovered a little. But not to the Hall: he wasn't going to return there.

Now that he was free, he needed to stay that way. He needed to expose and defeat Tarmo Holt.

DAG STARED OUT at the sea. Waves crashed against the rocks that were strewn along the shoreline, sending spray high into the air.

"The spring is just where Pavil said it would be," Calder said as he joined her at the edge of the cliff.

"Good," she replied. "Then we should stay here tonight." They could simply refill their waterskins, that should give them enough water to get to Tarklee, but only if they didn't run into any trouble. Neither of them wanted to count on that.

"I'll gather firewood," Dag continued. She turned and headed down a slight slope, back towards the road. Other travellers had stopped here, although not recently. Grass grew inside a ring of stones someone had gathered to create a fire pit, and bushes that had been cut back to allow a wagon to be pulled off the road showed new growth.

Dag grabbed a few fallen branches from under the nearest trees and dropped them by the fire pit. Once she'd gathered all the branches that were close, she headed into the thick stand of trees.

Her footfalls were muffled by a layer of pine needles, but there were plenty more branches on the ground, no doubt breaking off after being weighed down by ice and snow during the harsh winters.

Once she had an armful, she retraced her steps to the camp and dumped the wood with the rest that she'd gathered. She pulled out the grass that had grown in the middle of the circle of stones and started laying out kindling for a fire.

"It's far too rough out there to fish," Calder said as he came down from the cliff. "So it's Pavil's rations for supper." He dropped the two full waterskins on the ground and opened up the pack of food, pulling out a pot, the tea, and two wrapped packages.

They ate a cold supper of cheese and dark bread, washed down with tea. Once they were finished, Calder went to rinse the pot and mugs out at the spring.

Dag walked the few steps up to the edge of the sea and looked out across the waves. The sun was setting, and the water was tinged red and orange. As she turned to head back to the fire, her Trait activated as something almost caught her eye. She stared as the sun sank and the sky turned indigo. There—just along the horizon.

"*Skit.*" She rushed back to the fire and with a stick, quickly scattered the burning wood.

"What's wrong?" Calder asked. She looked up to see him holding a dripping pot in one hand.

"I need to smother the fire," Dag replied. Using the stick, she gouged the earth and scooped up a handful of dirt and tossed it onto the smouldering embers. "There's a ship. I don't want them to know anyone is here."

"A ship," Calder repeated. "You think it's the pirates?" He dropped the pot and knelt, helping Dag scoop up dirt and pile it on the fire.

In a few moments, the fire was out, and smoke no longer wafted into the air.

"Come on," Calder said. "Let's see if they noticed us."

Dag nodded and followed him to the cliff, grateful that Calder hadn't needed a long explanation the way Inger always did. Then she felt badly for thinking that of her sister; that she was too much effort.

She knelt beside a windswept pine tree and looked out across the water. Calder was on the other side of the tree's thick trunk.

"It's the *Bright Breeze*," he said.

"You can tell for certain from this distance?" Dag asked. She knew it had to be the *Bright Breeze*, but part of her wanted to be wrong.

"Yes," Calder replied.

"Where do you think they're heading?" Dag asked. And what was Inger going to be complicit in this time?

"There's nothing between here and Tarklee," Calder replied.

"Then Tarklee is their next target," Dag replied softly. "We need to get there as soon as we can." She turned and met Calder's gaze.

"They won't make it to Tarklee before dawn," he said. "And so far, every attack has been at night. I think it's safe to assume they won't change tactics now."

"So, we have until tomorrow night," Dag said. "To get to the harbour and warn them."

"I'll top up the waterskins," Calder said and headed back towards the camp.

Dag stared at the ship for a few more moments. It was too far away for her to even see movement on the deck, let alone individuals. But she knew that Inger was there. She sighed and joined Calder. He handed her one of the waterskins along with a bag of provisions.

"We should each carry our own supplies," he said. "Just in case."

Dag nodded and looped the bag and waterskin over one shoulder and settled them against her back. *Just in case*, Calder had said. What he'd meant was in case they had to split up. She didn't want to think about what could separate them, not when they were heading in the same direction as the ghost ship.

"Let's go." She took the lead, keeping her eyes open as she headed off along the dark road.

In the day the road had hugged the coastline, allowing cool sea breezes to reach them; now it went straight through tall stands of pine trees. She'd forgotten how unrelenting the insects could be.

She heard Calder's hand slap against skin, and she sighed. She'd had a glimpse of the sky a couple of dozen steps back and thought it was closing in on midnight. At this rate, they'd reach the farms at the outskirts of the city an hour or so before dawn.

"Will Ansdottir sail through the night?" she asked Calder. "Or will she anchor somewhere?"

"There's nowhere to anchor," Calder replied. "Not on any chart or map that I've seen."

"A way through the Teeth doesn't exist on any chart either," Dag said. "But we did it. Ansdottir has done it many times."

"You're right." Calder reached out and grabbed her arm, and

she turned to face him. "Ansdottir probably can find a place to anchor, which means they won't make Tarklee harbour tonight. That gives us some time before they attack."

"That sounds an awful lot like you want to make a plan," she said. He shrugged. "All right," Dag continued. "Let's make a plan. What is she targeting?"

"The same thing she targeted already: warehouses and ships." He smiled and picked up the pace. "And I know who we need to tell to be ready for her."

Dag had to hurry to catch up to him. When she did, she fell into step as they walked through the dark woods towards Tarklee.

A HAND SHOOK his shoulder, and Gustav snapped awake. The old man who called this corner home gestured to the bridge, and Gustav nodded his thanks. He'd used his Charisma on the old man and had shared what little food he had. In exchange, he'd promised to let Gustav catch a few hours of sleep while he watched for a young man crossing the bridge.

Gustav turned in time to see someone step from the bridge onto the South Tarklee side of the river. He dropped his chin to his chest: it was Vilis. His fellow student passed him, and Gustav rose to follow.

Since he had a good idea of where Vilis was heading, he was easier to follow. It was near dawn, and the sun was hovering at the horizon by the time Vilis knocked on the door and entered the warehouse. Gustav crept up to the window, but instead of voices, he heard the sounds of running feet followed by a muffled cry.

He quickly slipped through the door and into the warehouse, pressing his back against the door as his eyes adjusted to the dim light.

Was Vilis being attacked? Had something gone wrong?

Then the smell hit him. Blood and shit; and clouds of flies buzzing around it all. Someone or something had died here.

The sun peeked in through the window, illuminating a bucket on a table just outside of a doorway that led into a smaller room. A black trail led from there to an open door at the far end of the warehouse. Vilis stumbled out of the door, a hand over his mouth. He leaned over and retched, allowing Gustav time to dash into the small room.

Vilis headed towards him: had he seen him? No, Vilis went to the bucket, but after peering into it, he tipped it over. It was empty.

Gustav edged out of the room, reached his arm around Vilis's neck, and tightened his grip.

"Don't kill me, I won't tell," Vilis cried. He struggled, trying to loosen his captor's grip, but Gustav had learned how to fight from the same instructor and had sparred with Vilis many times. He was prepared for, and able to counter, all of his training mate's attempts to get free.

Finally, Vilis stopped struggling. Gustav grabbed a bloody shirt from the table and used it to tie Vilis's hands behind his back. Then he spun him around.

"Gustav! What are you doing here? You have to help me . . ." He paused. "Was it you? Did you kill her?"

"Kill who?"

"I don't know her name, but she's dead. In the back."

"She works for Tarmo Holt?" Vilis flinched at Holt's name, making Gustav think that he *knew* that what he was doing was wrong.

"I, I don't know."

"I'm pretty sure you do," Gustav said. "Since you met Holt here the other day. What are you giving him? What are you taking from Joosep's office and handing over to Tarmo Holt?"

"Nothing," he said. Gustav wanted to believe him, he really did but then, because of his Trait, he always wanted to believe Vilis. And because that reminded him how easy it was for people to like him because of his Trait, he did his best *not* to believe him.

"Do you know where Joosep is?" he asked.

"No."

This time he did believe Vilis; which meant that Tarmo Holt didn't trust him enough to let him know where he was keeping the Master Intelligencer.

"But you know that Holt has him," he said. Vilis didn't even bother to protest. "Or has he killed him already?"

"He's not hurting him," Vilis said. "He promised. He's just giving Joosep time to reconsider."

"Reconsider what?" Gustav frowned. Did Vilis really believe

Tarmo Holt was going to let Joosep live?

"Backing him to be permanently named Grand Freeholder."

"That's . . ." He was about to say impossible, but it made sense. Holt wanted to keep his position.

"Joosep will never allow it," Gustav said. "So if he hasn't already, Holt will have to kill him."

"He promised," Vilis insisted.

"I'm sure he did," Gustav replied. "Does your Trait make you believe liars? Or does it just make you a good one?" He grabbed Vilis's bound hands and pushed him towards the small room. He didn't think Vilis knew anything more about Joosep, and the longer Gustav stayed here, the more likely someone would come to investigate the smell. Or to meet with the dead woman, the way Vilis had.

"Someone will come, eventually," he said as he shoved Vilis into the room. He shut the door and jammed wood into the gap between the door and the floor. Vilis might even be able to get out by himself, but it would be long after he was gone.

He dropped the scarf beside the old man as he passed him and crossed the bridge. It would have been better, safer for him, if he'd been able to kill Vilis, but that wasn't something he could do. But now Vilis knew that Gustav was in the city, free, and trying to find Joosep. Would he tell Holt? Would it make any difference if he did? Gustav was already taking all the steps he could to be careful and stay safe.

THEY'D SPENT A few hours travelling through the farmland that bordered the city, and now, at midmorning, they were in a densely populated part of South Tarklee, nearing the river.

"You said North Tarklee?" Dag asked.

"Yes," he replied. "The Merchant Adventurers' office is there." They represented the owners of the ships the pirates likely wanted to destroy, if their targets at Nurmi were anything to go by.

"We need to cross the river soon," Dag said. "We should take New Bridge. It's in a rougher part of town."

If they crossed the river there, they'd be walking past the Hall, and anyone who might recognize either of them, in less than an hour. Dag's Trait meant that she probably wouldn't be noticed, and he'd been at sea for so long that few people knew him, so they might not need to worry. But he knew enough not to trust his Luck to keep them from being recognized.

"All right," Calder said. Despite growing up in the Hall, he hadn't spent much time in the city.

Dag led the way down a lane and headed west. The buildings they passed were progressively more dilapidated the farther they went. They turned north toward the river and New Bridge. Ahead of them, a group of people had gathered in the middle of the street.

"I'll find out what's going on," Dag said. She walked to the edge of the crowd and stopped to talk to a man. After a few minutes she returned to his side.

"Someone's been killed," she said, eyeing the crowd. "Under unusual circumstances—What? Don't let him see me." She turned to face him. "Tarmo Holt is here."

"Where?" Calder scanned the crowd, but he didn't see the Grand Freeholder. Was the man wearing a disguise? All he saw was a man in typical business attire who seemed to be asking questions of a woman at the centre of the crowd.

"I don't see him," he said. "Is he still here?"

Dag turned and looked around. "No. He's gone."

"I think we need to find out who owns that warehouse," Calder said. He didn't wait for Dag and instead, he strode up to the edge of the crowd. People edged out of his way as he made his way to the side of the man talking to the woman. She was a guard and wore the Swyford emblem on her cloak.

"I need to see inside," the man said.

"No one is allowed in that building," the woman replied. "We'll be investigating on behalf of the Clan Freeholder."

"I must see inside," the man said. "On behalf of my master."

"Is he the owner of this building?" the woman asked. "If he is, then I need his name."

The man frowned. "I need your name. My master is a very important man, and he will not appreciate you interfering with his property."

"His property is the scene of a killing," the woman said. "You can see my badge number clear enough. Your master is more than welcome to lodge a complaint with my Clan Freeholder. But you are not getting inside that building."

"I'll lodge the complaint myself," the man said. He frowned, jammed a hat onto his head, and stormed off.

"Good," the woman muttered. "At least then I'll know who owns this building." She turned to answer a question from someone else, and Calder felt a hand pluck at his arm. He looked behind him to find Dag pulling at him.

"Come on," she said.

He followed her through the crowd to a wider street that was lined with a few bedraggled vendor carts—he wasn't sure he wanted to know what they were selling—and a handful of beggars. The street led to the bridge.

"I think Tarmo Holt owns that warehouse," he said. "Someone wanted inside very badly, on behalf of his master: who is a very important man."

"Then it's a good thing I was able to get inside and take a look." She blew out a breath. "Someone was killed. It happened a day or so ago, and it was messy." She met his eyes. "The warehouse was empty. Whatever it was being used for, it wasn't to store goods. The body was at the far end, near what looked like an old stable." She paused and met his gaze. "And the body was not Joosep."

"But you think he was there," Calder said. "You think this is where Holt was holding Joosep."

"Yes. My Trait was triggered by a shirt. It was balled up and filthy, but I recognized it as Joosep's. I think he escaped by killing whoever was guarding him."

Calder nodded. He hoped it was true and that Joosep was free, but it didn't change their mission. "We still need to warn them about the ghost ship."

"I agree," Dag said. "Let's go."

CHAPTER 7

THE DRIED BLOOD on his trousers was attracting flies. Joosep shooed them away as he stared at the small door that was set into the crumbling wall.

He was so weak that it had taken him most of the day to travel a distance that should have only taken two hours. But he was here, finally. And now he was afraid to enter; afraid to find out whether this safe haven he'd put in place had kept Arnor safe.

But it would keep *him* safe. He'd be able to sleep, finally, and drink his fill of water. Food might pose a problem: he couldn't remember the last time he'd directed Arnor to replenish the stores of journey bread, pickled cabbage, and dried sausage.

When the street was empty, he shuffled across it to the door.

After a quick glance to make sure he wasn't being watched, he reached high above the door to a block of stone. It shifted when his fingers touched it, and eventually, he was able pull the stone out. The key was there, and his hope that his assistant had made it to this sanctuary evaporated.

He unlocked the door and entered a short hallway. No lamps had been lit, and he closed his eyes in grief: Arnor wasn't here. When Holt's comments had made it clear that he hadn't captured Arnor, Joosep had hope that his assistant had found safety. It was still possible that Arnor had fled the city and was safe somewhere far away. He hoped so: he would love his help, but he wanted him safe even more.

Joosep placed the key on a small table and spent a few minutes getting a lamp lit. Once that was done, he headed to the privy.

Much like in the Hall, a series of pipes brought water inside, although here they were fed from cisterns on the roof. Joosep filled the tub before stripping off his clothes and stepping in.

The water was lukewarm, and he sank into it gratefully. It was a luxury: even with the cisterns, water would need to be rationed. But he needed to be clean in order to feel human again.

His captivity had stripped his humanity from him: he knew that and had realized that it was happening. But that's also what had allowed him to survive. He touched the wound that hiding the shard of pottery had left in his side; it was now surrounded by the bruises his jailor had given him before he'd killed her.

If a shred more humanity had been left in him, he might not have been able to do that: live with pain in order to seize his chance and then fight to the death. And death for either of them would have sufficed; would have ended his captivity.

He gently rubbed his feet trying to both soothe and clean them; under the dirt was dried blood. The water was murky by the time he stood up and pulled the stopper that sent the water rushing through another set of pipes and out into the river.

Once he was dry, he found a clean pair of trousers and a shirt. Only then was he ready to see what supplies were available.

And that's when he realized that someone else *had* been here. A used mug sat next to a pot of cold tea. Joosep smiled as he felt the stove: it was still slightly warm. Arnor must have been here earlier today. Too tired to stay awake and wait for him to return, Joosep drank two mugs of water and ate three slices of the journey bread he found in a cupboard.

He lit a lamp as a signal to Arnor before heading into the small sleeping chamber and stretching out on one of the two cots. In moments, he was fast asleep.

For a second, he thought he was back in the stable; that the light that shone down on him was his jailer, coming to taunt him with a few drops of water. But his raging thirst had abated, and he was warm. And then he remembered that he'd killed his jailer and had escaped.

"Arnor?" His voice, unused for so many days, was a soft croak, but it was loud enough to wake his assistant, who was on the cot across from him. He was dressed and was sprawled on top of the covers, so he'd probably fallen asleep while waiting for him to wake. His eyes opened, and he sat up.

"Thank Nyorden you made it," Joosep said, each word stronger than the last. "I was worried."

"I was worried!" Arnor said. "Can I get you anything? Water? Tea? Soup?"

"Tea," he replied. "Haven't had that since I was taken . . . how many days?"

"Eight," Arnor said. "I'll make some tea and bring it to you."

"No, we need to get started." He sat up, but instead of rising, he leaned his head against the wall while Arnor left, taking the lamp with him. A few minutes later the lamp came back, and Arnor placed a steaming mug on the narrow table between the beds.

"Here, drink this."

"Thank you." He sipped the tea, enjoying the warmth that it spread throughout his body. "I meant to get up. There's so much to do."

"I know," Arnor said. "But I need to make sure you're well." He took the mug from him and set it back down on the table.

"How long was I asleep?"

"Eight hours that I'm aware of," Arnor said. "It's close to midnight, and I came back late mid-afternoon. I saw the light, and then I found you. You can't believe how glad I was to see you. Even though you look terrible."

"I'll recover," Joosep said. He had to, there really was too much to do. "But the key. It was in its hiding spot."

"Oh, that." Arnor looked sheepish. "I'm not tall enough to reach it, so I always just used the one you kept in your desk. I had it with me."

"Did they come for you?" he asked, when what he meant was had they tried to hurt him.

"No," Arnor replied, scowling. "I left as soon as I couldn't find you. Someone betrayed you; a student I think, but I don't know which one."

"Vilis. I saw his handwriting on a list of instructors Tarmo Holt showed me."

"Holt knows who the instructors are?" Arnor asked.

"Not all," Joosep replied. "I know which list Vilis found."

"Thank Nyorden. But some are compromised," Arnor said. "Along with some of the students." He frowned. "I saw him," Arnor said. "Right before I left. Vilis. I might have been able to stop him, if I'd stayed." He looked away. "I don't have a Trait, so I was extra careful. Maybe too careful."

"No such thing," Joosep replied. "You're alive and in the exact place where you can be the most effective." He sighed. "As am I, finally." His eyes drooped shut, and he felt the mug being taken away. Then the light was gone, and he sank into another deep sleep.

DAG STARED AT the building that sat next to the pier. According to Calder, it was the main office of the Merchant Adventurers. It was still a few hours before dawn, and the office was dark. Calder shifted beside her, and she looked over at him.

It was her watch, and he was asleep.

As they travelled the streets away from the warehouse in South Tarklee they hadn't heard any rumours of an attack. Word of a ghost ship would travel fast, so they felt safe assuming that the pirates hadn't attacked. Not yet.

They'd kept to the rougher parts of South Tarklee until dusk; people were likely to ask fewer questions there. They'd each managed to grab an hour of sleep during the day, but it hadn't made up for the sleep they missed last night. Once the sun had set, they'd crossed over to North Tarklee and made their way to the port area.

Dag had found this hiding spot a few hours ago, and Calder had offered to take the first watch, but although she was exhausted and had closed her eyes, Dag didn't think she'd actually slept.

Her worry about an attack by the ghost ship went far beyond what it meant for the Fair Seas Treaty Alliance: because Inger was on that ship. Dag was caught between concern for her sister's safety and anger and despair that she was now an enemy of the Alliance.

Someone walking along the pier stopped at the door to the

office, and after a moment, they entered. A minute later, a light showed in the windows.

"Calder," Dag whispered. "Someone's there." She reached out to squeeze his shoulder. He shifted at her touch but didn't stir, so she shook him.

"At the office?" Calder mumbled.

"Yes, they lit a lamp." She stood up and stretched, trying to work the kinks out of her cold and cramped muscles.

"It's early for someone to be there," Calder said from her side. He stifled a yawn and she turned back to the pier.

Light streamed out of three windows now: more than one lamp had been lit.

"Would they have a meeting at this time of day?" she asked. "The fishermen aren't even here yet." Merchant Adventurers dealt with shipping, and as far as she could tell, none of the ships in the harbour, or the barges that carried the goods up the river into the city, were stirring.

"I don't know, let's find out." He led the way past the stack of barrels they'd been hiding behind and out onto the pier.

Dag stopped behind him when he paused in front of the door to the office. Instead of knocking, he reached out and pushed the door open.

"Do you have your patch?" he asked her. She nodded. "Good." She followed him into the well-lit building, closing the door once they were both inside.

"Hello?" Calder called. "I wish to speak to the Master Captain."

"Oh, it's too early for him." A man wearing a dark shirt and trousers came out of another room. "He won't be in for hours. Do you have an appointment?"

"No, and I need you to call him here immediately," Calder said. "It is extremely important."

"On whose authority?" he asked, frowning.

Dag pulled her patch out of her waistband and held it up.

"On the authority of the Fair Seas Treaty Alliance," she said. "We are both agents, and this harbour is in danger."

"Let me see that," the man said, reaching for the patch.

Something about the way he held himself made Dag snatch her patch back. She stared at him, and he glared back at her. That was not the behaviour of a low-ranking worker dealing with a situation above his station.

"Who are you?" Dag asked, "and what are you doing in this office?"

"I have duties here," the man replied.

The itch started between her shoulder blades. In light of his belligerence, his clothing seemed more out of place than she'd thought before.

Calder sent her a questioning look, and she shrugged. Her Trait was telling her that this man was hiding something. She tried to step past him to look into the room he'd been in, but he blocked her way.

"Are you interfering with an agent of the Alliance?" she asked. "You never did say who you were. What are you hiding back there?" The man pushed her, but she was ready for it. She grabbed his arm and swung him past her, forcing his back into Calder. Calder grabbed both of the other man's arms and twisted them behind his back, holding him tight as he struggled to break free.

"I'll be right back," she said to Calder and stepped into the next room. And into chaos. It was an office, but it was in the middle of being ransacked. She studied the room: they'd interrupted him before he'd been able to find what he was looking for. She leaned out the door to look at Calder.

"He's been looking for something," she said. The man scowled as he struggled against Calder's hold on him. "I don't think he found it."

"Can you?" Calder asked.

"I'll find something," she grinned. "I can't promise if it will be what *he* was looking for."

"I'll see what I can learn from our friend here," Calder replied.

Dag stood in the middle of the room and slowly turned, scanning as she went. What had been hidden here? She paused. Something about the way the light hit one plank in the wall made her walk over to it. Yes, there was a hidden compartment. She pulled the plank away from the wall, revealing a sheaf of papers.

She leafed through them. They were all titles to ships, but why would they be hidden? Wouldn't the owners need to be on record? Except the owner of every single ship named here was the same. Tarmo Holt. A secret. Why else had they been hidden?

She replaced the plank and selected one ship title: the *Tazeyar*, named after the god of water. She knelt beside a pile of documents that had been tossed onto the floor. They looked very similar to the one she had in her hand. She flipped through them: yes, here it was, the *Tazeyar*. And Tarmo Holt's name was not on this title.

She kept aside the two papers for the *Tazeyar* and stuffed the rest of them inside her shirt.

"I have what we need," she said as she re-entered the main room, waving the papers. "Two title papers for the same ship. At least I assume it's the papers that are duplicates and not the ships."

"Is that what you were looking for?" Calder asked their prisoner. The man scowled but didn't answer.

"I'll take that as a yes," Dag said. "And I'm not so sure the Master Captain will be interested in hearing our warning."

"Why?" Calder asked.

"The papers hidden in his office," Dag said, "give title of all of these ships to Tarmo Holt. But the filed records show that they belong to someone else."

"Then it's just as well no one contacted the Master Captain," Calder replied. "We can still take this piece of *skit* to the Harbour Master, at least he—" He stopped speaking and stared out the window. "We're too late."

Dag turned, and a flare of light hit her face as a ship anchored in the harbour blazed into flames. "*Skit!*"

"Hey!" Calder shouted.

Dag turned in time to see the man Calder had been holding bolt away from him and race out of the building.

"I think this is what we need anyway," Dag said, holding up the papers. "I'll find the rest of the duplicates while you raise the alarm."

"Yes." He spun and ran out of the building while Dag went back into the office. She'd found a third duplicate ship title when the bells started ringing.

CALDER WATCHED PEOPLE rush to the waterfront. One dock was on fire, along with a couple of barges that were close to the mouth of the river. The ghost ship was a dark shadow lit by the dozen or so flaming vessels that were anchored out in the harbour. Shouts could be heard coming from the burning ships, and Calder hoped everyone on board was able to get to safety. Most sailors could deal with whatever the sea sent their way: storms, high waves, lack of wind, but fire on a ship terrified even the bravest souls.

Dozens of fishing boats were being rowed out into the harbour to pick up survivors: the ships were beyond saving.

Three ships that were anchored closest to shore were untouched. Calder thought that they would be targeted next, but the ghost ship ignored them and instead sailed towards the far side of the harbour. His focus narrowed on the three ships as his Trait was triggered. Why those ships were spared was important.

"I found them all," Dag said as she joined him. "Duplicate ownership titles for fourteen ships. One batch saying they all belong to Holt, and the other papers, the ones that had been filed properly, showing multiple owners. I think Holt wanted them in his hands instead of hiding with the Master Captain."

"That sounds likely," Calder said. "So, our friend who escaped works for Holt."

Dag grinned. "Holt won't like it that we have these." She waved the papers.

"We need to find out if the three ships there," Calder pointed to the intact ships, "are included in those papers."

"In the meantime, we need a place to hide," Dag said. "And figure out our next steps."

Calder sighed. "Especially since our would-be thief got away. Even if he has bad news to deliver, he'll know that keeping the fact that he saw us from Holt would make things worse. Tarmo Holt will soon know that someone in Tarklee knows about him." He turned, and Dag fell into step beside him as they made their way from the pier and into the streets of North Tarklee.

The farther they got from the waterfront and the cleanup from the fire, the emptier the streets were. It was still not quite dawn. Calder rubbed a hand across his eyes. He needed a proper sleep, and he was sure Dag did too.

"There's a wayfarer hostel a few blocks from here," he said to Dag. "We could get some rest there." He thought they had enough coin: hoped they had enough coin.

"I have a better place in mind," Dag replied. "Mine and Inger's apartment at the Hall."

"That doesn't sound safe," Calder said.

"Nowhere is safe," Dag replied. "But we'll slip in and stay a few hours. I need something from Joosep's office."

"What?" Calder didn't see how anything could be so important that they would risk being seen in the one place where they were most likely to be recognized.

"Joosep's notes on Tarmo Holt," she said. "He's behind all of this, and we need to know what Joosep found out about what Holt is doing and why."

Calder stopped and put a hand on Dag's arm. She turned and met his gaze. "Your Trait?" She nodded, and he sighed. "All right, get us there without being seen."

"That's my specialty." Dag grinned and led the way down a narrow street.

He never would have even noticed the small door set into the corner of the wall if Dag hadn't stopped in front of it.

"It's a back way into the Hall," she said. She reached above the door frame and pulled a stone out of the wall and grabbed something that was hidden there.

She held up a key. "I don't think Joosep knows I know about this." She fitted the key into the lock and pushed the small door inward before replacing the key above the door and pushing the stone back into place.

Calder followed her through the door and into a narrow hallway. The walls were stone, the blocks rising unbroken on either side. Dag shut the door and locked it, leaving them in the dark.

"I'll lead," she said. He felt her hands on his arm as she edged past him. He gripped her hand, and she slowly led them forward.

This early, the Hall was still and silent, and they didn't run across anyone else in the corridors. Calder hoped it was because of the early hour and not because the Intelligencer school was closed or disbanded in Joosep's absence.

Light filtered towards them, and when they reached the source, Dag paused to crane her head around a corner. With a quick backward wave, she sprinted ahead. Calder followed her along a short hall and through a door she opened. Once inside, she shut the door and leaned against it, her ear pressed to the wood.

Calder put his back to hers and scanned the room for threats.

A couch and a couple of chairs were pushed against the wall, and a long, low table sat in front of them. Two open doors opposite each other led off the sitting room into bedrooms, he assumed. Hooks near the door held a coat and an empty pack, and a pair of slippers were askew below it.

The room looked like it had been searched. A carpet had been pulled off the floor and was piled in a corner; a shelf was empty, its contents, books and papers and small knick-knacks, were scattered on the table.

"I don't think anyone saw us," Dag said.

He heard her sharp intake of breath, and when he turned to look, she was frowning.

"I wonder what Holt's people thought to find here?" he said. "Is anything missing?"

Dag walked around the room, studying the disarray. She peered through each door before stopping in the middle of the room. She closed her eyes and spun slowly before opening her eyes again. "Nothing is missing," she said. "Not that there's anything here to find."

"Good," he said. "If they searched here, that might mean they didn't find what they were looking for in Joosep's office."

"They didn't touch Inger's room," Dag said. "I guess they really do trust her."

"It could be because she's not an Intelligencer," Calder said. "They might be targeting us."

"I suppose," she agreed but didn't seem convinced.

"You need to go while it's still early," Calder said. "If you really think that you can find what Joosep hid in his office."

She snorted, and he knew he'd taken her mind off her sister, for now. "Of course, I can find it. As long as it's still there: as long as Joosep didn't destroy it. Are you staying here?"

"No, I have someone I want to see, if I can. An old instructor."

"Can you trust him?"

"Her, yes," he replied. "She was here at the Hall long before Joosep was put in charge." He hadn't heard that Nadez had left the city, but she had always kept her plans to herself. Which was one of many reasons why she and Joosep didn't get along. And why she and Calder, who didn't make plans, did.

"All right," Dag said. "We'll meet back here in two hours." She met his eyes. "And if one of us is not back by then, the other has to get to safety and try to stop Tarmo Holt from doing whatever he's doing."

"Agreed." Calder nodded even though he already knew that if he was the only one who made it back safely, he would try to find Dag. "Let's go."

He followed Dag out into the hall. At the second intersecting corridor, he touched her arm and gestured left. She nodded and pointed right. After making sure the corridor was empty, they split up, heading in opposite directions.

GUSTAV PULLED THE hat down lower. He'd been looking for a place to sleep when the bells started ringing. He'd followed a group of sailors to the docks and then tucked himself under a low tree branch to watch as people tried in vain to save the burning ships.

Most of the dock had been spared, although a section that jutted out into the bay had burned. Fishing boats filled with half-dressed sailors landed nearer the shore on the undamaged part of the dock. The survivors of the burning ships huddled together and stared out at the remains of their homes and livelihoods.

Flames illuminated a pale ship and cries of a ghost ship carried across to him. But it didn't look like a ghost ship: the sea parted before its prow, and the sails flapped in the wind. It sailed past a burning ship, and flames backlit figures darting across the deck and climbing amongst the sails. A pale woman stood at the prow, next to a solidly built figure. Then the ghost ship slipped past the burning ship, leaving only the pale woman visible in the night.

If he hadn't been staring at the deck of the ghost ship, he would have missed it. The pale woman pulled a dark covering or cloak over her and all but disappeared. But she hadn't completely covered her hair, and he was able to track her as she headed to the side of the ship.

A dinghy! They were lowering a small boat from the deck of

the ship, and instead of being white, like the rest of the ship, this boat was dark.

When no one seemed to pay attention to him, he slipped out from under the tree and joined the crowd.

A ghost ship didn't paint its dinghy black. Pirates must be in that boat. Who else would destroy the ships in the harbour? And he had a very good idea who the pirates were coming to meet. The same man they'd met with in the past: Tarmo Holt.

Gustav intended to be there too, to confirm that Holt was meeting with the pirates who had just attacked Tarklee Harbour. And if possible, he'd find out what else they were planning.

Joosep's office showed traces of being searched, but the evidence of it was subtler than the signs left in her and Inger's apartment.

Drawers were not quite closed, and books were slightly crooked on the shelves. She'd been in Joosep's office enough times to know that both he and his assistant Arnor were meticulously neat.

But had they found Joosep's notes on Tarmo Holt during their search? She couldn't imagine Joosep not hiding them, not when Holt had legitimate access to any place in the Hall, including the office of the Master Intelligencer. So where would he have hidden them?

With her hands on her hips she looked around the room. There were a few places she'd taken note of when she'd been in here with Joosep, so she started with them.

The back wall of the bookcase did have a secret compartment, but all she found there was a small purse full of coins. She tied the purse to her belt: it wasn't what she was looking for, but coin would be useful all the same.

She turned the desk chair around and pulled the brass corner fitting from the wooden strut off the back. There was a small indentation that looked like it had once held a key, but it was empty now.

She sat down in the chair in order to see the room from Joosep's perspective. Would he want to be able to see the place where he'd hidden his most secret information? Her Trait wasn't showing her anything obvious. Unless . . .

She left Joosep's office and went out to Arnor's smaller work area. Immediately, her eye was drawn to the floor beneath the desk. She had to move it: one foot of the desk rested on the flagstone that had caught her attention, but once she did, it was easy enough to pry the stone out.

That was what she'd noticed: the stone was shiny on one side, as though it had been polished. And in a sense it had been; it had been polished by fingers gripping it to lift it out.

She set it aside, shaking her head. This small detail was so obvious to her, how could Joosep miss it?

She paused. What if Joosep thought his Trait was stronger than it was? What if he assumed that he didn't overlook hidden things when he did? Because if he could miss that the shiny flagstone revealed a secret, it was possible that he'd missed signs that signalled Tarmo Holt's actions were not in the Three's best interests. Questions for another day: right now, she had secrets to uncover.

She pulled out a wrapped bundle and quickly uncovered a notebook. She flipped through it to make sure it was what she was looking for: Joosep hadn't named Holt, but a few details confirmed that the notes were about the Grand Freeholder.

She tucked the notebook under her shirt and put the wrapping back into the hiding place. Before replacing the stone, she did her best to scuff the shiny edges, then she set the flagstone into place and shoved the desk back to its original position.

Was there anything else? She wouldn't have another chance to search this office, but she was running out of time: the Hall would be stirring. She took another look around Arnor's work area, but nothing else caught her attention. She had to assume that she'd found everything that was important.

After a quick glance to make sure the outer hall was empty, she left and headed back to her own room. And Calder, she hoped.

CALDER BLEW OUT a breath. It was almost time to meet Dag, and he still hadn't been able to find Nadez. He knew she'd left the Hall, but he had no idea where she was living now. It wasn't as though he could stop anyone to ask if they knew where the former Intelligencer was. If he didn't find her soon, he would have to leave this task undone, even though she was the one person he trusted to notify all Intelligencers, students *and* instructors, of the dangers posed by Tarmo Holt.

Despite no longer working for Joosep, Nadez kept up with the workings of the Intelligencers and the Alliance. If she was missing because she'd gone into hiding, it might mean that she already realized that something was wrong. Or perhaps she'd simply become more reclusive since the last time they'd spoken.

He peered around a corner. This was the only other place he knew to look for her. She'd shown it to him once, long ago, when they had been talking about home.

Calder had arrived at the Hall at the age of six, so to him it *was* home. But Nadez said that home was where he was from not where he was now. Then she'd taken him out into the city and had shown him this small stable.

It had been her father's she'd told him, and the only part of a small lodging house he'd owned that was still standing. Nadez had bought it as soon as she could afford to. She'd chuckled when she'd told him that the coin had come from expenses she'd been given for an assignment. She'd completed the task quickly and had used the coin that was left to buy this place.

Calder had found out later that she'd never been punished over her use of that coin. And that to this day, Joosep, who had learned about her deception and reported it, was angry about both her misappropriation of the coin, and that she hadn't been disciplined for it.

The little stable looked abandoned though, so he was surprised when the door didn't open.

"Get over here and off the street," a voice barked. He turned to see his old instructor glaring at him from one side of the stable.

"Come on," Nadez said, "before you're noticed." She stepped around the corner, and Calder hurried to catch up to her. She slid three planks to one side and motioned him forward. Calder stepped past Nadez into a dim space. She silently slid the planks back over the opening, cutting off the light. She grabbed his arm.

"What trouble have you brought to me this time?" Nadez said in his ear.

He smiled at her old greeting. "I would like to say that it's not my fault." His former instructor snorted at his usual excuse. "But it is trouble. Serious trouble."

"I expected as much." Nadez sighed and brushed past him. "Come along."

Calder followed her to a small room. Light spilled in from a small window set high on the far wall, illuminating a sleeping pallet, a couple of chairs, and a table that was strewn with papers and scrolls.

"Joosep hasn't been seen for over a week, and now I hear that a couple of instructors have gone missing," Nadez said. She sat down on one chair and gestured to the other. "I know that you were one of the last Intelligencers to meet with Joosep."

Calder positioned the chair to face her and sat down. She looked tired. Her grey hair was scraped off her face into one thick braid that hung down her back, and her usual black shirt and trousers sagged on her wiry frame.

"Yes," Calder said. "I've heard from him since. A message was sent to him that was intercepted by his captors."

"His captors? You know that for a fact?"

"I do," Calder replied. "Joosep replied to that message: it was in his hand writing, but there was no baisa included in the money that was sent, and the message was coded. Tarmo Holt has captured Joosep."

"Holt!" Nadez frowned. "He was always too ambitious for my liking."

"He's working with pirates," Calder said. "We—I'm not sure what his plans are, but I don't think he has any intention of stepping down as Grand Freeholder."

"Hmm," Nadez said. "Pirates. I'm not surprised. The man has always been willing to do anything for power. Rumours were that he threatened to expose secrets of his biggest rival for Grand Freeholder, therefore clearing his path to the position. I couldn't find proof, and Joosep told me that he would manage him." She shook her head. "It seems that Joosep was wrong and he couldn't, *didn't,* manage him." She looked up and met Calder's eyes. "Who else is part of your *we*?"

"Another Intelligencer," Calder said. He trusted Nadez, but should he tell her about Dag? If he did, would he have to tell her about Inger too?

"All right," Nadez replied. "You don't need to say a name.

Besides, there aren't that many of you, so I'll figure it out eventually. How do you know about the pirates?"

"I was on Strongrock when the *Neas*, Holt's ship, put into port."

"Strongrock pirates: so, Margit Ansdottir is in the thick of this too, then." Nadez sighed and glanced away for a moment. "This is a task I never sought out," she said. "I turned down being Master Intelligencer once, but in Joosep's absence, I suppose I have no choice." She picked up a notebook and grabbed a quill and removed the stopper of an ink bottle. "Report."

Chapter 8

Gustav crept closer to the traps and nets laid out beside a fisherman's small boat. He'd had to make a wide circle around the buildings that ringed the bay in order to follow the black dinghy to the small dock it was now tied up to. Two of the people in the dinghy stepped out, and when the hood of a cloak slipped, he had a good look at a woman with white blonde hair and an annoyingly familiar face. He was trying to remember where he'd seen her when his view of her was blocked by a very large woman.

She stepped onto the dock like she owned it, and Gustav admitted that he wouldn't be willing to fight her for it. Because she carried herself with such authority, he paused instead of creeping closer. And that saved him.

"Captain," a voice said from the other side of the stack of traps. "What have you done?" A shadow stepped into view, but Gustav didn't need to see a face to recognize Tarmo Holt.

"What we agreed on," the large woman replied.

"That was not what *I* agreed to," Holt said. He walked a dozen steps and stopped just short of the dock. "You destroyed the wrong ships." Holt sounded angry, but the woman he'd called captain smiled.

"Fire is a tricky thing," she said. "You know that. I'm here to collect what I'm owed."

"I should keep it," Holt said. "Your incompetence has cost

me more than your payment."

"If you want to keep the three ships we spared, you'll give me what's due to me." The captain took a step towards Holt, who shrank away from her. "And I don't like being called incompetent."

"What do you call bringing her?" Holt gestured to the blonde woman. "Her presence was not part of any agreement."

"She knows the place better than I do," the captain replied. "And I like her."

"She has other ties that I do not like," Holt replied.

"Give me what's owed and we'll both be gone," the captain said. "And you'll still have three ships in Tarklee Harbour."

Holt frowned but held up a satchel, and at the captain's urging, the blonde woman approached him and took the bag when he held it out to her. She handed it to the captain.

"I have another task for you," Holt said.

"I thought I was incompetent?"

"No one else can do this," Holt said. "And you will enjoy it."

"Will I?" the captain asked.

"Yes. The sailor named Rahm. Find his people."

"I know the Rahm you mean. He's a fine sailor," the captain said. "A real shame that he wouldn't join me. What do you want done when I find his people?"

"Dead, starving, burned out of their homes; I really don't much care," Holt said. "But I want Rahm to know that there are consequences for crossing me."

"Should I look for him as well?"

"No, leave him for me," Holt said. "Along with the woman he's with. When I find them, I want to be able to tell him that his family has been destroyed."

"You're not touching one of mine," the captain said. She pulled the blonde woman closer to her. "What's mine stays mine."

"Just make sure she doesn't cause trouble for me," Holt said. "I'll send word when I need you again." Without waiting for a reply, Holt turned and left.

Gustav stayed crouched where he was until the women on the dock stepped back into the black dinghy and were half way to their ghostly ship. Then he made his way into streets that were starting to fill with merchants getting ready for the day's trade.

DAG PACED IN front of the door. She should have left by now. The two-hour mark had passed with no sign of Calder, and she was afraid that now it was too late in the day to sneak out of the Hall unnoticed. Or for him to return safely.

What could be keeping him? Had he been caught? She turned and strode the few steps across the floor. She'd save him if he'd been captured. They were a team now: they'd become one the minute he'd rescued her from Ursa and Hanne, and she wasn't leaving without him. The door jiggled as someone tried to open it, and Dag rushed over to it.

"Calder?" she whispered. When she heard his answer, she flicked the lock and moved aside to give him room to enter. Once he was inside, she relocked the door. She pressed her forehead against it for a moment before turning to face him.

"I'm sorry I'm late," Calder said. "I wasn't sure you'd still be here."

"I almost wasn't." She should be angry, but all she felt was relief. She repressed the urge to throw herself into his arms and walked past him to the sit in a chair. "Were you late because of your Trait?"

"I don't think so," Calder replied. "It took some time to find the person I needed to speak to."

"Your old instructor," Dag said. "What news did she have?"

"A couple of instructors are missing," Calder replied. "And she's appointed herself Master Intelligencer in Joosep's absence."

"What? Does she think Joosep is dead? I'm certain that he wasn't the person killed at the warehouse."

"She hasn't heard anything about Joosep," Calder said. "We *know* that he was alive and being held by Holt a few days ago, and we *think* he might have been able to escape that warehouse. But realistically, we have to be prepared for the worst. At least now someone is in charge of the Intelligencers and ready to work against Holt."

"Who is she that she can put herself in charge? Does she know all of the instructors?" Joosep always kept the students and instructors in separate training groups. She didn't think even the instructors knew all of the students.

"Yes," Calder replied. "She was chosen Master Intelligencer years ago, but she turned it down. That's how it fell to Joosep."

"Oh, I heard rumours . . ." She frowned. "I think Joosep mentioned her once; not by name but as someone who wasn't following his orders."

"That's her. She's been staying informed about the organization ever since she left the Intelligencers."

"Why?" Dag asked. "Did Joosep know?"

"I doubt he knew," Calder said. "And I don't think I was the only one, but I told her things in order to get her opinion. Nadez has a tremendous understanding of politics."

"And Joosep doesn't," Dag replied. "Which is one of the reasons Tarmo Holt's actions never caused him any concern."

"Yes." Calder leaned against the door for a moment before stepping away. "I think it's safe for us to leave now, but the question is where do we go?"

Dag rose and padded to the window of her sleeping chamber and pulled the curtain open an inch. The sun was up and although it was still early, she could hear sounds of carts being wheeled through the streets below. She went to the doorway and leaned against it.

"I think we should wait until nightfall," she said. "And rest until then. You take Inger's room." She gestured with her chin. "I know of a safe place where we can go: another one of Joosep's secrets. However, I've never actually been to it, and I don't think it wise to search for it in daylight." Without waiting for a reply, she eased back into her room, closed the door, and sat down on the bed.

She heard the sound of the other door closing and sighed. Sleep was the best idea, really, but she'd been abrupt because she felt awkward with Calder. They'd shared a bed at Pavil's small house, but that had somehow seemed more innocent than this. Perhaps it was the fact that they'd been with Pavil, or perhaps it was that just now she'd been so afraid that Calder had been captured. She wanted nothing more than to hold him close. But that could jeopardize their mission. So instead, she stretched out on top of her bed and tried to fall asleep.

CALDER STRETCHED AND then sat up, dangling his legs off the side of the bed. He couldn't remember the last time he'd slept in such comfort. Maybe not since he'd left the Hall and began his Intelligencer career. He certainly didn't have a bed this nice at his mother's house. He snorted. A life on the sea forced you to get used to sleeping in hammocks strung three deep and ignoring the snores and farts of the rest of your crew.

He rose and threw on his clothes before padding to the window. It was dusk. He'd slept for about ten hours. He yawned. But he'd needed it. Dag had been right to have them stay here. It was as safe as anywhere could be; it had already been searched, and both occupants were known to be missing.

He opened the door into the main room, and Dag looked up from where she sat at the table. A notebook sat in front of her along with a mug of tea and a stack of papers.

"I've made tea," she said. "But there's nothing to eat. Oh, and I've changed into clean clothes, but I doubt there's anything here that will fit you. Sorry."

"Thanks. Tea is more than I expected. And I can still clean up a bit even without a change of clothes." A smaller door rested between the two rooms. "I'll be right back." He headed to the privy. There was no shower, just a tub, and he looked at it longingly, but in the end decided on a quick wash. His stomach grumbled, and he ignored it as he rejoined Dag.

He sat down and picked the mug up from the table and took a sip. "Thank you." Dag nodded but didn't say anything.

"You could have woken me up," he said into the silence.

"We couldn't have left anyway." She shrugged. "There was some activity out in the hallway: I think because of the fire in the harbour. It's been quiet for over an hour now though." She got up and pressed her ear to the door and nodded.

"Still quiet," she said when she returned to the table and picked up the stack of papers. "Ownership papers for fourteen ships," she said. "Every single one has a duplicate that lists Tarmo Holt as the owner." She tapped the papers. "My Trait says that this is important, but I don't know why."

"He's either hiding that he actually owns the ships, or he's going to somehow steal them from the true owners. Are any of the owners the same?"

"No. Each person owns a single ship." She sighed. "I'll find the truth eventually, but I want to know now."

"And what did you find in Joosep's office?"

"An account of Joosep's dealings with Tarmo Holt," she said. "He started documenting all of their meetings a few months after Holt became Grand Freeholder."

"Do you think he knew even then that he didn't trust him?" Calder was surprised. "Joosep never once implied that he was worried about Holt." But could some of his missions have targeted information about Holt's shipping concerns without him knowing it? He'd have to think about that.

"Nor to me either," Dag said. "But I did only have the one assignment. To see what kind of man the next Grand Freeholder was."

"Huh. Well, we won't figure it out from in here." He eyed her. "Will we?"

"No. It's time to go." She stacked the notebook and papers, grabbed a small pack from a peg by the door, and shoved them in. Then she looped the pack across one shoulder.

"You know a safe place, you said."

"I do. Joosep has a hiding place. I saw the plans for it once. I know which street it's on, but what it looks like from the outside? I expect I'll know when I find it."

"You mean you hope your Trait can find it," Calder said. Smiling, he held up a hand to stop her from disagreeing with him. "That was not a criticism. I was just enjoying you using your Trait the way I use mine. And I trust your Trait the same as I trust mine." He stood up and joined her at the door. "I'll stay a pace or two behind you. Just in case."

"No argument?" Dag asked. "About why I should go first?"

"You're the one who lives here. I assume you know the safest route out of the Hall?"

She nodded. "I do but being back in the Hall reminds me that Inger seems to question every decision I make."

"I see." And he did. As he followed her out into the hall, he wondered that he hadn't seen them argue more. They were probably opposites in more than just their Traits. Maybe there was a good reason for Joosep to not train Inger, especially if it meant she and Dag would expect to work as a team. Opposite Traits would cause nothing but friction while complementary Traits like his and Dag's could increase their chances of success.

Dag did know a little-used exit, and sooner than he expected, she led them out a small door and into a deserted dead-end alley. It was dark, but he smelled what he hoped was nothing worse than a stinking pile of kitchen waste. It sat a few feet from the door, and he heard rodents skitter away from it.

Dag signalled for him to stay behind her, and he crouched by the door as she jogged to an intersecting street. She peered around a corner and then waved him forward.

Looking past her shoulder, he saw a wider lane that had a couple of hand pulled merchant carts pushed up against a building. The carts looked worn, and someone huddled underneath one of them. Even from where he stood, he could see that the cloth covering it had been patched many times. Probably a pair of vendors taking turns safeguarding their meagre livelihoods while they got some sleep.

Dag turned and met his eyes and signalled that she would go first; he lifted his chin in response. She pulled her hood up over her hair and stepped away from the side of the building and into the street. She walked calmly, her head high, not looking at the carts as she passed them.

She was almost at the next cross street when the person under the cart stood up and stepped into the middle of the street, facing Dag, watching her.

Other than to pull a scarf tighter around their shoulders, the person didn't move, but something about the way their attention was fixed on Dag made Calder's focus narrow. As soon as his Trait activated, he rushed toward the shrouded figure.

"HEY! LET GO of me!" Gustav thrashed against the arms that pinned his own to his side. At least now he was certain that it was her: the woman from the ghost ship. At the sounds of his voice and struggle, she retraced her steps.

"He was under the cart?" she asked.

"Yes," a man answered beside his ear. "He was staring at you."

"But not following?" The woman peered at him, and he gave her his widest smile.

"Good evening," he said. "I did see you go past my cart and was wondering if there was a chance to make one last sale tonight." He smiled and dropped his head in a bow as low as possible while being held the way he was. When he raised his head, his smile faltered. The woman was frowning at him: his

Charisma wasn't working. How could that be?

"I have a piece of blue silk that would set off your blonde hair wonderfully," he said, trying to infuse his Trait into the words.

"You may have seen a piece of silk once," the man growled into his ear. "But there isn't one in that sorry lot of threadbare goods."

"How do you know what colour my hair is?" the woman asked softly, and Gustav cursed himself. A hood covered her hair, but he'd known it was the same woman he'd seen this morning. She pulled a hank of white-blonde hair from beneath her hood.

Suddenly, she laughed and pulled her hood down.

"He's one of us," she said. "Or at least a student. Gustav, right?"

He was so surprised that he barely noticed that his arms had been freed. "How do you know?" Even if they were Intelligencers, they shouldn't know who he was. Was that what Vilis had found in Joosep's office? A list of every Intelligencer and student? But that still didn't explain how *she* knew *him*.

"My Trait," she said. "And yours is . . . being likeable?"

"Charisma," he replied before he could stop himself. How did she know?

"We're too exposed," the man said, and Gustav turned to look at him. And his heart sank. A Pilalian. He was probably from the ghost ship too.

The woman scanned the lane for a moment. "This way." She led them past the carts in the direction opposite to the one she'd been travelling. A few feet farther, she pried a board loose from a ramshackle building that leaned against a stone wall. The Pilalian pushed him inside a small, narrow opening. Before his eyes could adjust, the other two crowded in beside him.

"Gustav."

Even in the dim light, her hair shone.

"Do you know where Joosep is?"

"No," he said, suddenly even more confused. Tarmo Holt had Joosep, didn't he? "You should have asked Tarmo Holt when you met him this morning."

"When I met . . ." She looked over his head. "Inger." She turned back to him. "Where did you see . . . me . . . and Holt."

"At the docks, right after the fire." He paused. "Why don't

you know? That wasn't you?"

"My sister," she said. "My twin." She sighed. "She's working against us. I'm Dagrun Lund, and this is Calder Rahmson. We're both Intelligencers: we're trying to find Joosep and figure out what Tarmo Holt is up to."

"You really are Intelligencers?" Should he doubt them? He was so relieved to find some fully trained Intelligencers working against Tarmo Holt that he was worried he would trust them too easily. "Prove it."

His companions each pulled their patches out and showed him. He pulled his own from where he'd tucked it into his waistband and sighed. He would trust them.

"Gustav Gunnarson," he said. "Pleased to meet you Dagrun Lund and Calder Rahms—"

"Rahmson," Calder said, but Gustav barely heard him.

"Rahm is your father," he said. "I heard them, this morning. Holt told you, I mean your sister, and someone he called captain to find people close to a sailor named Rahm. He didn't care if they were killed or starved as long as he could tell Rahm that they had suffered."

"*Skit*!" Calder said. "Was the captain a large woman?"

"Yes," Gustav replied. "Acted like she was in charge, even with the Grand Freeholder."

"Skit, skit, skit." Calder slapped a hand against the stone wall. "Ansdottir is looking for my family."

"I'm so sorry," Dag said.

"That's you?" Gustav asked. "Rahm is you?"

"That's the name Tarmo Holt knows me by," Calder replied. "And Margit Ansdottir, captain of the pirates."

"That's who she was!" The only thing that surprised Gustav was that the leader of the pirates was a woman. "I told Joosep that Holt was meeting with pirates."

"How did you know?" Dagrun asked.

"And why did you tell Joosep?" Calder finished.

"I, uh." Joosep had called it a secret mission—did that mean he couldn't disclose it to Intelligencers? He had already decided to trust them. Besides, these two seemed to know more than he did. "Joosep asked me to use my Trait to get close to Tarmo Holt. At least, to get close to someone who was close to Holt. So I did."

"You're what, year three?" Dagrun asked. "Was Joosep worried?"

"Year four," Gustav replied. "And Joosep said he needed my particular Trait."

"He must have been very worried to use a year four," Calder said, ignoring that Gustav's Trait had allowed him to actually accomplish his mission. "It was probably after we had both left the Hall. He didn't have much choice."

"I got him the information he needed," Gustav protested. "So I was the best choice."

"What else did you find out," Dagrun asked. "About Holt."

"That he was behind Joosep's disappearance," Gustav said. "And Vilis, one of my training mates, has betrayed the Intelligencers to Holt. I think he gave him the names of our training group and instructors. Maybe more. I found him outside Joosep's office one day with some papers."

"Vilis," Dag said. "Joosep tried to get him to lie to me. He wouldn't have found much to give to Holt." She paused. "So Holt knows a few instructors. It could be the ones who are missing. Do you know where he's holding Joosep?"

"No." Gustav shook his head. "I know where he *was* holding him. A warehouse across the river, in the run-down part of South Tarklee."

"Where someone was killed?" Dagrun asked, and Gustav nodded, wondering how they knew so much.

"I think that happened when Joosep escaped," Gustav said. "At least, I followed Vilis there, and a woman had been killed. Vilis didn't know Joosep was being held captive, but I'm pretty sure he was. And that Joosep killed that woman and escaped."

"That's what we hoped," Dagrun smiled, but Gustav didn't see anything to smile about. "We just may find him alive after all."

"Do you think you can trust him?" Calder asked, and for a moment, Gustav thought he meant him: then he realized that he meant *Joosep*.

"Of course, you can trust Joosep," Gustav said.

Dagrun looked at him with steady eyes before answering Calder. "Yes. What Gustav is telling us corroborates what I found in Joosep's notes: he was worried about Tarmo Holt but wasn't certain there was any need to do anything about him because his reign as Grand Freeholder was ending soon. I don't think Joosep was aware of Holt's plans."

"What plans?" Gustav asked. "Why is he working with the pirates?"

"Later," Dagrun said. "We need to find Joosep." She looked over his head at Calder. "And you need to warn your people."

"No," Calder said. "I need to be here."

"Calder," Dagrun said. "You're the only one who can do this. You need to warn them so they don't share the fate of Setberg and Nurmi."

Gustav sidled away from the intensity of his companions' conversation, his eyes flicking back and forth between them. He wasn't sure what the relevance of the two towns was, but it was making Calder waver. Finally, the Pilalian sighed.

"You're right," he said. "I think this is why he triggered my Trait. You two leave first. I won't be able to get a ship until closer to dawn anyway."

"Here." When Dagrun passed a small bag to Calder, Gustav heard the muffled sounds of coins. "My guess is that Joosep has more where he's hiding."

"All right," Calder said. He squeezed past Gustav and Dagrun to stand farther away from the opening. "Be safe."

Calder's voice was so soft that Gustav wasn't sure Dagrun heard it, but she nodded and closed her eyes before she pulled her hood up over her hair.

"Time to go, Gustav," she said to him. She eased the wooden planks up and poked her head out before gesturing for him to exit. She joined him a moment later and then, after turning to make sure he was following, she headed off down the lane past the carts.

DAG PEERED AROUND a corner. She could hear Gustav breathing behind her. It had been just under an hour since they'd left Calder. An hour that she'd been wondering if they'd made the right decision. She and Calder had talked about splitting up, about whether their Traits would work better apart, and she'd thought they'd answered that question. Now they'd separated. And, even though he felt his Trait was pointing him that way, because she'd said it first, because she'd convinced him to go north, she felt like she'd betrayed him.

She pushed her doubts away to concentrate on the task at hand: finding Joosep's secret safe haven.

This was the right street; she knew that much from the plans she'd glimpsed once. But was she in the right block? She closed her eyes and concentrated on her Trait, on letting it guide her next glance to find something hidden.

When she opened her eyes, her gaze fell on a small building a half a block away. She felt a telltale itch between her shoulder blades and smiled.

"I see it," she said to Gustav. "You wait here." She stood and sprinted down the street before he had time to answer. As she ran, she studied the door. There, above it. She reached up and pried a loose stone out. But no matter how many times she ran her hand across the cavity, she didn't feel a key. She blew out a breath. Joosep must have the key. She'd have to knock.

She rapped on the wooden door as quietly as she could. If he was asleep, would he even hear her? She paused with her back against the door, staring at the still dark and empty street. She shook her head at the corner Gustav was hiding behind, telling him to stay where he was.

Without turning around, she rapped on the door again. Then the silence of the night was broken by the sounds of footsteps coming along the street. Was Gustav hidden? Dag took three steps away from the door and crouched down in a shadow, her face concealed by her hood. Someone shuffled past her, unsteady feet kicking up dust.

Then they swung around the next corner and out of sight. She rose and wiped her hands on her trousers and turned back to the door. It was open; just enough for her to see a thin line of shadow between the wood and the stone that hadn't been there before. Slowly, she walked back to the door. By the time she got there it had opened enough for her to see an eye looking out at her.

"It's Dagrun," she said softly. "Looking for Joosep." The eye disappeared when the door closed. She heard something being undone, and then the door opened wider.

"Arnor," she said, relieved. "There's one more." She turned and made a motion, and Gustav trotted silently towards her. Arnor moved aside, and she entered a small space. Gustav joined her, and the door was shut.

"I was expecting Calder Rahmson," Arnor said. He picked up a lamp and led the way further into the building. "Not Gustav. Although it's always a pleasure to see him." He turned and beamed a smile at Gustav, leaving Dag to wonder if the younger Intelligencer had this effect on everyone but her.

"Joosep is sleeping," Arnor said. "You two can bed down in here tonight. Privy is through that door."

"Has he recovered from being held by Holt?" Dag asked. Arnor set the lamp on a table and turned to meet her gaze.

"No, he has not." He sighed. "He had just fallen asleep when I heard you knock. And unless this is an emergency, that there is something only he can do right this minute, I would prefer to let him sleep."

"Morning is soon enough," Dag said. "What's happening tonight will or won't happen without him."

"Thank you."

Arnor seemed truly relieved, and Dag guessed that he'd never expected to see Joosep alive again.

"You were here first, weren't you?" she asked him.

"Yes. By a few days. And I know your Trait, so I won't bother asking you how you found this place. Can't keep a secret from some of you." Arnor pulled a bundle of blankets from a low cupboard and gestured to a row of shelves and a sink. "There's a pump for water but not much to eat except for part of a dried sausage. Otherwise, wait for porridge in the morning." He gave a curt nod to her and smiled widely when his eyes fell on Gustav, before walking down a hall to a closed door. Once Arnor was gone, Dag pulled her pack off and set it on the table beside the lamp.

"Does everyone fawn over you in that way?" she asked Gustav. She found a couple of mugs and pumped some water to fill them. She took a sip from one and left the other on the table for Gustav. She grabbed the sausage and broke it in half, handing one half to Gustav. Her small piece was gone in a few bites.

"Yeah," he replied. He shoved the sausage into his mouth and took a moment to chew and swallow. "Because of my Trait, as you guessed."

"I didn't guess," Dag said. "I knew. And your Trait doesn't seem to work on me."

"Huh, you're right." Gustav grinned. "I think I like that."

"Really? What if I think you're a terrible Intelligencer?"

"Well, for one," Gustav replied. "Since I'm only a fourth year, and I've already completed one assignment successfully, I'm not sure I'd believe you. But I would want to know why you think that."

"That would make a difference to you?" Dag asked. She didn't really care what Gustav Gunnarson thought, but talking to him was keeping her from worrying about Calder.

"Sure. How can I get better if no one tells me what I'm doing wrong?" he said. "Besides, not everyone does like me, and I need to be prepared for those people."

"How do you know that not everyone likes you?"

"I was poisoned," he said, and Dag looked up in shock. "By someone in Tarmo Holt's household, we think. That is, Joosep thinks that's who did it." He stood up and stretched and yawned. "Now, if you don't mind, it's been a very long time since I slept indoors. I'm going to make the most of it." He grabbed a blanket, lay down on the floor, and rolled himself up.

Dag stared at him for a few moments before she too stretched out on the floor. She thought she'd have trouble sleeping; after all, Calder was alone, and she'd slept in her own bed earlier, but she drifted off after only a few moments.

CHAPTER 9

CALDER SCANNED THE docks. He'd been watching for hours, and all of the activity that he saw was for the cleanup after the fire.

Getting north to Cutterstown and his mother was going to be more difficult than he'd thought. Nothing indicated that any ships were about to set sail. And worse, the only three that hadn't been lost to flames were not the type of ship that would head up the coast.

He sighed. Not only did that mean the ghost ship had a head start on him, but trade was going to be disrupted. A number of log haulers, the type of ship that traded along the coast, had been lost to fire. What would people like his mother, brother, and sister do when no logs could be picked up and sold? Who would even buy their lumber with the shipyards destroyed?

Or did Margit Ansdottir and Tarmo Holt have worse plans for Cutterstown? Setberg had been deserted after its warehouses and docks were destroyed. It was smaller than Cutterstown, but not by much. He and Dag were pretty sure that the people had fled to Nurmi: not only had they not found bodies in the village, but Clan Freeholder Timonis had mentioned them. Would Ansdottir allow the same for Cutterstown? Would they be allowed to leave and head to Langin or even Tarklee? Or had Holt's order to destroy his family put everyone there at risk?

He had to warn his family. But even if he could find a ship

heading there, Ansdottir might already be ahead of him. He had to assume that using his father's name wouldn't keep her and her Unseen trait from discovering where his family lived.

A small boat much like the one he and Dag had used to escape Lavais Island sailed into view, and Calder's focus narrowed on it as his Trait was triggered.

The little boat docked near the mouth of the river, as far away from the Merchant Adventurers' office as possible. Were they trying to go unnoticed by that organization, or were they simply wary of the fire damage? And did it really matter? There was a boat and he needed it. If he sailed close to the coast, he should be in Cutterstown sometime late tomorrow.

No one paid attention to him when he stepped out from behind a stack of crates. He passed a group of fishermen, overhearing their worry that the fire had made it impossible to fish today. Another knot of men, merchants from the way they were dressed, were more subdued as they looked at the ruination of their businesses for at least the next year.

Calder wondered if they knew the worst: that the ships that were lost would not be easily replaced since the Lavais shipyards had also been destroyed.

Slowly, doing his best to be inconspicuous, he made his way to the dock where the small sailboat was tied up.

A sailor slumped at the shore end of the dock, and another sat beside the boat. The sails had been rolled up but not stowed: this boat was ready to sail. He grinned. But it would be with him at the tiller, not these men.

"Did you see the fire?" he asked when he was just a few steps from the first sailor. "It lit up the sky as bright as a full moon." He peered over the man's bowed head. The second sailor hadn't stirred at his approach.

"I wasn't here—You! Quick, get down!"

Calder ducked and met the sailor's eyes.

"Jaak," he said. "Well met."

"No, it's not," Jaak replied. He glanced along the dock to where the other sailor sat. "You can't be here. The captain's looking for you!"

"Tarmo Holt is looking for me," Calder said. "The captain's looking for my family. Which I don't appreciate."

"Yeah, all right, but she'll take you if she can get you."

"Yes, and then she'll still find my family," Calder said. Jaak hadn't given him away yet. Was he going to? Or . . . ? "Jaak, you never did like crewing for Captain Ansdottir. Would you consider changing sides?"

"There's only one side," Jaak said bitterly. "I don't know how you managed to escape the captain, but I doubt you can do it again. Then you'll die. I like you and all, but I don't really want to die."

"I'm not planning on dying," Calder said. "And there are two sides." He reached into his waistband and fingered his patch. Should he tell him? Would knowing that Calder was a Fair Seas Treaty Intelligencer make Jaak more or less likely to help him?

With his head still down, he looked around. There were still far too many people within shouting distance of Jaak. He didn't dare share that information with him—not yet.

"Do you trust me?" he asked Jaak, who sighed before nodding and looking away. "Good. Then come with me." He paused. "Or at the very least, don't get in my way."

"Where are you going?" Jaak asked, and Calder had hope because Jaak hadn't said no.

"Probably in the wrong direction," Calder said, "because I plan on making sure my family is safe."

The sailor stared at him for a moment before his shoulders slumped.

"Seems like trying to win against the captain is a bad idea," he said finally. "But I suppose you did beat her once already. I really hate being on her crew. Burning ships with sailors on board makes me sick. I hate always destroying things. Most days I think anything, including dying, would be better, so yes, I'll come with you."

"Excellent choice, Jaak," Calder said. He was actually a little surprised. The most he'd hoped for was that Jaak wouldn't interfere when he took the boat. "What about the sailor over there? Do you think he'll step aside while we sail off in that little boat?"

"He won't fight us, but he'll tell the captain I went willingly. Next time she sees me she will kill me."

"Then you won't go willingly," Calder said. "Stand up." He looped an arm around Jaak's neck and loosely grabbed his arm and twisted it behind his back. "I'll be as gentle as I can," he whispered into his ear. Then he started marching him toward the other sailor. He shook his head when they were able to stop a foot away from the man without him waking up.

Calder kicked the sailor in the calf. "Wake up!" he said. "You're lucky I didn't kill you in your sleep."

"Jaak," the man said. "You all right?"

"Shut up," Calder said. "I do the talking. Get away from my boat."

"No."

The sailor looked more angry than afraid, and Calder decided he had to change that. He reached out and punched him in the jaw.

"I said get away from my boat." He tightened his grip on Jaak. "Or I'll kill your mate here, and then you're next."

"Go ahead," the sailor said. "We've all sworn to die for our captain."

"Have you?" Calder said. "I guess you'll be happy to die first." He pushed Jaak towards the other sailor, and before either of them could recover, he jumped behind the other man and grabbed him. He didn't worry about being gentle when he pulled his arms tight behind his back.

"What do you say," he said to Jaak. "Are you willing to let this man die for his captain?"

"No, please," Jaak said. "Don't kill him."

"What's in it for me?" Calder asked.

"I'll do whatever you ask," Jaak said. "No trouble, just don't kill him."

"You don't want our captain after you," the man snarled. "She's got all the pirates and ships on the Pale Sea at her command. You won't be safe anywhere."

"I'll take my chances." Calder pushed the struggling man down onto the dock and straddled him. Now that his hands were free, he was able to grab a length of rope and tie his captive's hands together.

"You," he said to Jaak. "In the boat. I'll take the tiller."

Once Jaak was in the boat, Calder untied the lines and jumped in. He pretended to tie Jaak up before he unfurled the sails. "Tell your pirate captain that I'm a better pirate," he called as the boat skimmed away from the dock.

JOOSEP STRETCHED AND groaned when his joints and muscles protested. He looked over at the other bed, but it was empty. Arnor was up and about, as usual. No doubt making him tea and porridge. He sat up and swung his legs out from under the blankets, cursing his weakness under his breath.

A week with little food and water had depleted his body and left him with no energy. Despite two days of plenty to eat and drink—he snorted—and near constant sleep, he could still barely get himself out of bed.

He put his feet on the floor and stood on unsteady feet, dragging a blanket with him. He chilled easily, and since he would no doubt be back here soon after breaking his fast, he saw no reason to expend the energy to change out of the loose trousers and shirt he'd been sleeping in.

He cocked his head. Was that conversation? Was Arnor talking to someone? He leaned against the door. Yes, he heard a mumbled voice that was not Arnor's. It sounded like a woman.

Nothing in the tone of Arnor's voice seemed alarmed or afraid or worried. But who was he talking to?

"Joosep," Arnor called softy. "Oh good, you're awake. I thought I heard you." The door was pushed open, and Arnor stood in front of him with a huge smile on his face. "We have company." Arnor leaned towards him. "Dagrun Lund and Gustav Gunnarson have found us."

"Dagrun?" Joosep was shocked. "Dagrun Lund is here, in North Tarklee?"

"And right *here*," Arnor replied. "Just down the hall. Come on."

"And Gustav too?" He was even more surprised, and grateful, that the lad had made it to relative safety. After Holt told him he knew about Gustav, he'd been worried that he'd already killed him. "And what of Calder? Is he here too?"

Dagrun was standing when he reached the small living space. She shook her head.

"Calder went north," she said.

"But he's safe?" Joosep asked.

"So far."

Dagrun's frown told him that she wasn't sure that Calder would remain safe, which meant his reason for going north was important—and dangerous. Joosep let Arnor help him over to the sofa, and he struggled for a moment to catch his breath. Even the short walk had tired him. He gratefully accepted the tea Arnor handed him, and he took a sip.

"I am so thankful that the two of you found us," he said once he'd set his tea down on the table beside him. "Dagrun, did you and Calder receive my message?"

"We did," Dagrun sat in a chair opposite him. "Just hours before the pirates set fire to Lavais Port." She reached for a pile of papers that were on the table. "We travelled along the coast of Swyford, where they attacked both Setberg and Nurmi. Now they've set fire to ships in Tarklee Harbour."

"Fire? What?" Joosep reached for his tea, ignoring the way his hand shook when he picked it up. This was no time for his body to give out, there was much to hear. And too much to do.

"We," Dagrun started. "Calder and I, think that the pirates are destroying shipping in the entire Pale Sea region. The shipyards on Lavais are gone, as are most of the ships that were there along with many that were anchored in Tarklee. These," she waved the papers, "were hidden in the office of the Master Captain of the Merchant Adventurers. Duplicate ship ownership papers. All of which show Tarmo Holt as the owner."

"You think he's working with the pirates to control shipping on the Pale Sea? To what purpose?" Joosep asked.

"We have some theories," Dagrun replied. "Calder and I. I'd be curious to see if any of the ships named here have been spared from fire," she said.

"Tarmo Holt was angry."

Joosep looked over at Gustav, who had paused while eating his porridge. "When did you see Holt?" he asked.

"This morning." Gustav put his porridge down. "When he met with the pirate captain."

"He was angry at more than Calder?" Dagrun asked.

"Yes." Gustav nodded. "At the pirate captain. He said that she destroyed the wrong ships and that he wouldn't pay her. But then she threatened to set fire to the last three ships, and he did pay. That's when he asked her to find Rahm's people."

"Destroyed the wrong ships," Dagrun repeated. "Meaning she destroyed some of these ships." She held up the papers. "Did she say why?"

"Just that fire was tricky. She didn't seem sorry though."

"Huh. I'd still like to know which ships were spared and which were destroyed," Dagrun said.

"I'll go," Gustav said. "I already have a disguise and a few people who will vouch for me. And asking what ships are still afloat won't seem too odd a question, under the circumstances."

"Yes," Dagrun said.

"No," Joosep said a moment after her. He met her eyes. "He's not trained."

"He's been training himself," Dagrun replied. "Besides, he's right about it being a pretty innocuous question to ask the day after ships and docks burned. He can go now and be back with the information before I've even completed my report to you."

"It's that long?" he asked.

"Yes. Calder and I, using our Traits, have uncovered quite a lot."

He sighed. He'd need a nap soon, despite the tea. Which meant that there was even more time for Gustav to fulfil his task than Dagrun thought.

"You're sure?" he asked Gustav. "I do not want to put you in jeopardy."

Gustav shrugged. "I've already been in jeopardy. We all have been. And that's part of the job, isn't it?" He put down his bowl and grabbed a scarf that had been looped over a peg by the door. "The names of the surviving ships," he said. "What else should I look for?"

"Anything to do with Captain Margit Ansdottir and her crew of pirates," Dagrun said. "Or my sister Inger." She turned to him. "Inger is with the pirates. They are using her Trait to distract everyone from what they are doing."

"They are?" He didn't see how Inger Lund's Trait could be used for anything, which is why he'd never tried to train her. Could he have missed something?

"Yes. When all eyes are on Inger, they sail in close enough to set the fires." Dagrun stared at him, and he squirmed at the blame in her eyes.

"Gustav," he said, pulling his gaze away from Dagrun. "You should leave now, while it's still early." If he and Dagrun were going to argue, he preferred that the lad not witness it. She'd been angry at him at Inger's departure: how much angrier was she now that her sister was apparently in league with pirates?

"I'll be back in an hour or so," Gustav said with a grin.

"I'll make sure the way is clear," Arnor said. He eased past Gustav and into the hall, and the lad followed.

"I know you're angry," Joosep said once the other two were gone. "But I need more tea and some porridge, if it's made, before I can deal with it."

"All right." Dagrun grabbed his mug and took it to the counter along with her own. She poured more tea and had pulled a bowl off the shelf by the time Arnor returned.

"I'll get that," Arnor said as he took the bowl from her. He scooped some porridge from a pot, added a spoonful of honey, and brought it over to him.

"He's still very weak," he said to Dagrun as she placed both mugs of tea on the table. "And will need to sleep again once he's eaten." Arnor sat down on the sofa beside him. "Eat," he said.

Joosep nodded and spooned some porridge into his mouth. He was tiring already; Arnor had been correct about him needing to sleep soon. But there was so much to know.

"I am sorry," Dagrun said. "I forgot that you've had your own ordeal. And since Arnor is here, should I assume that Tarmo Holt knows who the rest of the Intelligencers are?"

"No," Arnor replied. "We think he only knows of Gustav's training group and instructors."

"Which is why I'm so happy to see him safe and sound," Joosep said around a mouthful of porridge. "Holt told me that he knew Gustav was one of mine. I'd already had the lad spy on him, and he wasn't happy about that. Especially since he befriended his daughter to do it."

"Gustav told me he'd been poisoned by someone in Holt's household," Dagrun said. "Is there another Intelligencer or student you wish to contact?"

"To warn?" Joosep ignored Arnor's frown when he set his spoon down. "I wish there were."

"No, warning them is being done," Dagrun said. "I meant is there anyone we can pass messages through in order to share information and coordinate our activities."

"You warned them?" he asked. "How?"

"Calder spoke to one of his old instructors," Dagrun said. "He didn't tell me her name, but apparently she was once offered your job."

"Nadez Norup!" It was a testament to how surprised and tired he was that her name popped out of his mouth before he could stop himself. "And she agreed to act?" That surprised him even more. The woman was notorious for only doing what was in her best interest. And using whatever resources she could get her hands on; even if they weren't hers to use.

"So she told Calder," Dagrun replied. "According to him, she agreed to take up the position she turned down so long ago." She shrugged. "I know you and this Nadez woman haven't always gotten along, so I hope this isn't a problem. We . . ." she paused. "Calder and I weren't sure you were alive."

"And I nearly wasn't," Joosep said and shivered. He let Arnor pull his blanket higher up on his shoulders, and he tried to suppress a yawn. Then he grinned. "You used a word that even yesterday I hadn't expected to use myself any time soon," he said. "Hope. Nadez and I may not have always seen eye to eye, but knowing she's agreed to step into this fight gives me hope."

"So, we now have two Master Intelligencers at work," Dagrun said.

"And Tarmo Holt won't see that storm heading his way."

GUSTAV PULLED HIS scarf higher over his nose, right up to his eyes. The fires had been extinguished, but the confusion on the pier had grown as more people arrived. Crowds of people milled about surveying the damage and wanting to know what was going on.

He'd attached himself to a group of merchants who were asking after goods from specific ships. He explained that he was a peddler with a cart looking for information on what wares might have been destroyed. One merchant recognized him, and they let him stay with their group as they searched for their own answers.

And they found quite a few. These merchants were worried most about the ten locally owned ships that were destroyed. Another three had escaped undamaged. Gustav had the names memorized; he wasn't about to write anything down, not if he wanted them to believe he was a peddler with a cart.

He did learn who owned the warehouses and the goods that were stored in them. And everything he'd heard so far made him think that the fire had spared not only three of Tarmo Holt's ships, but his warehouses too.

A familiar figure strode through the crowds, and Gustav tucked his chin to his chest.

"Grand Freeholder Holt," one of the merchants in Gustav's group called. "Have we a full tally of the damage yet?"

Holt stopped a few feet from Gustav and scanned the small group.

"I am sorry to say that we do not," Holt said. "But it looks as though we have all lost much this day." Holt tipped his hat and walked on.

Except for him, Gustav thought, *Holt seems to have lost very little.* He waited until Holt was occupied with another group of people, men who were much better clothed than even the merchants Gustav was with, before slipping away.

As he left the dock area, he saw a group of Pilalians. They were dressed for the sea with bare feet and vests over knit shirts. A few had gold hoops hanging from their ears. Wondering if they had different news, he headed towards them.

"Watcha looking at," one of the Pilalians said as he came even with them. "Never seen a Pilalian before? We don't like folk staring."

"I didn't mean to," Gustav said with a smile. At the answering smiles on the five dark faces that were turned to him, he widened his grin. His Trait was working. After dealing with Dagrun Lund, he'd been a little worried. "I have met Pilalians, but you look like you might have news . . ." he lowered his voice, "about what really happened last night." He gestured towards the harbour. "It doesn't make sense to me."

"Nor to us," a woman replied. "And we were there."

He'd had a year's worth of lessons in Pilalian: not enough to understand every word, but he caught the curses and worry in the comments a couple of sailors made.

"No one has asked us anything," the first speaker said. "Until you."

"As you can see, I'm not with any official office," Gustav replied. "I'm just trying to find out what happened so I can figure out how it will affect my trade. The *officials* won't care about me, so I have to look out for myself." He sighed. "Just as I always have."

"I know what you mean," the woman replied. "That's why I

left for the sea. It's a lot simpler to follow your captain's orders than try to figure out politics."

"I'm on my own," Gustav said. "With no one to tell me which way to step to avoid the skit. Did you see what happened last night?" he prompted.

"It were the strangest thing," the woman said. "A ghost ship sails right past us. There was a ghost woman on deck: it were the spirit of the ship, is what I think."

"A spirit and a ghost ship. No one I talked to has mentioned this."

"It weren't no ghost ship," a third Pilalian stepped forward. "I told you, I saw a crew on that ship. Dark like us and wearing all dark clothes."

"It were a ghost ship," the woman insisted. "All white, and a spirit standing on the bow had white hair and skin and wore a long white robe that flowed all around her."

"A dark crew, I tell you. That's why they sailed right past us. They recognized that we were the same as them: Pilalian."

"What about the other two ships that weren't set on fire?" Gustav asked. "Did they have Pilalian crews too?"

"Not that I know of," the first Pilalian said. "Some Pilalians were aboard Sapphire Sea owned ships that were lost, but the crews weren't *all* Pilalian. They targeted the ships that were carrying timber. That's why they burned so fast and so hot and the flames jumped to some of the other ships."

"How do you know they carried timber?" Gustav asked.

"Other than how fast and hot they burned?" the Pilalian asked. "'Cause of the type of ships they were. Log haulers are smaller and wider across the beam. Makes them good for transporting timber around the Pale Sea but not very good for handling the weather you run into when you sail to the Sapphire Sea."

"I see," Gustav said. "What were you carrying?"

"Food. Mostly from the Sapphire Sea. The other two ships not set ablaze? Probably the same. Those ships were built for long voyages too, not short hauls along this coast."

"If it wasn't a ghost ship, then who would have burned the ships and why?" he asked. "Who could have even managed it?"

"Pirates," the man who'd seen a Pilalian crew said. "Margit Ansdottir and her pirates. They could have done this. Rumour has it she can sail through The Serpent's Teeth. Pretending to be a ghost ship would be easy for her."

"Pirates steal," the woman said. "No one stole anything. And no one can sail through the Teeth. Now we best be off to find our captain and see what his orders for us are."

"Pirates do more than steal," the man muttered as he trailed his group towards town.

As Gustav watched them head away, he had to agree with the last man: pirates did more than steal. They met with the Grand Freeholder, for one.

CALDER STARED UP at the sky: it was clouded over, but he thought it was close to noon. He and Jaak had taken turns sleeping and sailing last night, and now they'd soon be passing Langin. Byholt's capital city straddled the mouth of the Three Rocks River. The fishing boats should have returned to shore by this time in the day, so there would be fewer people out to notice them sail past. Despite the number of times he'd done it lately, sailing this type of boat long distances wasn't usual.

He'd debated trying to warn the town about the pirates, but in the end, he trusted Gustav's information. His family was the main target, not Langin. He'd warn them on his return trip.

"Did you catch anything yet?" he called to Jaak, who was leaning over the port gunwale trailing a make-shift net in the water.

Jaak hauled in the net: he'd made it by untwisting the strands of a spare length of rope he'd found and knotting them together. As fishing nets went this was small, so neither of them were expecting much in the way of a catch, so when silver flashed when the net landed in the bottom of the boat, Jaak let out a whoop.

"Caught a couple of pike!" Jaak said. He plucked the fish from the net, shook it out, and tossed it back into the sea. "Let's see what else I can get before we make for land and a fire. Unless . . . ?"

Calder shook his head. "No, we'll cook these. Let's leave eating raw fish for when we can't land." He steered them out a little farther from shore to stay out of sight of Langin. The wind was filling the sail, and they were making good time, but a ship like the *Bright Breeze* would be much faster, especially with

Margit Ansdottir at the helm.

Had she uncovered his identity and found out where his family lived? Not for the first time, he wondered if they were racing to view the destruction of Cutterstown and not to save it. He would see to his family anyway, if that was the case. And make sure that the pirates paid, somehow.

Despite his Trait, he could never assume that Luck was going to work in the way he wanted it to, or help events turn out the way he hoped.

"There's a boat straight ahead," Jaak called from the bow and started pulling the net into the boat.

Calder peered past him to what looked like a small fishing boat. It wasn't moving, and the sail was rolled up and tied to the mast.

"Stay low," Calder said to Jaak, who pushed the fish and the net to one side and lay flat in the bottom of the boat. "It's probably out of Langin. Let's hope we don't see too many other boats out here."

Calder steered the sailboat in between the fishing boat and the coast. When he was close enough to see the lone occupant of the other boat, he raised a hand in greeting. His wave was returned, but the fisherman didn't make any other movement.

He sighed and kept a smile on his face as the two boats came even. An older man with weathered features nodded, and then they were past him.

"Just a fisherman minding his business," Calder said softly to Jaak. "He didn't seem alarmed, so I assume Ansdottir didn't come this close to shore. At least not today."

"Maybe they're heading back to Strongrock," Jaak said. "And they'll get the *Vassan* before heading north."

"Then it means we will be in time to warn my family and Cutterstown," Calder said, although he didn't think Ansdottir would do that. She'd used this ship and crew to attack Tarklee; there was no reason not to use it to attack Cutterstown.

"And she for sure knows where you're from?" Jaak asked.

"No, but she'll find out." Ansdottir's Unseen Trait would help her get the information. And Inger knew who he was. Had he mentioned where he was from to her? Had Dag? He had to assume Ansdottir would find his mother's home.

Jaak shrugged and sat up. "I'll try for some more fish, and

maybe we can land and eat now that we're past Langin," he said.

"How much longer until we reach Cutterstown?" Calder asked. He made the trip home a few times a year, but Jaak had spent years sailing these waters, shipping out on vessels that hauled timber from the Woodlea forest to Lavais ship builders.

"I think another half a dozen hours," Jaak said. "But I'm no navigator."

"I'll stop in an hour," Calder replied. "We should be well past any villages near Langin by then, so get fishing."

CHAPTER 10

"How are we for supplies?" Dag asked Arnor. Joosep was resting: apparently that was how he'd spent most of his time since he'd arrived here. Arnor said that he hadn't spoken about what he'd endured at Tarmo Holt's hands, but he was weak and thin and covered in bruises. Dag was grateful that Nadez was willing to step in and lead the Intelligencers since, through no fault of his own, Joosep wasn't capable.

"Water is supplied by a cistern on the roof, so as long as it rains, we'll have enough. Our food stores are low," Arnor frowned, "we'll be out of everything but salt fish in a matter of days."

"I'll do something with the salt fish," Dag said. When Arnor raised his eyebrows, she shrugged. "I watched Calder do it a couple of times, and it tasted all right. Do we have enough coin to buy more supplies? I gave most of what I had to Calder." She scratched her head. "And is a bath allowed?"

"In the name of Nyorden, please have one," Arnor said. He went to a cupboard and came back and handed her a cloth. "But keep it to half a tub. We can't use all the water on bathing."

"Thank you," Dag replied. She'd cleaned up and changed her clothes while in her old apartment, but she hadn't dared a bath. Even she could tell that her hair smelled terrible.

She took the cloth with her into the privy and ran the water into the tub before stripping down and stepping in.

The water was warm from the sun, and she sighed and sank into it until she was completely submerged.

Far too soon, she was scrubbed clean and had no excuses to stay in the tub. She stepped out and pulled the stopper, letting the water drain out. Her hands smoothed out the worst snarls in her hair, and after rubbing her skin dry with the cloth, she put her clothes back on. She draped the cloth over the lip of the tub to dry and returned to the main room.

Gustav was back and sitting at the table drinking from a mug.

"Is that tea?" Dag asked. "And is there more?"

Arnor nodded, poured another mug, and set it down beside Gustav.

"Thank you." Dag sat down and wrinkled her nose. Now that she was clean, she realized how strongly the youth smelled.

"Should we wait for Joosep to wake up?" Gustav asked.

"No, we can fill him in later." She pulled the stack of ship ownership papers over to her. "Which ones were spared?"

Gustav flipped through and pointed out two papers: two ships that secretly belonged to Tarmo Holt that had not been set on fire by the pirates.

"Were there any ships spared that weren't listed on one of these papers?" she asked.

"The *Neas*," Gustav replied. "Everyone seemed to know that it's Holt's ship." He picked up another four papers. "And these four ships that secretly belong to Holt were destroyed along with a couple of ships from the Sapphire Sea."

"These four must be why Holt was angry with Ansdottir," Dag said. "Are any ships out at sea? Is there any way to know?" She had no idea how many ships should be in the harbour at this time of year. She wished Calder was here: he might know.

"Maybe," Gustav agreed. "Some of the ships that were burned were carrying timber."

"How do you know that?"

"Well, all right, I don't *know*." Gustav shrugged. "But a group of Pilalian sailors said that's what they thought. Almost half of the ships that were destroyed weren't built for sailing to the Sapphire Sea, and all three of the ones that were spared, are."

"Huh." Dag flipped through the papers. There were descriptions of the ships, of course, but she didn't know enough about ships to be able to tell if these could sail to the Sapphire Sea. Something else that Calder would know.

"One of them said he saw Pilalians on the ghost ship," Gustav said. "He thought that was why the ship they were on was spared." He pointed to a paper. "But they were on this ship, and it belongs to Tarmo Holt."

"It does look like ships are the target," Dag said. "Along with shipbuilding in Lavais Port."

"But why?" Arnor asked from where he leaned against the counter. "So that Holt has the only ships?"

"It will cripple trade on the Pale Sea," Dag said. "If there's no shipbuilding, then no one will need timber. And even if they do, there are fewer ships to transport it. And most of the surviving ones belong to Tarmo Holt." She looked over at Gustav. "What were the ships that were spared carrying? Do you know?"

"The Pilalians said their ship was mostly carrying food," he replied. "They figured the other ship from the Sapphire Sea was carrying much the same."

"And Tarmo Holt has warehouses in unexpected areas of the city," Joosep said from the hall. He shuffled over and sat down heavily on a chair. Arnor quickly poured him a mug of tea.

"That's what I've heard," Gustav agreed.

"The warehouse," Dag said. "Where—" She was about to say where the murder took place, but then she remembered that Joosep was the one who had committed it to escape and save himself.

"Where you were held captive," she finished. "That was empty. Do you think Holt plans on filling it with food?"

"Probably." Joosep took a sip of tea, and Dag drained her own.

There was something here. She itched between her shoulder blades: her Trait telling her to look deeper.

"We, *I*, need to find out every single warehouse that Tarmo Holt owns," she said. "Especially any that don't list him as the owner on record." She resisted the urge to rub her back against the chair to ease the itch. "Who else has stores of food?"

"You think this is what he's hiding?" Joosep asked.

"I think he's hiding many things," Dag replied. "Including why he's doing this."

"He wants to hold onto power," Joosep said. "That's

obvious."

"Yes, but how? I don't think Holt is planning on securing any kind of vote." She paused. What if he was planning on forcing a vote? Would the ghost ship help him? Or was it just a way to destroy ships and shipbuilding without fingers being pointed at him and the pirates?

"Calder and I thought Holt might be trying to disrupt trade," she continued. "Then he could use his ships to make himself even richer and more powerful. But what if he wants more than that?" Would he be ruthless enough to do what she thought he was doing? To put so many lives at risk in pursuit of his goals?

"The ghost ship set fires in Nurmi just as Calder and I arrived there," she said. "Ships were lost along with warehouses, two of which belonged to Clan Freeholder Timonis."

"You think that this is Holt's way of ruining Timonis' chance to become the next Grand Freeholder?" Joosep asked.

"I'm sure Tarmo Holt is happy to harm Timonis," Dag replied. "But I think he was after what was in the warehouses: grain to get Nurmi through the winter. I met a grain seller who told me that all the grain set to arrive before winter has been spoken for, so replacing it is not possible. Unless people are able to pay a very high price and are willing to let others go without."

"And now Tarmo Holt owns the ships that can bring in more grain from the Sapphire Sea," Joosep said.

"Maybe he already owns most of the grain in the region," Dag said. "In his warehouses. That would allow him to control much of the food the Fair Seas Treaty Alliance countries need to survive the winter, along with the means to distribute it." She ran a hand through her hair as the rest of them absorbed her comments. The itch between her shoulders had subsided. So that was it; that was the secret Holt had been hiding.

"I think Tarmo Holt is planning on staying in power by withholding or supplying food," she continued quietly. "He'll get the votes and support he needs. What Clan Freeholder would stand by and let their people starve?" Even if it meant giving in to a tyrant.

"He's been planning this for a very long time," Arnor said finally.

JOOSEP SIGHED AND lay back down on his narrow bed. He could

hear Arnor in the main room, probably tidying up. Four people in such a small space meant that things—dirty mugs, papers, clothing—piled up. He was grateful that Arnor was willing to tackle all of these small issues before they became big ones.

Both Dagrun and Gustav had gone out. Dagrun was going to try to find out more about Tarmo Holt's warehouses.

Gustav had left with a list of food to buy and a handful of coins from the pile he'd hidden here over the years. It used to seem like a lot, and it had been difficult to amass so much, taking a few coins out of the Intelligencer budget every month. Now he worried that it would last only a few weeks. He very much feared that they would need to hide here for a lot longer than that.

Arnor was right: Tarmo Holt had been planning this for a very long time. And he'd done it all right under Joosep's nose. Joosep, with his Unseen Trait, *should* have seen this. How could this have happened?

He snorted. It happened because he'd been deliberately blind to Holt. One of the arguments Joosep had with Nadez so long ago was about the role of Intelligencers. He thought they should gather information, interpret what they found, and then let their superior, the Grand Freeholder, make any decisions and take any actions they deemed necessary.

Nadez had always insisted that Intelligencers worked on behalf of the Fair Seas Treaty Alliance, not on behalf of any one Grand Freeholder. She'd always advocated for a more active role for Intelligencers. That they had all the information they needed to act, that action should be taken as soon as issues were discovered, and that early action would minimize any damage and lessen future problems. And that by doing so, Intelligencers would reduce any risk that they would be used for political purposes.

She'd also always said that she'd rather explain a hasty decision than live with the consequences of one that came too late.

He shook his head. Nadez had been proven right. If she'd accepted the role of Master Intelligencer, none of this would be happening. She would never have let Holt continue unchallenged for so long, would never have assumed that he would simply step away from the Grand Freeholder position after the next election.

At least she was working with them now: something that no one could ever have predicted. All Joosep could do was hope that Tarmo Holt would be taken by surprise by a still formidable Intelligencer organization and that he would have no defence against Nadez and whatever actions she took.

And Calder was on his way North. Holt couldn't have predicted that either.

With Luck, Calder would save not just people, but food stores and ships that did not belong to Tarmo Holt. It wouldn't be much against what had already been lost, but fewer desperate people come winter would be a blessing.

Exhausted, Joosep closed his eyes. He'd made some very big mistakes, but he had to hope that his team, that Intelligencers he had trained and prepared, could minimize the number of innocent people who had to pay for them.

CALDER SAILED THE little boat as close to shore as possible. The weather was favouring them: Luck, he thought as he looked up at the cloudless late afternoon sky.

They were very close to Cutterstown; he recognized the rocky point that jutted out into the sea. It acted as a natural break wall, keeping waves that were swept along by storms from the south from overwhelming the town's pier.

They had yet to see the ghost ship, but he had to assume it was on its way here by now.

"Would Ansdottir hide somewhere north?" he asked Jaak. "And attack at night?" His mother lived north of Cutterstown. Would the pirates find her before he could warn her?

"Maybe," Jaak said. "There are some coves up near the White Wood."

Calder smiled. "That Pilalian crew won't like the cold."

"They'll put up with whatever the captain asks them to put up with," Jaak said, and Calder's smile faded.

He was right: Margit Ansdottir ruled her crew completely. And it wasn't all discipline, like when she hung Hanne the spy on Strongrock. She had their respect as well; who wouldn't want to ship out with the captain who could navigate the Teeth? That tale alone would allow any sailor to drink his fill for free all over the Sapphire Sea.

Although he wasn't sure what she would do about sailors who did that—who talked about her skills—Margit Ansdottir didn't strike him as someone who liked her secrets to be told.

"Shorten the sail," he called, and Jaak scrambled to untie the sail and roll it up until only half the canvas remained. The boat slowed as they came even with the last small stand of evergreens on the point. They would soon be able to see Cutterstown, and their little sailboat would be visible to anyone looking this way.

Jaak scrambled up to the bow and leaned out over the water.

"No sign of the *Bright Breeze*," he called before he inched back to him. "And there are three log haulers; two are anchored offshore, and one is tied up at the pier. It looks like they're loading it."

"Good," Calder said. "I think we're in time." He nodded at Jaak, who let the rest of the sail out. The boat skimmed along the water, and soon he could hear men singing as they worked on the dock. A few heads turned their way, but for the most part, they were ignored as he maneuvered the little boat close to the pier. A boy of about ten waved, and Jaak threw him the line. The boy caught it and pulled them in.

"Thanks," Calder said to the boy. He dug around for a small coin, and with a nod, the boy pocketed it and wandered off, no doubt looking for his next opportunity to make some money.

"We'll find my brother first," he said to Jaak once the boat was secured. He led the way along the dock towards a small huddle of buildings. "After that, I need to visit my mother. She lives a little farther north."

"Your brother is a logger?" Jaak asked.

"He has been," Calder replied. "But now he works in the office. He's a local Freeholder." He looked over at Jaak. "And I guess now is the time to tell you that my name isn't Rahm. It's Calder Rahmson. Rahm is my father."

Jaak grinned. "That was smart, telling the captain a false name. No wonder she's not here yet. That makes you harder to track down."

"I should have used a name that has no relation to me," Calder said. "Because she will track me down."

"She would anyway," Jaak said. "She's got a knack for things like that."

"Yes," Calder agreed. A knack—a Trait—but he wasn't going

to explain that to Jaak.

He paused in front of the door to the Cutterstown Freehold office. His family and a few close friends knew he was an Intelligencer, but the rest of the town did not. He'd leave it to his brother to explain how he came by his knowledge, if anyone asked.

He pulled open the door and entered, followed by Jaak.

"Calder!"

"Noak," Calder replied and grinned as the older man embraced him. "It is good to see you." Noak had been a family friend for decades: Calder always thought he'd hoped for more from his mother once Rahm had gone back to the sea, but his mother seemed happy with her life just as it was.

"Yakop should be back soon," Noak said, stepping away from him. "He's just overseeing the loading."

"Good, I have news that can't wait too long." Calder turned to Jaak. "This is Jaak, a former shipmate. Meet Noak, the most senior Freeholder in Cutterstown."

"You make it seem like a real accomplishment," Noak said. "When the reality is, I just outlived the others. Glad to meet you, Jaak. Come on in, and I'll make some tea." Noak took a step away before turning back. "Unless you care for something stronger?"

"I'm tempted," Calder replied. "Noak is famous for his beer," he said to Jaak. "But we all need clear heads for my news."

"Huh." Noak headed to a doorway that led off the main room. "We haven't had much of any news. Not surprised it's bad when it gets here. I'll be back in a moment."

"You said that your brother is a Freeholder too?" Jaak asked.

"Yes, thanks to our mother." He led the way to a table surrounded by eight chairs and sat down. "My father joined the Merchant Adventurers the first time they visited the Pilalian town where he grew up. He tried to live here when he married my mother, but he was born to the sea and eventually returned to it. But he didn't forget us and always sent my mother coin. She took that money and bought land. She's technically the Clan Freeholder, but my brother manages everything for her."

"Here you are," Noak said as he returned with a tray and three steaming mugs. He set it down on the table and passed a mug to Calder and a second one to Jaak before sitting down in front of the last one. "Any news from here you need to know before Yakop shows up?"

"Yes." Calder wrapped a hand around his mug, enjoying the warmth. "Have any ships other than log haulers berthed here in the last day or so?"

"No." The door opened. "Ah, here he is," Noak said.

Calder stood up as Yakop entered. His brother stopped and frowned before closing the door. He barred the door before greeting Calder with a hug.

"I may not like what you have to tell me, but I am happy to see you," Yakop said. "Do I have time for tea?"

"It's already made," Noak said. "You sit, and I'll get it."

"You're right," Calder said. "There isn't much time. Pirates are on their way here as we speak."

"Why?"

"They're burning ships and winter food stores." Calder shook his head. "They've already attacked Lavais and burned the shipyards to the ground. Setberg has been abandoned, and warehouses and ships were destroyed in Nurmi."

"What? Why?" Yakop frowned. "Never mind, that doesn't matter right now. I'll sound the alarm and call in the council."

"There's more," Calder said. "Because the captain of the pirates also has a personal grudge to fulfil here. Against my family."

"Oh Calder, this is exactly what I always worried about."

Calder shook his head. "I'm sorry," he said. "I'm going to warn Mother and try to convince her to come back here with me, or at the very least, take some precautions."

"Good luck," Yakop snorted. "I'd rather stay and fight off pirates."

Noak returned with another mug of tea, and Yakop took a single sip before standing up. "There's no time for tea after all," he said. "Come along, Noak. We need to sound the alarm and get the contents of the warehouses to safety. If we lose that food, we'll starve this winter."

"And you need to move the ships," Calder said. "Send them north. Jaak here can go. He's familiar with the captain of the pirates, so I think he can help them stay one step ahead."

"Familiar?" Yakop asked.

"Yes sir," Jaak replied. "I've been part of her crew. Not by choice, either."

"Calder, you do know how to bring trouble." Yakop shook his head. "Jaak, with me then. Calder, I'll see you in the morning, or will you be back later?"

"The pirates could attack tonight," he replied. "So, I'll be back later. Unless our mother decides otherwise."

"Otherwise," Yakop repeated with a smirk. "You mean if she decides not to let you live."

FROM THE STREET corner, Dag watched the warehouse. There were no signs of the murder that had happened here a few days ago, and no one seemed to be standing guard. Was it still empty, or had Holt filled it with food or other goods?

A woman passed by her, three small children trailing after her. None of them looked like they'd had a decent meal today. What would people like her do if winter came and there was no food even for those who could afford to pay a lot for it?

She squinted at the building: what would hungry—*starving*—people do if they knew that food was just a locked door away?

Had Tarmo Holt even thought that far ahead, or was he so insulated in his well-appointed apartment and fine estate that the plight of the poor never crossed his mind?

She blew out a breath. That was a thought for another day. Her task was to try to see that the future was different from the one Holt had planned.

She'd been here for hours, and no one had visited the warehouse: she should leave soon. There were other locations to investigate before she headed back to Joosep's refuge.

She'd just stepped into the street and was heading away from the warehouse, when a man passed her. She tightened her hood, making sure her hair was well covered. This man was better dressed than anyone else in this rough part of town, and she didn't need her Trait to realize that he didn't belong here. She slowed her steps as she turned a corner.

Yes, he was heading to the door of the warehouse. He unlocked the door and entered. Dag searched for a place to hide and then tucked herself in between a couple of bushes.

This time, she didn't have long to wait.

An overloaded cart trundled up the road, pulled by two women in tattered dresses. They pulled the cart up to the side of the warehouse and stopped. One woman stepped away from the traces while the other one wiped her hand across her forehead.

"Heya," the woman called as she headed to the door. "Goods are here."

"Quiet." The man stepped out and frowned at her. "Where are the men?"

"They be behind a bit," the woman replied. "You gonna help us unload?"

"No." He shook his head. "I'll tell you where to put everything." He stepped back inside.

"Sure," the woman said as she rejoined her mate. "That'll help things go fast. Come on," she said to the other woman. "Looks like it's up to us."

"Like it's never not," the second woman said and cackled.

They were carrying their second set of baskets inside when four more carts, pulled by men this time, arrived.

It didn't take long to unload the carts. As soon as a cart was emptied, it was hauled off down the road. The last cart left, and Dag stayed where she was.

She thought that the goods delivered today would barely take up a quarter of the space inside the warehouse. Were more goods expected, or had this shipment filled up an already partially full space?

Ah, there he was. The man peered out the door for a moment before he exited. He locked the door, pocketed the key, and walked away.

Dag let him get a few paces down the street before she stepped out to follow him. Instead of heading away from the river towards the wealthier part of the city, he stayed on the road that followed the river.

He led her to another warehouse. This time, men and women with carts were already waiting for him. One grumbled at his tardiness, but the rest wearily started hauling goods from the carts into the warehouse. This building was much smaller, and Dag thought it might be half full once everything was stored away.

It was late afternoon by the time the carts had all been emptied and dragged away. The man exited the warehouse a short time later, and Dag followed him out of the poor part of South Tarklee.

He stayed in South Tarklee, making his way to a tidy house that was one of a cluster of homes that lined a well-kept square. A small fountain splashed in the centre of the square and a couple of prosperous looking people strolled past it.

He walked right into the house, so Dag assumed it was his home or place of business.

Light flared inside, but there were no other signs of activity. After half an hour, since it looked like the man had no plans to leave this house tonight, Dag finally decided to leave.

To make sure she wasn't followed, she took a roundabout route back to Joosep's safe apartment.

She knew the location of two of Holt's warehouses, but what, if anything, should she do about it? If poor and hungry people living nearby knew food was being stored in their midst, would it make things worse? Riots were dangerous and could easily turn deadly.

She had no qualms about wishing for Tarmo Holt's death, but others would also meet that fate: desperate people who had so little to lose that they would risk what they did have—their lives—to feed their families.

A couple of sailors passed in front of her, and their familiar rolling gait made her stop, her heart clenching.

Calder was north, risking his life doing whatever he could to keep his family and their community safe.

Her family, her sister, was somewhere with the pirates, and Dag couldn't help Inger even if she wanted her help. But she *could* help her community. She could help reduce the amount of misery and death Tarmo Holt was planning on inflicting on North and South Tarklee.

So she would, no matter the risk to herself.

The road in front of the apartment was empty, so she crossed the street, reached up for the key, and entered.

GUSTAV SWIVELLED HIS head when he heard the door open and close. When Dagrun Lund walked into view, he relaxed.

Even though she'd left hours ago, neither Arnor nor Joosep had seemed worried about Dagrun, so he'd tried not to be. But he knew how dangerous it was to work against Tarmo Holt.

"There's stew," he said. "It should still be warm."

"Thank you." Dagrun found a bowl and ladled some stew into

it. "I take it your trip to get provisions was successful?" she asked as she sat down at the table across from him. She lifted a spoonful of stew into her mouth.

"Yeah," he replied. "Arnor thinks we have enough food for a week or so." He peered at her. "As long as you do something with the salt fish."

"Sure," she nodded. "I'll change the soaking water as soon as I finish this." She ate another spoonful of stew. "It will be ready to cook tomorrow."

While Dagrun ate, Gustav stared down at the paper in front of him. He'd written down every person's name from the duplicate ship ownership papers. Now he was trying to remember if he'd either met or heard about them during the time he'd befriended Saulia Holt. He didn't think so, but what if he was missing something?

"Has Joosep been up?" Dagrun asked as she pushed her empty bowl away.

"He was out here for a while when I got back," he said. "But he went back to bed. Did you find anything?"

"Goods are now being stored in the warehouse where Joosep was being held," Dagrun said. "As well as in another warehouse in South Tarklee." She grinned. "And I know where someone who works for Holt lives."

"We should put that all on a map," Gustav said, excited now. "I can draw one."

"I can do better than that," Arnor said from the door into the bedroom. "This place was intended as more than just a safe haven." He walked past the table to the kitchen area and knelt down.

Gustav craned his neck, but all he could see was Arnor's back. He heard a scraping noise, and Arnor backed towards them. When he rose, there was a blank space where part of the wall had been.

"I'm going to need to look around here a little bit," Dagrun said. "I missed that."

"Joosep does have a Trait," Arnor said. He lifted the lid of a wooden box, pulled out a few rolls of paper, and tossed one to Gustav.

Gustav untied the string and unrolled the edge of a map. He unrolled it further: it was a map of the Pale Sea. There were dots along the coast indicating towns and villages as well as lines drawn on for rivers. And a large circle represented both North and South Tarklee.

"And the city itself," Dagrun said. She'd unrolled a second roll of paper and spread it out on the table. He leaned over to see a detailed map of Tarklee—right down to individual buildings.

"If Joosep has records that tell us who owns every building," Dagrun continued. "I will be very impressed."

"He does," Arnor said. "The records for the entire city are vast, so we guessed which information was important to keep here." He shrugged. "Copying everything in Joosep's office would have taken all of my time."

"But the records exist?" Dagrun asked, and Arnor nodded. "How is Joosep?"

"He's resting," Arnor said. "But he's better. I think part of it is the relief that you both are here. He's very hopeful that you two, along with Calder and Nadez, can stop a catastrophe."

"Someone has to."

Gustav looked up at the anger in Dagrun's voice. "You think Joosep caused this?" he asked. "He was held by force and tortured. Do you really think he wanted this to happen?"

"No," Dagrun replied, her voice hard. "But he didn't stop it when he could have, long before Tarmo Holt was in a position to kidnap the Master Intelligencer and not have to worry about facing any consequences. Joosep must have seen that Holt couldn't be trusted, yet he did nothing."

"You don't know that," Gustav said. "How could you have any idea what Joosep should have known about Holt?"

"Because he and I have the same Trait," she said "Anyone I meet, I know if they have secrets. My guess is that Joosep does too."

Gustav looked away first. He'd had no idea what Joosep's Trait was. So Dagrun Lund had the same one as the Master Intelligencer but stronger; that didn't mean she knew more than him.

"Dagrun is correct." Joosep joined them at the table, sitting down heavily in a chair. "I've spent some time today trying to pinpoint when I first realized Tarmo Holt was trouble, and I think it was the first time I met him." He shook his head. "I did not realize he was dangerous until much later, and that is my fault." He sighed. "But that will not help us. Information will. Report."

Gustav thought Joosep was talking to him, and he opened his mouth, but then Dagrun spoke.

Chapter 11

"Anything else?" Joosep leaned over the maps. Arnor had fastened them down onto the table, side by side, and the number of red marks indicating places where Tarmo Holt and his pirate allies had attacked almost overwhelmed him.

Dagrun had implied that he'd been so compliant that he might as well have been one of Holt's accomplices. He didn't believe he'd been that remiss, although he certainly held some responsibility. He shook off his self-recriminations to concentrate on a solution.

"Calder will make sure Cutterstown is safe," Dagrun said.

"Will he? You're certain?" They couldn't afford to make plans based on assumptions and then find out those assumptions were wrong.

"Yes, but all that changes for us is that we don't need to send anyone else."

"How can you be so sure Calder will succeed?" Gustav asked.

"His Trait," Dagrun said. "It's—"

"It's a strong one," Joosep interrupted. "I believe it will make the difference."

"It's Luck," Dagrun said. "Good Luck."

"That is not your secret to tell," Joosep said. He was stunned and angry. Not revealing another person's Trait was one of the most basic principles of his Intelligencers. It was the very basis of how he led them. In his opinion, disclosing Traits put everyone at risk.

"Calder won't mind as long as it helps us," she said, glaring at him. "I already know everyone's Trait. And if you expect the people in this room to help plan Holt's defeat, then I think we *all* need to know each other's strengths and weaknesses."

Joosep stared from Dagrun to Arnor to Gustav before settling on Dagrun. He frowned. He didn't think she was right, but he didn't have the energy to argue. "I suppose it might help. We do need to discuss any and all ideas: I can see how knowing what assets and advantages we have would be helpful. I can ask Nadez to find specific people; Intelligencers and students whose talents we want to use." He turned to Gustav. "We'll need another list started."

It took another half hour to catalogue everyone and their Traits. After the first few minutes, Joosep stopped arguing with Dagrun. She had different names for many of the Traits, but she also had very different insights as to what they did and how they could be used. In the end, he named the person and described their Trait, and Dagrun completed it.

He still didn't like revealing Traits, and he would make certain that piece of paper was destroyed when this was done, but it sounded as though Gustav was the only person in this apartment who hadn't already known most of this information.

"That's it," he said. He rubbed a hand across his chin. He was tired, but he needed to eat before heading back to bed.

"Another name," Dagrun said. "Inger Lund."

"No," Joosep said. "She's not an Intelligencer. And you said yourself that she's joined the pirates."

"I'm not giving up on her," Dagrun said. "But you can put her on a separate list of Traits we may need to guard against."

"There are others with Traits?" Joosep asked.

"Yes. Captain Margit Ansdottir has at least two. An Unseen Trait strong enough that she can navigate a ship through the Teeth and another one that has to do with Keeping what's hers. And Ursa Ozlinch the innkeeper on Strongrock has a really strong Keeper Trait."

"Keeper," Gustav said. "What does that do?"

"It instils loyalty," Dagrun said. "At least from what I've seen: Ansdottir has the absolute loyalty of her crew. It also seems to make her hate losing anyone or anything. And usually she doesn't have to."

"Is that what's happened to Inger?" Joosep asked.

"What happened to Inger," Dagrun said, "is that *you* made her feel as though she didn't matter. So yes, she was open to someone who appreciated her talents, including her Trait."

"What's her Trait?" Gustav asked in a soft voice.

"Seen: the opposite of mine because she's my twin. But I was selected by Joosep to be an Intelligencer and Inger was not."

"Her Trait is not useful," Joosep said. "And I allowed her to live here with you."

"Yes, she was always very aware that she was *allowed* to be here," Dagrun said bitterly. "Now the pirates have found a use for her Trait, and she can't resist being useful even if they are thieves and murderers."

"I didn't know," Joosep said. "How could I have known? I didn't see any way to harness her Trait."

"Which is why Traits shouldn't be such a secret," Dagrun replied. "Why having one single person who knows all the Traits and makes decisions based on their own *very limited* knowledge should never be allowed to happen again."

"I suppose." Joosep closed his eyes. He would admit his responsibility for Tarmo Holt not being restricted in any way, allowing him both the time and opportunity to plan all of this, but his decision to not train Inger Lund? Just because pirates found a use for her Trait didn't mean she should have been trained as an Intelligencer. "I have always concealed Traits so that they could remain unknown and therefore a surprise," he continued.

"You didn't even try to figure out what Inger's Trait does," Dagrun said. "She can lie."

Joosep looked at her in alarm. "That's not possible," he said. "At least, it shouldn't be."

"So I thought," Dagrun replied. "Because that's what you told me. But I saw her lie. So did Calder."

Joosep wasn't sure knowing that would have made a difference to him, but he wasn't going to fight with Dagrun, not when he needed her so much. And he had such little energy to spare. He stifled a yawn, inwardly cursing his frailness. He might never recover from being imprisoned by Tarmo Holt. "I apologize. I am far too tired to be able to think as clearly about this as I need to." This time, he couldn't contain his yawn.

"We'll finish up here," Arnor said as he helped him rise from the chair. "You get some rest."

As Joosep shuffled to the bedroom, he heard Arnor whisper something to the others. He couldn't tell what he said, but he knew his assistant was angry. He should tell him not to be, that Dagrun's anger towards him was partially deserved and that he'd been blind in so many ways. And that he could fight his own fights. But he was too exhausted. Instead, he shut the door and climbed into bed, hoping that there was a way to fix the mess he'd allowed to happen.

CALDER WAVED TO Jaak, who stood at the stern of the last log hauler as the three ships headed north. He shoved the tiller over and turned the little sailboat closer to the shoreline.

He'd helped get the log haulers ready to sail. It hadn't taken the captains of the three ships long to agree to sail north, not once Calder told them how many ships had been destroyed in Tarklee and Nurmi. As he watched them sail away, he saw buckets being lowered into the sea. They would store sea water on deck in case Ansdottir spotted them.

The *Bright Breeze* was faster and nimbler than these loaded-down log haulers. Ansdottir would easily catch them, and once caught, setting them ablaze would be simple.

Yakop was handling the removal and storage of the food. It was being taken to the clearing created by last year's logging harvest, along with as much cut and dressed timber as they could manage. Even if no ships could be built, no one wanted to lose the summer's harvest. At the worst they could sell it as firewood. Warm and hungry was better than cold and hungry, if it came to that.

Cutterstown had to prepare for more than just an attack by sea. A landing party didn't seem out of the question, not when Ansdottir was after his family. Calder also assumed that the pirates would target what they'd destroyed in Nurmi and Setberg: warehouses and the docks and ships needed to fill them.

But enough was being done that he felt he could leave to warn his mother. He didn't relish explaining to her that his choice of life had put her at risk. She wouldn't be happy, and his sister might be afraid. But that didn't mean he was going to avoid this duty.

He recognized a couple of landmarks: the stream that fell twenty feet into the sea; a sand bar that stretched across the mouth of a small cove. He rounded a point and saw it—his mother's cabin. It wasn't home: despite what Nadez had told him years ago, this hadn't been his home since he was six. That didn't mean it wasn't a welcome sight.

No one was outside when he docked at the small pier that jutted out into the shallow bay. A skiff was tied up; his mother and sister used it to hunt for clams when the tide was out.

The smell of smoke drifted to him, but he didn't see anything out of place when he looked at the cabin. He shrugged and walked past the racks of drying fish, the reason why he knew how to cook it so many ways, towards the smokehouse that was tucked into the trees behind the house.

"Calder?"

It was his sister. "Berna."

"What's happened?" his sister replied. She held out her arms, and he walked into them and hugged her. "You were here just a few weeks ago. Is everything all right?"

"Not really," he said. He ignored her questioning look and stepped away from her. "I need to talk to you and Mother." So much had happened that it was hard to believe he'd been here within the last month, just before Joosep sent him after Dag.

"Did you see Yakop?" she asked.

"I did. He's taking precautions in Cutterstown."

"Precautions! That sounds like something interesting is happening. Maybe I should finally take him up on his offer to move there," she paused, "despite his plans to marry me off."

"I'm sure any match would be to his benefit," Calder said.

"He tells me it would be to mine," Berna said. "I wish I had a Trait so I could study in North Tarklee, like you did. I'm afraid life as the wife of a Freeholder would bore me."

"Don't wish a thing like that." Lauma Strauskas, his mother, stood in the door to the smokehouse, her hands on her hips and a frown on her face. "To have a Trait. You know what had to happen before Calder was taken away."

"Mother," Calder said. He stepped over to her and placed a kiss on the cheek she turned to him. He would have stepped back, but she grabbed him and held him as she stared into his eyes.

Finally, she nodded and let go. "Trouble, that's why you're back so soon." She turned and started walking towards the cabin. "And you'll tell me all about your new love." She spun around. "And don't pretend there isn't one, not to me."

"Is it true?" Berna caught up with him. She took a look at his face and grinned. "Of course, it's true, Mother always knows. Although Nyorden knows how she does."

He knew how, he thought as he let his sister guide him into the house. His mother had a Trait. She must because she always *did* know. And now he wondered that he hadn't realized that before; that no one had realized that before. And then he thought of Inger Lund, a woman with a Trait that Joosep considered useless. Perhaps Joosep had considered his mother's Trait useless as well.

He smiled. Although if his mother hadn't wanted to become an Intelligencer, no one could have forced her.

He wasn't sure if the inside of the cabin had even been cleaned since he'd left. The blanket he'd folded was still hanging over the desk chair, and there was a pile of dishes in the kitchen. Fish stew bubbled on the stove. He walked over to it and sniffed. Perhaps he could still save it from blandness. He searched the shelf and found some pepper and a shrivelled clove of garlic.

"Leave it," his mother said. "Berna? Tea, please."

His mother sat down at the small table, and Calder sat across from her. He picked up a torn net and tidied it up before setting it to one side. He'd inherited his habit of fixing any little thing that crossed his path from his mother. But the difference between them was Calder liked to finish anything he started. His mother tended to start, get interrupted, and then never return to that item again.

"So, you met someone?" his mother prodded.

"Yes." There was no sense pretending he hadn't, even though he had no idea what his relationship with Dag was, or would turn into. "She's an Intelligencer."

"*Skit*," his mother said. "The only thing worse than that would be a sailor like your father."

"A sailor like me, you mean," Calder said. "So, you agree that I'm Lucky to have met her." It had always struck Calder as odd that his mother, a woman who had happily left her own marriage behind, was so very keen on her children finding spouses.

"Luck." His mother almost spit the word, evidence that she had no idea that she had a Trait. "I hate that word."

"No, you hate that it's my Trait," Calder replied. At times, he thought he should just stay away, since every visit home brought her loss to the surface. "And that Hakon, my opposite, was Unlucky."

"Yes, and then they took you too." His mother glared at him as though it was his fault that he'd gone to North Tarklee when he was six.

"Here's the tea," Berna said as she placed the pot and three mugs on the table. She grabbed a jar of honey and sat down between Calder and his mother. A position she'd held ever since she was born.

"Now, I think we need to find out what *precautions* Yakop is taking in Cutterstown," Berna said. "And why Calder came to visit."

Their mother scowled but nodded, and Calder smiled. He'd been gone before his sister was born and had only been an occasional presence as she grew up. But at sixteen, Berna was on her way to becoming a strong woman. His gaze went from his sister to his mother. He supposed she'd have to be, to hold her own in this house.

"Pirates have attacked Lavais Island," he said, starting with the incident that would have the most far-reaching effect here. "They burned the shipyards to the ground, along with any ships in the process of being built and log haulers that were in the harbour." He held up a hand when his mother would have spoken. "Then they did the same in Nurmi and Tarklee: log haulers and Merchant Adventurer ships were destroyed, along with warehouses full of food. Nurmi lost their winter supply of grain. I'm not sure of the exact losses in Tarklee, but they were significant."

His mother took a deep breath and placed her hands flat on the table in front of her. The fact that she hadn't said anything meant that she understood what his news meant.

"Yakop's precautions?" she asked finally.

"Moving the food stored in the warehouses to a safer place."

"Safer," his mother repeated. "Not safe."

"The pirates are after more than just the destruction of Cutterstown's food and ships," Calder said. "They are after my family: they are after you."

He mother shut her eyes as though in pain, then she nodded and met his gaze.

"I'm sorry," he said.

"Yes, I'm sure you are, but that will not help us."

"What will?" Berna said. "Should we go to Cutterstown?"

"I don't know that it will be any safer than here," Calder said. "But I have a small boat, and I can take you both south. Or north if you prefer." He'd promised Yakop he would return to Cutterstown, but his brother would understand that he was at their mother's mercy.

"I didn't mean to be safe," Berna said. "I meant to be effective! Would it be better to add our strength to Cutterstown instead of using it to defend ourselves here?"

"I am not leaving," his mother said. "I will die here if that is what my fate holds."

Calder blew out a breath. He would not argue with her about this. His mother's legendary stubbornness would either get her killed or save her. He wished he could transfer some of his Luck to her.

"Will you at least hide?" he asked.

His mother's smile chilled him. "Sure," she said, "but I prefer to think of it as lying in wait."

"And I'll go to Cutterstown," Berna said. "That's where you're heading, isn't it? In case there is a fight?"

"Yes." He looked from his mother's calm face to his sister's excited one. He hadn't really expected anything different. "After we eat. I'd prefer to meet whatever is coming with a full belly. Even if it is that bland slop you call fish stew."

"Stop that," Arnor said to her. "He's far too frail to be burdened with your anger."

"Burdened with my anger," Dag repeated. "I need him to understand exactly what's happened, what he's *let* happen, so that he can help us figure out how to fix it."

"So a few ships have been burned," Gustav said. He smiled, which made Dag think he was trying to use his Trait—his

Charisma—on her.

"Don't bother using your Trait on me," she said to him. "And if you think it's only a few ships, then you haven't been paying attention to what the marks on the maps mean." She jabbed a finger. "The Lavais Island shipyards have been destroyed. Calder said that there were two Master Shipbuilders: if they are dead, it may be years before another ship is built there. Here."

She pointed to Setberg and Nurmi. "Setberg's warehouses were burned, and the village has been abandoned; in Nurmi, all of the grain they had stored for the winter has been destroyed. A road along the coast leads from Nurmi to Tarklee. If it's not already jammed with hungry, frightened refugees, then it soon will be. The numbers are not huge, maybe a hundred or one hundred and fifty people, but they will have no shelter in Tarklee. No food, no water, no means of earning a wage."

"You spent some time there in South Tarklee," she said to Gustav. "What do you think will happen when one hundred and fifty desperate people arrive there?"

"Fights," Gustav said. "The people who live there will fight to hold onto the little they have. The new people might move to North Tarklee."

"Yes, they might try that. But what if Tarmo Holt doesn't allow them to cross into North Tarklee?" she asked. "These people are Swyfordians. He could say that they are Swyford's problem. He might even argue that since Timonis can't manage his own country, he should not be put in charge of the Three."

"He wouldn't, would he?" Arnor asked, then he answered his own question. "Of course, he would. And he would use that as an excuse to keep Clan Freeholder Timonis from succeeding him as Grand Freeholder."

"That's what I think," Dag agreed. "Holt retains his position and there are an extra one hundred and fifty people stuck in South Tarklee. No food, no housing, no work. And winter just weeks away. What will happen next?" she prodded Gustav. The lad was training to be an Intelligencer and had been taught history. He should have an idea of what to expect.

"Sickness," he said finally. "People will die in the streets. Or they will riot, if they think there's anything to be gained by it."

"Yes, there will be sickness, and there will be riots." She paused. "And what's the one thing that will allow Holt to control everyone?"

"Food." It was Arnor who answered. "If he has food, he can basically decide who survives the winter."

"Yes, and not just this upcoming winter," Dag said, "if he really does own most of the ships capable of travelling to the Sapphire Sea. Oh sure, there will be Freeholders who will be doing their best to fish and grow and preserve as much food as they can, but most of the ships that traded within the Pale Sea were destroyed. If Holt forces the Freeholders into bad trade bargains in order to survive the winter, *he* will be the one who decides where that food goes as well."

"And he will," Gustav said. "He will do anything. I told you someone in his household poisoned me? I was a favourite of his daughter, and that's what was done. He and his people will do anything."

"Now you see," Dag looked over at Arnor, "why I'm angry with Joosep and need him to understand exactly what we're faced with."

"Are you sure that's what Tarmo Holt is planning?" Arnor asked. "It's hard for me to believe that Joosep missed something of that significance."

"I'm as sure as my Trait allows me to be," she replied. "And knowing how my Trait works, how Joosep's Trait works, I find it impossible to believe that he missed all that. And yet it seems he has."

"That's why," Gustav said. "That's why you weren't sure you could trust Joosep. You and Calder."

"Yes," she agreed, ignoring Arnor's angry looks. "We worried that Joosep had either helped Holt, or he had been so woefully tolerant that it ended up being the same thing. Joosep has been complicit in Tarmo Holt's plans to remain in power, and indeed, increase the amount of power he wields."

"He's not to blame," Arnor protested.

"He is." Gustav nodded. "He didn't act when he could have. Joosep asked me, a student, to spy on Holt. He knew that Tarmo Holt was up to something. I think he'd known for a long time, months or even years, before he gave me that assignment."

"And he still he didn't confront Holt," Dag said. "Not even when you were poisoned."

"Oh, all right," Arnor said. "He's complicit but not to blame. Does it matter?"

"Not as long as he recognizes that," Dag said. "And takes steps to make sure that the same situation never happens again." She sighed. She felt her shoulders relax as some of the angry tension melted away. They needed to start making plans.

"Gustav, you said something earlier that gave me an idea," she said, "when you were talking about what the poor people of South Tarklee will do."

"Get sick," he said. "And riot."

"Yes. I think we can use the latter to our advantage."

"You want riots? Won't people get hurt?"

"Yes, probably," she said. She didn't like it any more than he did. "These are people who would riot anyway, and who could blame them, when they are starving? I just want to help them pick the right places to riot."

"Tarmo Holt's warehouses," Arnor said. "You want the list of who owns what in North and South Tarklee so you can find out which are Holt's warehouses."

Dag picked up the paper that held the names of the ships and the people who supposedly owned them. "I'd also be interested in finding out if any of these people own warehouses across the city," she said. "Holt might have acquired more than ships from them. How do we get that information?"

THE PIER WAS dark by the time Calder sailed into the bay at Cutterstown. Berna crouched in the prow, and as soon as the boat was close enough, she jumped out onto the wooden planks and tied the little boat to the dock.

"I'll meet you at Yakop's," he said to her. "After I take care of the boat." Berna nodded and headed along the pier.

Calder pulled the sail down and stepped onto the pier. He lay the sail out flat and ran a hand along it, checking that it was dry before folding it and tucking it under the stern seat. The rigging was next; he checked each rope, making sure that nothing was frayed or tangled. He needed this boat if he was going to get back to Tarklee. And Dag.

His mother had pried very little information out of him about Dag: partly because he'd had years of experience in telling some of the truth but not all of the truth, and partly because there wasn't much to tell. He had no idea if Dagrun Lund wanted anything to do with him: if what they'd shared had simply been because they'd been safe, finally, and without a task. He snorted. Being warm and dry and bored wasn't why he'd bedded her, but perhaps it was why she had bedded him.

He stepped from the pier onto land and paused to look at the huddle of buildings in the centre of Cutterstown. The Freehold office was dark, so he headed towards his brother's house.

"Calder." Someone called from the shoreline at the edge of town.

He turned to find Thorben, his brother's oldest friend, staring out at the dark sea.

"Do you really think we'll see pirates tonight?" he asked. He held up an unlit lamp. "I'm to signal if I see anything. Rina's across the bay doing the same."

"Maybe not tonight," Calder said. He stared out at the darkness. The only thing he could see were the crests of waves as they broke close to shore. "But they will come one night." Margit Ansdottir would find his family, he was certain of that. All he could do was hope it would be sooner rather than later. He needed to be here when she came, but he also needed to be back in Tarklee, with Dag, figuring out how to stop Holt.

"We'll be ready," Thorben said. "How will we know it's the pirate ship?"

"It's painted white," Calder replied. "And it will look like it's being sailed by ghosts, but it's not. It's being sailed by Pilalians."

"Your father's people?" Thorben laughed. "Did they ask you to join?"

"They did, actually," he replied. "I told them no. Now, I'm off to find my brother."

"Yakop's talking strategy at his house," Thorben said. "I'm sure they would appreciate any help you can give."

"I hope I can help." He turned back to the path.

When he knocked, his brother opened the door and pulled him inside.

"Good, you made it," he said. "Berna's here along with Noak. But you're the one who knows the pirate captain. We need you to tell us which ideas will work."

Gustav followed Arnor through the dark city. He didn't

recognize any of the winding streets and lanes they travelled until they passed the small wooden building where he'd first spoken to Dagrun and Calder. It wasn't until Arnor led them to a small door and unlocked it that he realized this was where Dagrun and Calder had been coming from.

Dagrun was right, to a certain extent. Keeping too many secrets could harm their ability to challenge Tarmo Holt, but he could see Joosep's point too. Vilis had betrayed them; if he'd known more, he would have told it all to Tarmo Holt. As it was, his actions only exposed a few people, not the entire Intelligencer organization. Who knew what the Grand Freeholder would have done with that information?

Arnor eased open a small door. Peering over his shoulder, Gustav recognized Joosep's outer office.

"The records are kept in there," Arnor said, waving a hand at the door to Joosep's office. "You keep watch and stop anyone from entering until I'm done." He paused and sighed. "It will take me at least an hour to find and copy the ownership records of all the people who owned the ships."

"All right. Who might come here?" he asked. "I mean who would have a legitimate reason to be here?" He was confident that he would be able to bar any trespassers from this office, but keeping someone out who had a right to be here would be harder.

"At this time of night?" Arnor's grin flashed in the dark. "No one. Not even me." He pulled a ring of keys from his pocket and used one to open the door. "Do we need a signal in case someone tries to get in?"

"Since no one else is allowed," Gustav said. "The only signal you need to listen for is a fight. I'll make as much noise as I can." He'd use his Trait first, of course, but if that didn't work, he would fight, if he had to. His training included self-defence, which was more training than most people got. And probably more than any opponent would expect.

Arnor simply nodded, slipped through the door to Joosep's office, and disappeared from view.

Gustav found a dark corner a few steps from the door and settled his back against the wall to wait and watch. Two things he'd had a lot of practice doing in the past week.

JOOSEP REACHED UP and put the key back in its hiding spot, wrapped his cloak tighter around his shoulders, and set off into the city.

He'd waited until Gustav and Arnor had left and Dagrun was asleep before stealing out of his room. Gustav wouldn't have believed that despite his infirmity only he could do this task, and Dagrun, well, she probably wouldn't trust him to do this alone.

She was right, in a way, that more than just he should have the knowledge of the Master Intelligencer. But the person who needed that knowledge wasn't her.

Nadez was the one he was willing to share it with; the person who had the skills and maturity to take up the responsibility of his position as Master Intelligencer. Who, it seemed, had already taken it up.

Now, he was going to make sure that she truly had, that she was finally willing to aid the Intelligencer organization. He wanted to confirm for himself that there was someone to replace him if he failed, or more likely, if his health never returned and he could not physically perform the tasks that needed to be done.

During the past few years, he'd thought that Dagrun Lund could be trained to succeed him. Unlike Nadez, who had no Trait and never fully trusted them, he believed that Traits were essential to an Intelligencer. And the Unseen Trait was superbly suited for a Master Intelligencer. Not only did it help uncover secrets, it helped uncover Traits.

But he'd also envisioned having years to groom Dagrun for the role. He couldn't imagine handing her that responsibility now, not when her sister had been compromised, and Dagrun was so angry that she blamed him for it.

He was willing to accept responsibility for some things, but Inger Lund falling in with pirates was not one of them. Most people had fulfilling lives without having a Trait. Inger could have had one as well, if she'd been content to do that. Instead, she'd chosen to live at the Hall, with Dagrun, and forfeit any type of normal life.

Of course, his preference, since he wanted to keep tabs on every person with a Trait, was for her to live at the Hall. He might even have encouraged it, but he'd never forced her.

Unfortunately, he had never seen a use for her Trait. Even now, he didn't think he'd been wrong. He supposed it might have made both her and Dagrun more loyal, but he felt he'd done more than required by allowing her to live at the Hall with her sister.

He peered around a corner at the deserted street, wondering if Nadez was still frequenting her old haunts now that trouble was here or if she'd found some new hideouts.

He headed down the street trying not to go either too slow or too fast for this time of night, but his weakness betrayed him. By the time he was at the next cross street, he was exhausted and winded.

He leaned against a building, taking deep breaths, worried that he'd made an error in judgement. For the past few days, all he'd been able to manage, all he'd *had* to manage, was moving from the bed to the table to eat and then back to bed. He hadn't even had to cook the food he'd eaten.

Somehow, being able to manage that had made him think he could do so much more.

He heard a sound behind him, and his heart raced. Had he been caught? The footsteps passed him, and he sagged in relief. No one was following him, no one had discovered him.

He sighed and took in a few deep, slow breaths, trying to calm his breathing and slow his heart rate.

For a moment, he'd been back in the cell, waiting for one or another indignity to be visited upon him. He squared his shoulders and stepped away from the building and back into the street.

Two more blocks to go, that was all. If Nadez wasn't there, he'd use another route and head back to the secret apartment.

He stared at the small stable. It looked like it had been abandoned for years, but it was Nadez's own secret safe spot. The very thing they'd argued about for years, ever since she'd used Intelligencer funds to purchase it. And hadn't been disciplined for it.

"It looks like no one is home," a voice whispered in his ear. "And no one is, since I'm out here with you."

He turned to find Nadez Norup staring at him. There was no trace of humour in either her voice or her face.

"We need to talk," he said.

"Yes, we do," she replied. "And although I am happy to see you alive, I am wondering why you're out here in the middle of the night tramping around for anyone to see and hear."

"I did not tramp!" He was offended that she would accuse *him*, with his Unseen Trait, of giving himself away.

"Then explain to me how this Intelligencer could track you and find me first?" Nadez stepped aside, and to his alarm, he saw Dagrun Lund staring at him from a shadow.

"You followed me?" he asked. "How dare you!"

"I told you the time for keeping secrets is past," she said. She nodded to Nadez. "We need to share information and then figure out what to do with it."

"I agree," Nadez said. "This way." She led the way, not towards the old stable, but down a narrow alley that stopped at a small fence. She pushed on the fence, and a section of wood swung inward. Nadez gestured for him to enter, and when he hesitated, Dagrun swept past him. He followed her into a dark passage. He heard something close, and then light bloomed from behind him.

"Keep going straight," Nadez called out softly.

In front of him, the back of Dagrun's head was illuminated as she headed down the passageway. Joosep followed her for two dozen steps before the passage spilled them into a larger room.

Using the lamp she held, Nadez lit a second lamp and set them both down on a stone slab that took up most of the floor space. A bundle of blankets was heaped in a corner, and a bucket sat on the floor.

"I wasn't expecting guests, so I have nothing to offer except for water," Nadez said, gesturing to the bucket. "The dipper is on the table. Sit down."

"Not until I know why an inexperienced Intelligencer is questioning my authority," Joosep said, glaring at Dagrun. "Or have you decided to betray us and join your sister?"

"Sit down, I said." Nadez picked up the dipper and scooped up some water.

She took a sip before handing it to him. He wanted to refuse it, on principle, but he was thirsty and his energy had flagged. He took a drink and deliberately put the dipper down without offering it to Dagrun.

"That's too petty even for you," Nadez admonished. She

refilled the dipper and handed it to Dagrun, who took a sip before setting it back down. "No wonder Dagrun came to talk to me."

"She can't be trusted," Joosep said.

"I'm still not sure you can be," Dagrun replied. "Because not an hour after we agreed that we needed to share information, that keeping too many secrets helped Tarmo Holt more than it helped us, you sneak away."

"To meet with my colleague," he said. "Who is my equal, and therefore this has nothing to do with you."

"Which you could have explained to me," she countered.

"You would never have allowed me to leave alone." Joosep couldn't believe he was being challenged. And by someone who'd completed just one assignment and had then run away, chasing her sister.

"Secrets," Dagrun said, "will get us all killed."

"Will you two stop squabbling?"

He looked across the slab of rock to find Nadez staring at him, a smile on her face.

"You think this is funny?" he asked.

"No." The smile slid off her face. "Too many lives depend on what we do. But it does remind me of why I left once you'd been promoted to Master Intelligencer. Although I never voiced my opinion of your choices as openly as Dagrun is doing." She nodded to the younger woman and sat down.

Dagrun sat as well, leaving Joosep standing, staring at Nadez. He abruptly sat down on a wooden crate that had been placed beside the stone slab.

"I thought it was because you didn't trust Traits," Joosep said. "I thought it meant that you needed to work alone. That taking direction from me and trusting my Trait had finally become too much for you. That you didn't want the job."

"I didn't want the job," Nadez agreed, "which meant I felt it not fair to remain and challenge how you performed it. You know I never agreed with some of your ideas, especially that all Intelligencers needed a Trait. But mostly it was because you thought the best approach was to gather intelligence and pass it along. And keep all of your secrets to yourself. Too much secrecy and too little action was how I saw it. I couldn't stay and be part of that; couldn't watch while you, in my opinion, made so many mistakes. So, I left."

Joosep stared at her as her words sank in. She'd left because she didn't believe in him, because she'd thought he'd make mistakes; that he'd fail. And he had.

GUSTAV RUBBED A hand across his eyes, trying to keep them open. Arnor had been in Joosep's office for over an hour, and he was worried that it would be dawn before he was finished and they could return to the apartment.

If there were too many people on the streets, they might be forced to find a place to spend the day and wait for dark. It wasn't a problem: he knew a handful of places where they could hide, but it meant a whole day that Dagrun didn't have this information. A whole day when she couldn't be planning the next steps in the fight against Holt.

Because although Joosep was the Master Intelligencer, in his mind Dagrun Lund was the one who could save them all from Tarmo Holt.

Even Joosep admitted that he'd been wary of Holt, even suspected the man was hiding something the day he met him. And he did nothing. All those years, and he did nothing.

And Holt had done much.

Had he laughed at them? When he met with his pirates, had Tarmo Holt laughed at how pathetic his Master Intelligencer was? At how useful he'd been in aiding Holt's cause? That could be how he'd convinced Vilis to betray Joosep and work with him. By telling him that Intelligencers were being mismanaged into uselessness and that he would make them relevant and important.

Gustav shook his head. Even though he'd been proud to help, proud to be given an assignment by Joosep, he was only half trained. And because of that, he'd been put into danger: he'd ended up being poisoned. He was lucky he hadn't died.

The door opened, and Arnor poked his head out. Gustav checked the halls before he stepped out of the shadow and met Arnor as he exited Joosep's office.

"I got what we needed," Arnor said. "Let's go."

Gustav nodded and followed Arnor back through the small door, and they let themselves out into the alley.

Soon they were back in the safety of the secret apartment.

"Where's Dagrun?" he asked. He'd expected her to be sleeping in the main room: her blankets were on the floor, but she wasn't in them.

"Joosep is gone too," Arnor said from the hallway.

"There's no sign of a struggle." Gustav shuffled the papers on the table. "And nothing is missing. I think they went on their own, even though they didn't leave a note."

"Joosep isn't well enough to go out," Arnor said.

"Apparently, he didn't agree," Gustav replied. "Hand me that list you made."

He sat down. He was tired, and he had to admit that he was a little worried about Joosep and Dagrun being gone, but worry wouldn't help. What would help was mapping any warehouses that were on Arnor's list: making sure that they had information to direct the riots. Riots that would happen whether or not Joosep and Dagrun returned, if he had anything to do with it.

Chapter 12

"It's too close to dawn," Calder said. "I don't think they'll attack now." His brother stifled a yawn, and Calder fought the urge to copy him.

"Then we have time to create the defences?" Yakop asked. "Do we need to worry about them scouting us?"

"If they do, all they'll see is that they can't land," Calder replied. He stood up and stretched, trying to work the stiffness out of his limbs. "And that will be almost as good as sinking their ship." Idly, he wondered which scenario his Luck would allow. "Let's get the loggers busy submerging the logs. Each one has to be anchored to the bottom. I don't want them tied together like a raft."

"And sharp objects nailed into them, yes," Noak said. "So they can't just walk across them."

Calder nodded. "And uneven depths: I'd like some, especially closer to the open sea, to be far enough below the surface that even waves won't uncover them." He didn't expect Margit Ansdottir to steer her ship into a submerged log, but they might get Lucky and sink a dinghy if the pirates launched one.

"Come on," Yakop said to him. "You can tell them what you want yourself. I'm not letting you go to bed while the rest of us do all the hard work."

"I visited Mother," Calder said. "I consider that extremely hard work." He followed his brother outside anyway. For one, the logging camp would have breakfast ready soon. At least he would be able to eat, and he needed food almost as much as he needed sleep.

Bjorn, the lead logger, stood a head taller than Calder, and although he had the blond hair of a northerner, he spent so much time outdoors that his skin was almost as dark as his.

"You sent the ships away," Bjorn said when Yakop introduced him. "How am I supposed to pay my men?"

"Right now, I'm more worried about keeping them alive," Calder replied. "Pirates have already destroyed the Lavais shipyards. Now they're coming for the ships and food."

"You're saying that Lavais is gone?" Bjorn looked at Yakop. "Is this true?"

"Yes," Yakop said. "My brother saw it with his own eyes. There is no one left to buy your timber, and other than the three ships we sent north, there is no way to get it there."

"Pirates," Bjorn said. He turned his head and spat. "Have no respect for the hard work of others. So, you are here just to tell me the news?"

Calder laughed. Bjorn had reacted to what he'd been told as though he always expected bad things to happen. But *he* had Good Luck on his side. "Of course not! We're here to get you to help us defend against the pirates."

"And kill some?" Bjorn asked.

"If we're lucky," Yakop said. "But in order to be lucky we need to be smart. And we," he gestured to Calder, "are very smart."

"Better to be lucky," Bjorn replied. "But my men and I will help you. What do you need?"

"Enough logs and timber to fill the bay," Calder said. "Each one with a separate anchor—either a large rock or something else that keeps them submerged and secured to the bottom. And nails or shards of glass or crockery, anything sharp really, driven into them so that a man in bare feet can't walk across them."

"Noak will supply the rocks and sharp objects," Yakop said. "He's organizing the townsfolk now."

"And what will my men do for the rest of the day?" Bjorn asked. "Once we are done this little project. There is no point in felling more trees if Lavais is gone."

"There are paths along the shore that lead to town," Calder said. "Use your imagination and make them impassable. Maybe make it a contest. Your men like a challenge, don't they?"

"They do," Bjorn said with a laugh. "Come, we will discuss more over breakfast."

"Breakfast, finally," Calder replied. He winked at Yakop and followed Bjorn to a tent.

"I'VE ASKED THE students and instructors not to change their routines too quickly," Nadez said. "In case Holt has people watching. But they will leave when they can." She met Dag's eyes. "And until he showed up," she gestured to where Joosep sat propped up against a wall, "I assumed that Joosep was either dead or still being imprisoned by Holt."

They were in the small room still. Dag sat across from Nadez while Joosep sat along the wall behind them. Dag was pretty sure Joosep was asleep, although it was possible he was simply pretending to be. She gave herself a mental shake. She should trust him, shouldn't she? Then why this feeling of doubt? She frowned.

And although her Trait was activated, it wasn't telling her to not trust him; it was her head and her heart that were wary because Joosep had allowed this to happen. His actions and inactions had led to Tarmo Holt being in a position where he could coerce every single person in the Fair Seas Treaty Alliance countries into doing exactly what he wanted.

What was almost worse, Dag wasn't sure he truly accepted the role he had played in allowing this. And if Joosep didn't accept it, he could make things worse instead of better. *That* was what her Trait was warning her about.

"What about Vilis?" Dag asked, forcing her attention back to the conversation. "Did you speak to him?" Joosep didn't flinch at Vilis's name, so he might truly be asleep. "That's the training group that has been disclosed to Holt."

Nadez frowned. "The instructors are missing, but whether they've been taken or are in hiding, no one knows. The girl is safe, but I haven't heard any news about Vilis or the other boy everyone likes so much."

"Gustav," she said. "He's with us. Vilis is the one who betrayed his group to Holt."

"I'll keep an eye out for him," Nadez said. "But I expect he's dead by now. He won't be of any more use, and he knows more than Holt would find comfortable." She shook her head. "You'd think Intelligencer students would be smarter than that." She nodded to Joosep. "And how is he?"

"He's been through a lot," Dag said. "It took its toll physically." And that was true. She couldn't imagine what it took to escape captivity like that; to be desperate enough to kill to free yourself. But she refused to let Joosep's suffering overshadow his responsibility for the current situation.

"And mentally?"

"He's tired, but I think he's fine," Dag lied. She wasn't sure Joosep was capable of leading the Intelligencers through this crisis, but she wasn't going to say that in front of him, even if she did think he was asleep. "We're all relieved that you stepped in when you did. Especially Joosep."

Nadez snorted. "I think he liked the idea of it more before he met with me and it became real." She lowered her voice. "Where's Calder?"

"There was a threat to his family," Dag said. "He's gone north to warn them. He'll be back as soon as he can. He doesn't know where the hidden apartment is, so he may come looking for you." She paused and looked away. "Tell him I'll be by every few days."

"Will you now?" Nadez grinned. "Calder was always my favourite."

"I will," Dag kept her eyes averted away from the older Intelligencer, but she knew she'd already figured out something about her and Calder. "We should keep in touch for safety and because we need to tell each other our news and plans."

"Plans? You have some?" All trace of humour was gone from Nadez's voice.

"A beginning of one, yes," Dag said. "If the others have been able to gather the information we need, there will be riots in the next few days."

"Where?"

"That's what we hope the information tells us," Dag replied. "We want it to be at warehouses scattered across the city."

"Let me know if you need any help starting these riots. There may be other activities we want to hide among unrest like that."

Nadez stood up. "I think it's time for me to wake Joosep up. If you don't want to be seen, and *I* certainly don't want you to be seen leaving my little hole in the wall, then you need to go now."

Joosep was groggy, and Dag had to guide him every step of the way back to the apartment, but they made it without being noticed, she thought.

"You're back," Gustav said. "Good." Arnor rushed past him and helped Dagrun lead Joosep to a chair. The Master Intelligencer sighed as he was lowered into it.

"What did you do to him?" Arnor said.

"I followed him," Dagrun said. "And then I helped him get back here safely." She sounded tired, and Gustav got up and put the water on to heat. He didn't want Dagrun to bed down until he'd shown her what he'd mapped out.

"You followed him?" Arnor asked. "Why? Because you don't trust him?"

Gustav kept his eyes averted, afraid they might betray him. He had no desire to fight with Arnor, but he didn't trust Joosep as much as he trusted Dagrun. And knowing that he'd snuck out without telling Dagrun, made him trust the Master Intelligencer even less. His assistant was blindly loyal though, which he assumed was a good quality in an assistant but a very poor one in an Intelligencer.

"Because I didn't think he was well enough to be out on his own," Dagrun retorted. "And the fact that I had to practically carry him back means that I was right."

"Huh." Arnor didn't seem happy, but he didn't say anything more to Dagrun. Instead, he fussed over Joosep, helping him shuffle to the back bedroom.

The water was boiling, so Gustav made tea.

"Back from where?" he asked as he placed two mugs on the table. Dagrun eyed him before joining him.

"Back from seeing Nadez Norup," she said. "Something we need to do regularly. Thank you." She took a sip and closed her eyes.

Gustav sipped his own tea, allowing her a moment to relax. "I don't trust Joosep either," he said softly.

Her eyes flew open and met his. "Why?"

"He's blind to his own faults," he said. "And he doesn't trust his own Trait." He paused. "I recognize it because that's how I feel at times." He sighed. "Mostly since I met you. My Trait doesn't work on you, so I worry that if it's stopped working on everyone, what will I do?" He wouldn't be able to be an Intelligencer: that was the real fear.

She stared at him until he wanted to look away, but he didn't. Finally, she nodded.

"Thank you," she said. "That's the one thing that makes sense. That's why Joosep allowed Tarmo Holt free reign all these years. If he doesn't trust his Trait, there is no way he would act on what it was telling him." She smiled. "I still don't trust him, but for a different reason. I assume you made tea because you and Arnor found something. Tell me."

He liked that she didn't ask him to report; that would have been far too much like Joosep. Between them, they'd just agreed to watch Joosep: to work around him and, by extension, they'd agreed that Dagrun was now in charge. But she wasn't trying to be Joosep; she wasn't trying to become Master Intelligencer. She was just trying to keep their part of the world safe. The same as him.

"Arnor found dozens of properties that are owned by the same people listed on the duplicate ship ownership papers." He pulled a sheet out. "His notes indicate which are warehouses, which are houses and cottages, and which are workshops." He passed the sheet over to her. "I've marked them all on the map. Warehouses with an X, living quarters with a circle, and workshops with Ws."

Dagrun leaned over the map. "Each warehouse has another building near it," she looked up at him. "Guards?"

"That's what I'd do," Gustav said. "If the warehouses do contain food, and that is what Holt plans on using to gain and maintain control, he'd want to make sure they are protected."

"He can't afford to lose his leverage." Dagrun grinned, and he realized that she was not much more than half a dozen years older than he was. How long had she been a full Intelligencer?

"No," he agreed. "Which is why we're trying to take it away from him."

Dagrun yawned. "This is great, thank you, but I don't think we need to figure anything out this moment. I need to sleep, and I'd like to discuss this with Nadez." She yawned again. "I'll bring you with me. It's safer if we all know how to keep in contact."

"Sure." He stared down at the map until Dagrun returned from the privy and wrapped herself in the blankets. Only when he'd blown out the lamps and bedded down in the dark did he grin. He was helping! Him! He was a key member of the Intelligencer team that was going to save the city. No, not just the city, they were going to save all three of the Fair Seas Treaty Alliance countries!

CALDER HAD ASSUMED Bjorn was joking when he'd asked what his loggers would be doing for the rest of the day once they'd put the logs in place, but he hadn't been.

It was just after noon, and Calder had managed to steal a few hours of sleep, but he was bleary-eyed and knew he'd need a full night's rest soon.

He eyed the pile of logs that had already been stacked at the water's edge. Many of them had sharp metal spikes or bits of broken pottery embedded into them. He leaned over for a closer look and saw the tips of smaller nails. A few carts piled with rocks had been pulled up beside the logs, and now some of the townspeople were wrapping them in squares of what looked like fishing nets.

"We're about to start working on traps on the north and south paths," Bjorn said as he joined him. "Some of the men got excited about that challenge, let me tell you."

"Ask the ones working on the north path to wait," Calder said. "I want to move my sailboat to the point I would be grateful to have a clear path back here tonight."

"What are you planning, brother?"

He turned to see Yakop stepping off the pier and onto the sandy beach.

"I have to be able to access my sailboat," Calder said. "Once the logs have been set in the harbour, I won't be able to sail it from here. Eventually, I'll need to return to Tarklee, but before that, I'm going back to make sure Mother is all right."

"If it comes down to a fight between Mother and pirates, my money is on Mother," Yakop said. "She's a grown woman who was given a warning. The fact that she didn't take it isn't your fault."

"It feels as though it is. It always feels as though everything is," Calder replied. Yakop had the luxury of not being blamed for the death of a child and the loss of another. Even though Calder himself was the lost child. He'd been far too young to make any decisions, and he'd been scared and missing his twin brother. But since nothing he did made his mother smile, he had desperately wanted to please his father.

Looking back, he thought it was his mother's reaction to that more than anything else that had driven his father away. A man who came from a people who went to sea for most of the year had seen nothing wrong with sending his six-year-old son to live in a strange city and learn a strange craft. Even while the child and his mother had both been mourning the death of the twin.

"It still doesn't make it your fault." Yakop gripped his shoulder. "But say hello to her for me."

"If she'll let me," Calder replied. He sighed and looked up at the afternoon sky. If he was going to move the sailboat, he had to do it soon.

"I have work to do," Yakop said. "We'll talk later." Then he stepped back onto the pier and headed for the building that held his office.

"I'll tell the crew to hold off on the northern path until we hear from you," Bjorn said, and then he too left, leaving Calder alone.

For a few moments, he watched as loggers and townspeople got the logs ready to be submerged in the bay to guard the town against pirates. Then he headed for the little boat: time to move it somewhere he could sail away from even if the pirates blocked the exit from the cove.

He unpacked the sail and rigged it before pushing the little boat away from the pier. A gentle breeze took him to the point in just few minutes.

He stepped out of the boat and dragged it up onto a narrow strip of beach, close to a stand of trees. This time he didn't bother taking down the sail, and instead rolled it and tied it to the boom.

The path was just a dozen steps inland. He'd spent most of his summers at his mother's, and once when he was about ten and was almost halfway through his training, Yakop had brought him to this point. They'd eaten their fill of berries and had jumped in the water to wash the purple stains from their hands and faces.

The seawater hadn't saved their clothing though, and their mother had been angry. They had come in from the cabin to pick up supplies, and she'd made Calder give her any coins he had with him and used it to buy more shirting material. That had meant he'd had to work off his passage back to North Tarklee.

At the time, he'd thought she was being too harsh, but it had made him aware that there were consequences to even the most innocent actions. A lesson that had benefitted him ever since.

And looking back, he could admit that he'd been pretty full of himself and his Trait. He'd thought that he was special because he'd been taken away to be trained in the capital. And though he suspected that work he did on board the ship on the way home was of little value, it made him fall in love with life on the sea.

Calder crossed the path to the opposite side of the spit of land.

There was no sign of the ghost ship or any other vessel. He stared north, in the direction of his mother's cabin and where Jaak and the three log haulers had gone. Had they run into the ghost ship? Was that why Margit Ansdottir hadn't reached Cutterstown yet?

He turned down the path the led to town. If Jaak and the log haulers had been lost to Ansdottir, there wasn't anything he could do about it. What he could do was try to protect Cutterstown. And his mother, if she let him.

Too many things to do, he thought. Too many obligations keeping him from the one thing his heart wanted the most: to make sure Dag was safe.

When he emerged from the trees at the edge of town, he was greeted by a line of loggers. Bjorn waved, and he waved back and nodded.

"Let's get to it, you *karls*," Bjorn yelled. A cheer went up, and Calder laughed as loggers rushed past him and into the trees.

Then he went in search of a meal, which would be followed by the wait for nightfall and the expected arrival of the pirates.

JOOSEP ROLLED OVER and sighed. He should get up, but he wasn't sure he had the energy. And he definitely didn't want to face Dagrun Lund.

He'd fallen asleep during their meeting with Nadez, and he was horrified and embarrassed with himself for that. And for allowing Dagrun to lead him back here like a child. No wonder she thought to challenge him: he couldn't even stay awake for a key planning session.

And Nadez! Admitting that she'd always disagreed with his approach in front of a junior Intelligencer! How could she humiliate him like that?

He rolled over again and stared at the ceiling. Nadez and Dagrun seemed to think he'd failed, and for a moment, he'd believed them. His way of operating the Intelligencers may have given Tarmo Holt some time to plan, but it had also kept most of the Intelligencers, students *and* instructors, secret from Holt. Along with their Traits.

So, his habit of keeping all of the secrets to himself would now be instrumental in defeating Holt.

There was a soft knock on the door.

"Joosep?" Arnor called and opened the door a crack. "Are you awake? There's fresh soup if you are."

"I'm awake." Joosep threw the blanket off him. He wasn't hungry, but he knew he needed to eat if he wanted to regain his strength. He hated admitting it, but his foray out into the city last night had been far more physically taxing than he'd expected it to be.

"Come out when you're ready," Arnor said. "Dagrun and Gustav have gone out."

"In daylight?" he asked, but Arnor had already left, closing the door behind him. With effort, he swung his legs onto the floor and sat, his chest heaving.

How he hated being so incapacitated, so useless. He was lucky to be alive, he knew that, but this long convalescence was frustrating. And it was allowing others to usurp his role.

He was the Master Intelligencer—*him*—not Nadez nor Dagrun.

He shuffled out into the other room and sat down at the table. Arnor, his most trusted ally, was there with a bowl of soup.

"It's salt fish," he said. "It's all we have. But Dagrun prepared it using a trick she learned from Calder Rahmson, so it's better than my mother's cooking."

"Thank you." He grabbed the mug in both hands and sipped it. It was better than he'd expected, and not as spicy as he'd thought it might be, given what he knew about Calder. He finished the soup, and as soon as he put the mug down, Arnor picked it up and refilled it.

"Where are the other two?" he asked.

"Gustav has gone to procure more supplies, and Dagrun said she was going to head back to the house of one of Tarmo Holt's employees and see if he might lead her to something else of interest."

Arnor wasn't looking his way, so Joosep rolled his eyes. How would Dagrun know what was of interest? She had completed one single assignment while he'd been doing this for years. "Without asking me for my opinion?" he asked.

Arnor looked contrite. "I did check on you," he said. "But you were asleep." He frowned. "You overdid it last night, Joosep. You really should take more care."

"I will," Joosep replied. "But there are things only I can do; tasks and meetings I must see to myself. But next time I will take you with me."

"Me? Wouldn't it be better to take Dagrun? She's trained, and I'm not."

"Yes, she's trained," Joosep said. "So her skills would be needed for more important tasks than minding me." He couldn't trust Dagrun to not interfere, not when she'd done exactly that last night. Instead of him, the Master Intelligencer, giving clear instructions to Nadez, Dagrun had turned the meeting into a collaboration. That was not how this organization worked. Not under his leadership, and he was still in charge. "Besides," he continued, "I have all the skills she has and more; it's just that I'm still weak."

"Of course," Arnor said. "You know best."

"I do." He picked up the mug and drained the soup. "I'd like more soup please." Arnor beamed his approval and grabbed the mug from him.

He'd eat as much as he could, do whatever he could, to regain his strength. He had things to do, people to meet with. He was Master Intelligencer: he would decide what steps were appropriate to ensure the safety and integrity of the Fair Seas Treaty Alliance.

WHEN SHE COULDN'T stand it one more moment, Dag scratched at an insect bite. She'd been sitting under this small bush for over an hour and had yet to see anything unusual. If someone didn't exit the house soon, she'd leave and check the next place on the list.

She and Gustav had divided the map. Each of them would survey three or four of the secondary buildings to determine if their assumptions about every warehouse being guarded by people staying in these secondary buildings were correct.

But first, Dag had decided to spy on the house of the man she thought worked for Tarmo Holt, the man who had overseen the delivery of goods to the warehouses.

Except there had been no activity at the house: not even a lamp being lit. She stared at it. Judging by its neighbours, it should be a home with a family. Where were the workers who tended the yard or delivered supplies? Was there a family, or did the man live here alone? Did he even live here?

Someone walked past her, and when the itch between her shoulder blades started, she stepped out from her hiding place. The middle-aged man was reasonably well dressed, although his clothing wasn't rich by any means. When he stopped by the fountain, she kept walking towards him. She was about to stop when she saw the man she'd followed here the other day walking towards her. She kept her head down as they passed each other.

She expected him to go to the house; instead, he stopped beside the man at the fountain. They bent their heads together in conversation, but they spoke too quietly for her to hear over the burble of the fountain.

Dag patted her pocket and peered down at the ground, pretending that she'd lost something.

She retraced her steps slowly, counting on her Trait to keep the two men from paying too much attention to her.

"I must be reimbursed," the middle-aged man said.

"Keep your voice down," the other man replied. "You've already compromised me by coming here."

"My ship was to be spared," the middle-aged man said more quietly. "He promised. Now I have nothing and no way to rebuild my trade. I must be reimbursed."

"I'll talk to him and see what can be managed," the other man said. "And I will come to you."

"I would have been in the exact same ruinous circumstances if I hadn't risked everything and thrown my lot in with him." The middle-aged man frowned. "I've a mind to tell the Merchant Adventurers just what the Grand Freeholder has been up to."

"Then you will get nothing," the other man replied. "Besides, what makes you think they don't already know?"

"Pirates!" the middle-aged man spat. "And Holt is acting like he's the worst pirate of them all." He spun and walked back the way he'd come.

Dag kept her eyes on the ground. The other man slowed as he walked past her, but he didn't stop. With one last glance around, Dag hurried away from the small square and fountain.

Had Tarmo Holt lied and told people their ships would be spared and then had Ansdottir destroy them anyway? But Gustav had seen Holt angry with Ansdottir because his own ships had been set on fire. Perhaps the pirate captain had done this on her own and betrayed Holt. Either scenario meant that Tarmo Holt would have angry conspirators looking for compensation. Would Holt's control of all the food force them to back off?

Every time she saw something, she had more questions. She sighed. Right now, she had other buildings with other secrets to discover.

CHAPTER 13

A THIRD MAN let himself out of the small building, and just as the others had, he headed across the lane to the warehouse.

Gustav pulled his hat down lower over his head until his eyes were in shadow. There hadn't been any other activity at the warehouse: just the three men coming from the smaller building across the road and entering the larger one.

He blew out a breath. What he'd seen was enough to convince him that he'd been right: this warehouse had guards assigned to it. He had to assume that it already held food, which meant that it would be a good target for a riot.

Gustav waited another few minutes before rising and wandering away. This was the second building on his list; he hadn't seen anything suspicious at the first one. The next building was on the other side of the river, where his cart was, so he was going to use his peddler disguise when he spied on it.

He was just about to step onto Key Bridge when something about a person heading towards him made him pause. It was Vilis. It had been a few days since he'd seen his former training mate.

Wondering what Vilis was up to, Gustav jammed his hat low on his head and shuffled past the bridge. Once he was far enough ahead, he ducked into an alley and peered around the corner of a building.

Vilis was heading away from him, so Gustav stepped back

out into the street and started to follow him.

Vilis wasn't making any efforts to disguise himself as he walked through South Tarklee. At first, Gustav thought he was being so bold because he was officially working for Tarmo Holt, but when he got closer, he wondered if he was ill. The other student stumbled over a dip in the road and almost fell, grabbing a tree in front of a building to keep himself upright.

But he kept going, so Gustav followed.

They passed Freeholders Bridge, and Gustav frowned. This part of town was rich, and neither he nor Vilis would be able to remain unnoticed for long, not dressed as roughly as they both were.

Vilis slowed, and Gustav took a moment to really look around. He thought that some buildings around here were ones they'd marked on the map, although he and Dag had decided to concentrate their investigations in less wealthy neighbourhoods. It would be difficult for people with nothing, people willing to riot for something, to gather in large numbers in areas like this.

Gustav no longer cared what Vilis was doing here, and he let him get ahead of him. His own priority had changed: he wanted to determine what Tarmo Holt was keeping here.

He found a tree and sat down under it, trying to be as inconspicuous as possible, despite his threadbare clothing that identified him as an interloper in this neighbourhood.

He closed his eyes and pictured the map, wishing for Kaja's Memory. A building they thought was quarters for guards should be a few houses up and on the right. He stared at a two-storey stone building. It was well kept, just as the rest of the buildings that surrounded it were, but nothing Gustav could see was large enough for a warehouse.

"Get out of here!" someone yelled.

"I'm owed!" Vilis stood in front of the stone building that Gustav had been looking at, facing the open doorway. "I'm owed," he repeated.

"*Skit* like you always think you're owed something," a man called. He stepped out of the house and confronted Vilis. "Get back to your part of town before I call the Grand Freeholder's guard."

"I am owed," Vilis said, but this time Gustav heard the slur in his voice. "By Tarmo Holt. He promised me a position."

"Why would the Grand Freeholder promise the likes of you anything?"

A crowd had started to gather, and Gustav took the opportunity to join it, keeping behind the other people who had come to watch the confrontation.

"We had a bargain," Vilis said. He staggered forward into the man, who pushed him to the ground. Gustav sucked in a breath. Vilis was drunk!

"We had a bargain," Vilis repeated, now on his knees. "He promised."

Two more men emerged from the house. When they joined the one Vilis was arguing with, he nodded to them. The two reinforcements grabbed Vilis by the arms and hauled him back up to his feet.

"Let go of me!" Vilis yelled, his words slurring. "Stop. I'm owed."

"We'll take care of him," the man who'd been arguing with Vilis said to the crowd. "He's always been a bad drunk. We'll help him sober up and send him on his way."

"No!" Vilis cried. "Let me go." But the men who held him started pulling him towards the house.

No one from the crowd stepped in to help, and Gustav frowned. These men had argued with Vilis, and now they were dragging him off the street in front of almost a dozen people. Why wasn't anyone trying to help him? He touched the shoulder of a man in front of him.

"Do you think he'll be all right?" he asked.

"Not sticking my nose into the Grand Freeholder's business," the man said over his shoulder. "Not worth—" He stopped talking as soon as he saw Gustav. "Get back to your own part of town," he said and left.

Gustav shrugged. He couldn't really blame people for not wanting to risk the wrath of Tarmo Holt.

Now that Vilis was off the street, the rest of the crowd started wandering away.

The man who had argued with Vilis looked around before retreating inside the house. Once the door was closed, Gustav dashed along the side wall to the back of the house.

A small unkempt garden signalled that this house wasn't the same as its neighbours, and some overgrown bushes right below an open window offered a decent place to hide. A door to the left of the window opened onto a path that led to a privy at the back of the property.

"What do you want us to do with him?" a voice asked.

"I don't care as long as he doesn't turn up here again." Gustav recognized the voice of the man who'd argued with Vilis. "If Holt had been here, it's possible we'd all share the same fate."

"The crowd is gone," the first man said.

"Wait an hour," the one in charge replied. "Just to be sure. And I don't have to tell you that whatever you do, the body can't be found."

"All right."

Gustav blew out a breath. Should he leave Vilis to his fate? He had betrayed them all, but he'd spent years studying with him. Vilis wasn't all bad: he didn't deserve to die because of this one transgression.

But should Gustav risk himself to try to save him?

He sat for a while, trying to decide what he should do. He wanted to help Vilis, but in the end, he wasn't willing to jeopardize his information gathering tasks. Stopping Tarmo Holt was more important than the life of any one person, wasn't it?

Still unsure, Gustav decided to investigate a little more. If rescuing Vilis was easy, he would do it. If not? Well, Vilis had made his own decision to side with Holt.

He crept past the door to the far side of the house and peered around the corner. A window along the wall was too high up for him to look in without the risk of revealing himself. He was debating how safe that would be when the back door slammed open. He scrambled to the side of the house.

"Be quick about it," a man said.

Gustav peered around the corner. One of the men who had dragged Vilis into the house stood just outside the door, his back to him. He reached an arm back through the door and Vilis, pulled off balance, stumbled out. His hands were tied together in front of him and he overbalanced and fell into his guard. The man swore and pushed Vilis into the garden.

"I need my hands," Vilis mumbled. He raised his hands towards the guard.

Who swore again and reached over and untied him. "Don't go pissing yourself," the guard said. "It won't help." The door to the privy slammed shut behind Vilis, and the guard shook his head.

"Stupid drunk," he said. While the guard stared at the privy, Gustav wondered if he could disable him before he could call for help. He was still wondering that when the guard swore again and headed towards the privy.

"It don't take that long to take a piss," he called. "So you better come out right now." He reached the privy and pulled on the door, but it didn't budge. He banged a fist on it. "Come out now, before I get real angry."

The guard continued to pound on the door, and Gustav stood and got ready to run. He grinned. If Vilis was trying to escape, he was willing to help him.

Suddenly the privy door burst open, forcing the guard to back up. Vilis emerged holding a plank above his head. He swung it down and hit the guard on the head, and Gustav cringed at the sound it made. The guard grunted and toppled over. Vilis dropped the plank and looked around wildly.

"Here!" Gustav called out as loudly as he could. "This way." Vilis ran towards him. As Gustav hurried past the side window, he heard shouts coming from inside. Assuming that Vilis was behind him, he dashed out into the street. He ran a few steps before ducking into a narrow laneway that branched off the main street. It took him a few frantic moments to loosen a fence board. Vilis joined him, and together they pried the board far enough away from the fence that they could slip through it.

They were in a yard behind a large house, and as soon as the fence board was back in place, Gustav took off again. He led the way through back gardens and down lanes until the New Bridge was in sight. With an arm around Vilis's shoulder as though they were out for a drink, Gustav shepherded them to his cart.

"We'll be safe here," he said, sliding under the cart. Vilis joined him, laying down flat on his back.

"Thank you," he said. He threw a hand across his eyes. "I'm not sure why you helped me, but thank you."

"You would have gotten away," Gustav said.

"No." Vilis sat up. "I wouldn't have. I would have tried, but they would have found me."

"They still might," Gustav replied. "Here." He took off his hat and shirt and handed them to Vilis. "Give me your shirt. If you're dressed like me, no one will bother you as long as you stay under the cart."

Vilis tugged his own shirt off and put on Gustav's. "What about the cart owner?" he asked. "Will he chase me away?"

"That would be me," Gustav replied. He pointed at Vilis. "And now you. Don't let anyone tell you otherwise. I bargained for this cart a week or so ago."

"Huh. You've done better than me."

"That's because you trusted Tarmo Holt," Gustav said.

"Shhh." Vilis looked scared. "That's who wants me dead. And how do you know I trusted him?"

"I know that you gave him the names of our training group and instructors," Gustav replied. "And from what I overheard today, I know that he promised you something for your help and then didn't deliver."

"He's the Grand Freeholder! I thought it all right to give him the names."

Gustav shook his head and stared at Vilis until, finally, the other lad turned red and looked away.

"Fine, I didn't think it was right to give him the names. Joosep obviously hadn't, so that meant he didn't want Holt to have them." He paused and scowled. "I was hoping for an advantage. Your Trait gives you one, and it's the same for Kaja. All I have is a Trait that makes people trust me." He glanced at Gustav. "And my Trait is so weak that it hardly ever works. So yes, I made a deal with Holt."

"All right," Gustav said. "You stay here. If you're gone when I come back, I'll assume that you didn't want my help." He nodded to himself, his decision made. Whatever information Vilis had, it would be better if Dagrun and her Unseen Trait got it out of him.

He crawled out from under the cart and peered up at the sky, trying to figure out how late in the afternoon it was. Would she still be at their meeting place, or would she have returned to the apartment?

"How long will you be?" Vilis asked. "I'm not leaving, I just want to know how long . . ." he trailed off.

"Hopefully only a couple of hours," Gustav said. "But I might not be able to make it back until late." He needed to speak to Dagrun alone: if he'd missed their meeting, then getting her alone at the apartment might take time. If Joosep and Arnor were in the main room, that meant he would have to wait until they both went to their beds.

He nodded to Vilis and headed down an alley. And not once did he question why he was keeping Vilis's whereabouts a secret from Joosep. In his mind Dagrun Lund was the one who needed this information.

So FAR NORTH the days were noticeably shorter: Calder estimated that there was less than an hour of daylight left.

He waved to Berna, who sat watch on top of the warehouse and set out along the path back towards his small boat. Bjorn had given him a list of traps to avoid, but Calder didn't plan on setting foot on the path. He'd travel through the forest on the inland side of the path, to steer clear of the traps and keep away from the coast in order to stay out of sight of the pirates.

He wanted to arrive just before dark and find a good place to hide. He'd had some time this afternoon to fret about the boat, to worry that if the pirates found it, they would destroy it or worse, use it to sneak up on Cutterstown.

If that happened, he wouldn't be able to check on his mother. Or return to Tarklee—and Dag.

The strip of land was empty, and the boat was undisturbed when he reached it. The sky turned indigo as night fell. He searched for a place to hide that let him watch the sea, finally settling on a spot behind a boulder just a few feet from the water.

An INSECT BUZZED in his ear, and Calder jerked awake. *Skit*. His lack of sleep had caught up to him, and he'd dozed off. Carefully, he raised his eyes above the boulder, and immediately his focus narrowed on the water a few dozen feet from shore.

His Trait activated, he peered into the dark. Was that a light? Yes, a single lamp swung back and forth as the dinghy it was on was rowed to shore. Sailors, eight in all, stepped into the gentle surf, followed by a cloaked figure. The hood fell back, revealing blonde hair.

Inger.

Calder sank back down behind the rock. He didn't think he'd been seen. Such a small group was likely a scouting party, looking for a way to sneak up on Cutterstown and surprise them in the dark. But where was the ghost ship?

He risked another look past the beach, but if the *Bright Breeze* was out there, it was sailing without lights; something Ansdottir, with her Unseen Trait, would have no trouble doing.

One of the sailors remained with the dinghy, and the lamp had been turned down so low that he almost wasn't sure they still had it with them.

He heard the rest of the sailors head up the beach towards the path. Would they find his boat in the darkness? They didn't have a light, and he wondered if someone with an Unseen Trait was leading them. Then he remembered what the very first trap was.

He rose to a crouch. Would Dag forgive him if he let Inger die? He blew out a silent breath. He wouldn't forgive himself, so he doubted that Dag would.

He carefully picked his way among the rocks until he was close enough to the small group to hear them.

They were all Pilalians, except for Inger, and they were arguing in their native tongue. Looking nervous, Inger stepped away from them, her eyes scanning her surroundings.

Taking a chance, Calder stepped out from the shadow of a tree. It was just a moment, and then he hid again right away, but he thought he saw Inger give a quick nod.

In case she told her companions she'd seen him, he stepped behind a different tree. The Pilalians seemed to have come to an agreement because one after another they started along the path.

Inger loitered at the rear. The last sailor glanced her way before he followed the rest onto the path that led through the woods.

"I know you're here," Inger called out softly. She looked over her shoulder at the trail her companions had taken before she took a few steps towards the tree Calder had been hidden behind.

"Over here," he said as he stepped out onto the beach behind her.

She turned to face him, and he stared at the familiar yet

unfamiliar face: so like Dag but in small ways, so completely different.

"Why?" she asked.

"To warn you," he replied. "To not go down that path. Dag would never forgive me if you . . ." he paused. "Just don't go down the path."

"It's always about Dag," Inger replied. "Even out here, where I thought I was beyond her influence, it's about Dag."

"It's not on purpose," he said. He estimated that they had another few minutes before the crew came across the first trap. Unless one of them came looking for Inger before that. "I think it's because of your opposite Traits. I think it means you see almost everything differently."

"Then why can Margit Ansdottir make me see everything her way?" Inger said, and Calder was surprised at the bitterness in her voice. "She has the same Trait as Dag, so why don't I fight with her? How can she make me believe I'm doing the right thing when the moment I'm away from her, I know it's wrong?"

"You know it's . . ." Calder stopped. "Are you saying that you don't want to be with the pirates? Then come with me now."

"I can't," she replied. "She'll do worse things if I leave." She sighed. "And I can't be trusted."

"She has a second Trait," Calder said. "That's why you don't fight with her. It makes people loyal to her no matter what."

There was a scream from down the path, followed by a shout and wails of pain.

"They found the first trap," Calder said. "What are the pirates planning?" If Inger wasn't willing to leave Ansdottir, he didn't have time to persuade her. What was left of the landing party would be returning very soon.

"Will they die?" Inger asked.

"Some, probably," he said even though from Bjorn's description he was certain at least one would die. Some of the others could be maimed for life.

"Good. What about the path along the coast south of town? Are there dangers there too?"

"Why are you asking? So that you can tell Ansdottir? Or is she taking the other route into Cutterstown?" If Ansdottir was hurt or killed, would that make the rest of the towns along the coast safe? Was there another person, Charis maybe, who would take over and lead the pirates?

"She's on the ship," Inger said. "She's always on the ship. If the south path is clear, then the town could already be burning. And I will tell her, I won't be able to help myself."

"That's her other Trait at work," Calder replied. "Does she tell you anything? About what she's planning?"

"No." She turned her head as moans reached them, along with the sounds of people rushing back along the trail. "They're back." She met his eyes. "I won't tell them you're here. I won't say anything until Ansdottir makes me."

"Come with me," Calder said. "Now. I have a boat; we can sail away somewhere safe."

"No, you don't understand. I will betray you. As long as Ansdottir is alive, I will betray you." She smiled a sad smile. "But it helps knowing that it's because of a Trait. Now go, hide."

The sailors were close, and with no more time, he did as she bid and slipped into the shadows beneath the trees.

He watched Inger rush to the path and help a sailor limp onto the beach. One mangled foot was slick with blood.

Another two sailors helped each other into the clearing and collapsed in the sand, each one with a bloodied foot.

The moaning got louder as a sailor backed off the path, dragging a writhing man behind him. *He must have fallen,* Calder thought. The sharpened branches had penetrated his left thigh and arm, along with his feet. The last man dragged into the clearing hadn't fared as well.

He'd fallen as well: had possibly been startled when what looked like solid ground gave way, and he stepped onto pointed wood that ripped through his feet. But he'd fallen forward, and one of the sharpened stakes had penetrated his eye.

Calder slipped away through the trees, not bothering to wait to see them get back into the dinghy.

Hopefully the other landing party had met a similar fate. But Ansdottir was on the ship. Had she been able to navigate close enough to set fire to the town despite the submerged logs in the harbour?

CHAPTER 14

"WHAT TOOK YOU so long?" Dag asked when Gustav crawled through the gap in the fence and joined her. "Trouble?" She'd told herself to leave half a dozen times in the past two hours only to stay where she was, not willing to give up on Gustav. Not willing to believe that he was either caught or hurt or dead. And here he was, and she was too relived to be very angry with him.

"No, yes." He looked her way even though she was pretty sure he couldn't see her. "Maybe."

She'd found this hiding spot earlier. The fence looked solid, but someone had neglected to fasten all of the boards securely. There was just enough room between the fence and the wooden building behind it for a couple of people to fit. Not comfortably, but safely.

Dag rose onto her toes, trying to stretch out the cramp in her calf.

"Maybe?" she repeated.

"I ran into Vilis," Gustav said. "And followed him to one of the buildings marked on the map. One of the ones in a more prosperous part of South Tarklee."

"And?" She didn't trust the boy: he'd betrayed his fellow students along with his instructors. But she did want to know about the building. And what he was doing there.

"I think it's more than a barracks." He paused. "Vilis tried to talk to someone. He was complaining about not getting what he'd been promised. Then they took him inside. To kill him."

"Did they?" Dag asked. "Kill him? And what do you think he meant; that Holt betrayed him somehow? Or maybe he didn't actually fulfil Holt's request so therefore didn't earn whatever had been promised him?" Did Holt have even less information than they'd thought?

"I don't know what he meant," Gustav said. "But you can ask Vilis yourself. He was already escaping, so I helped him get away and hide."

Dag was so surprised that she couldn't speak for a moment. "He escaped?"

"Yes." Gustav chuckled. "He tore the seat off the privy and hit the guard with it. When he ran, I had him follow me. But not here," he said quickly. "I didn't tell him about anything. Not about the apartment, or you, or even about Joosep."

"But he's safe?" She already knew that she would talk to Vilis. And that the answer to the question of what to do with him would depend on what he said to her.

"He's under my cart," Gustav said. "He told me he was looking for an advantage since he feels that his Trait is weak and not very useful. That's why he gave information to Holt."

"I see. Well, let's go find out what else Vilis has to tell us," she said. "And well done. All of it, well done."

She followed Gustav out from behind the fence. The street beside them was empty, so Gustav led the way to his cart.

The lad was proving to be smart and resourceful even when not using his Trait. Dag was very impressed that he'd had the presence of mind not only to help Vilis but to keep everything else a secret from him. She understood a little better why Joosep had assigned the partially trained youth a mission. But he'd still put Gustav at considerable risk.

"I can't see him," Gustav said. "Is he there?" They were peering around a corner of a crumbling building at the cart.

"Yes," Dag replied. "I think he's asleep. Or pretending to be. I'll talk to him alone while you keep watch."

"All right." Gustav stepped back, and Dag rounded the corner.

By the time she reached the cart, she knew that Vilis had only been pretending to sleep. He didn't move, but she sensed that his muscles were tense, and his breathing was shallow. She thought he was afraid.

"Gustav told me where to find you," she whispered as she approached. "I'm coming under." She crouched and slid under the cart. "Hello, Vilis."

"Dagrun Lund." He seemed even more nervous now that he'd recognized her. He sat up and leaned his back against the building behind him.

"Yes, but don't worry, I know you were only doing what you were asked to do when you lied to me." She sat facing him, her legs crossed.

"Is Gustav safe?"

"Yes. He told me where he met you. I want to know what happened. Why were you not rewarded, where have you been all this time, and how did you know to go to that part of town?" She held his gaze until he looked away. "But first we need to be somewhere safer than here." She crawled out from under the cart. "Come on."

Dag waved Gustav forward.

"You head back," she said to Gustav. "I'm taking him somewhere safer than this. I'll be back . . ." She looked up at the sky: dusk had fallen. She should have enough time to question Vilis and get back to the apartment while it was still dark. "I'll try to make it back before dawn."

Gustav nodded and headed off in the wrong direction. Dag suppressed a smile at his caution.

The smile faded. His caution was why he was still alive when Tarmo Holt knew he'd been spying on him.

"Come on," she said to Vilis. "We have someone else to visit."

She knew better than to barge into one of Nadez's secret hideaways. Instead, she and Vilis propped themselves up against a wall between the two she knew about.

A short time later, Nadez approached them.

"Who is this?" she asked.

"Vilis. A student. I need to ask him some questions," Dag said. "But I want your opinion on his answers."

"And you need a safe place."

"And I need a safe place," she agreed. "To talk to him and for him after."

"We'll discuss the after," Nadez said. "Once we hear what he has to say. This way."

Nadez led them past the ramshackle stable to another narrow lane. At the back of the lane, she moved a rain barrel to expose a break in the wall behind it. Dag crawled in first, followed by Vilis. Nadez came last, turning around to drag the barrel back in place.

Flint struck stone, and a spark flared. A small flame blazed until Nadez dipped the wick of a candle into it. Once the candle was lit, she tamped out the flame.

"Pretty soon you're going to know all my secrets," Nadez said with a grin.

"You'll just find new ones," Dag said, impressed. She was the one whose Trait meant she should have secrets all over the city, and yet Nadez was the one who had them.

The candlelight flickered across three wooden walls opposite the stone one they'd crawled through. Four small crates clustered in the middle of the small space, and one corner held a folded blanket.

"Do you live here?" Vilis asked. He looked nervous as he stood a few paces from Dag.

"I could if I had to," Nadez said. "Sit down. I'm here to listen to your answers."

She sat down on a crate. Dag pulled one towards her and sat down as well. Vilis, with a glance in the direction of the exit, finally perched on a third.

"Vilis," Nadez said. "Before Dag gets started, I want the answer to one question: why is it you're not dead?"

Vilis gulped visibly, and Dag thought for a moment he wasn't going to be able to answer.

"I would be," Vilis said in a quiet voice. "If Gustav hadn't helped me." He looked down at his feet. "Tarmo Holt promised me that my weak Trait wouldn't keep me from progressing, that I could do important work for him as Grand Freeholder."

"But he was due to step down in a few months," Dag said. "Why did you think that he wouldn't?"

"Because he said he already had an agreement with Freeholder Timonis that he would stay on until Timonis was ready."

"Ready for what?" Dag asked. "I spent a month in Timonis' household, and he seemed to have all the votes lined up to be selected Grand Freeholder."

"I don't know," Vilis said. "I only know what Holt told me."

"All right," Dag said. "When did you realize that Holt wasn't going to honour your bargain?"

"Almost as soon as I handed over the list of students and instructors." Vilis looked up. "It was only my group, but the next day, they were all gone. Kaja, Gustav, and our three instructors. I was worried, so I went to Holt. Well, I wasn't actually allowed to see him. One of his men took my message. Three days later—*three days*—I was sent a note telling me that since I couldn't deliver what I'd promised, the list of every student, Intelligencer, and instructor, that I wasn't to bother the Grand Freeholder ever again." He paused and ran a hand over his eyes. "By that time, I realized that I'd made a terrible mistake. Joosep was gone, Arnor was gone: everyone I knew who was associated with the Intelligencers was gone."

"You were still in the Hall?" Nadez asked.

"No, by this time I'd taken whatever money I had and found a cheap room." He hung his head. "I didn't want to go home, not once I understood that I'd betrayed the school. But I didn't know what to do, so I got drunk."

"And then you went to see Tarmo Holt," Dag said. Vilis hadn't been able to supply Holt with a list of everyone. It was good to have that confirmed.

"Yes. When I was drunk, I got mad and . . ." he paused. "I guess I didn't care what happened to me. So, I went to a house where I'd met Loke, one of Holt's men."

"What did you want?" Dag asked. "What did you expect to happen when you got there?"

"I guess I wanted Holt and his people to know that I knew he'd defaulted on our bargain," Vilis said. "Other than that, I wasn't really thinking. But then I finally understood that they planned on killing me." He looked up and met Dag's eyes, and despite trying to use her Trait, she didn't see anything hiding behind his anguish. "I was never so happy to see anyone in my life than I was to see Gustav. A friendly face," he said quietly, "even though I didn't deserve one."

"And then he hid you and brought me," Dag finished. "All right. Nadez?" She looked at the other woman. "Your thoughts?"

"This lad can never be an Intelligencer," she said. "He should probably never have been accepted in the first place, Trait or no

Trait. But that's not his fault. I think he's telling the truth."

"I do too, and I agree with your assessment." Was the existence of a Trait the only thing Joosep looked for in an Intelligencer? Gustav and Vilis were close to the same age and were at the exact same stage of their training, yet Gustav had proven to be intelligent, resourceful, and discreet. Vilis had shown none of those qualities. And it had nothing to do with Traits.

"What do you think, Vilis?" Dag asked. It wouldn't help if the lad was determined to become an Intelligencer.

"If I were you, I wouldn't trust me," Vilis said. "Not as an Intelligencer."

"Then what do we do with you?" Nadez asked. "Or is it me that has to find a solution?"

"If you could, I would appreciate it," Dag said. "I have other things to deal with." Including adding the information she and Gustav had discovered to the maps. "But first I need Vilis to tell me everything he knows about Tarmo Holt, his people, including this Loke, and every single time and place where you met."

Other than the people in the house who had imprisoned him, the dead woman from the warehouse, and another man whose name he didn't know but who sounded like the man Dag had followed home from the warehouse, Vilis had very little information.

Dag crawled through the stone wall, rolling the barrel back in place once she was out. It was just after midnight. As she made her way back to the apartment, she thought of another dozen questions to ask Vilis. But her Trait hadn't been triggered by some secret the lad was keeping. Besides, Nadez would be spending some time with him; no doubt she would find out anything else worth knowing.

The key was behind the brick, as usual. Once she was sure no one was watching, she opened the door, returned the key, and entered the apartment. There was a single candle still lit, and Gustav was rolled up in a blanket on the floor.

Dag yawned as she leaned over the map, studying the recent additions made by Gustav. She'd just add what she'd found out today, while it was fresh, before getting some sleep.

"ANY CHANGE?"

Calder looked up as his brother joined him.

"No." He stared out at the bay where the *Bright Breeze*, its paint shining ghostly white in the moonlight, sat just beyond the logs that were scattered in the water. "But both dinghies have returned." The first dinghy, the one carrying Inger, had arrived when he did, almost two hours ago now. He'd been wondering ever since if Inger had already told Ansdottir that she'd seen him.

He expected Margit Ansdottir would be furious to know that the man whose family she'd been sent to destroy had instead mounted a defence, a successful one so far, to keep her from completing her task.

"Do you think she'll give up?" Yakop sat down on the roof beside him.

"Eventually," Calder replied. "I need to go check on Mother."

"I almost wish they'd find her," Yakop said with a laugh. "Mother will not go down without a fight."

"But she will go down," Calder said. His mother was stubborn and fierce and willing to fight for what was hers, but she was one woman against a ship full of pirates. Captained by an infuriated Ansdottir whose other targets were unreachable.

"That's the only terrible part of that whole scenario," Yakop said. "So, you'll go and help her in spite of herself."

"Yes. It's the least I can do for causing her such pain."

"*Skit*, she caused enough of it herself," Yakop said. "She's the one who gave in to Father when he suggested you go away. Trust me, I was young, but I knew she made him pay for that. She chased him to the sea and then never forgave him for leaving." Yakop put a hand on Calder's shoulder. "Then she did the same with you: she blamed you for going to North Tarklee when it was her and Father's decision. Then every single time you came home she made you feel like it was your fault. She even blamed you for Hakon's death. You were six! You don't owe her anything."

"I still feel responsible," Calder said. Although he knew the truth of what his brother said, it didn't make any difference. There were things his mother blamed him for that were not his fault, but it was *his* decision to go to sea, like his father, and he knew that had caused her pain. It had been his decision to spend his time in the Sapphire Sea rather than closer to home.

Oh sure, Joosep sent him places on assignment, but that was usually in response to suggestions he'd made.

No, his mother had made his life uncomfortable at times, but he'd done the same thing to her.

"They're doing something on deck," Yakop said abruptly. "Can you see what it is?"

Calder put the spyglass to his eye and swung it around to view the ship. Sailors were scrambling into the sails, readying the ship for travel.

"They're moving," Calder said. "No, wait." The sails were furled partway, and then the ship moved until the stern faced them. "They're preparing the cannon." He stood up. "They can't hit anything this far away, but it's possible that they could use it to clear a path through the logs." They'd need to be incredibly Lucky though.

Yakop stood up beside him, and they watched as the *Bright Breeze* maneuvered into position with the stern and its single cannon, facing the town. He saw the smoke first and then heard the boom of the cannon. One shot was all they took. Then the sails were unfurled and the *Bright Breeze* sailed out of sight.

"I think we made her angry," Yakop said.

"I know we did," Calder replied. The sky was starting to lighten. It was time for him to go find his mother.

JOOSEP STEPPED OVER the sleeping forms of Dagrun and Gustav. He glanced at the map that was spread out on the table, but that was all he did. That was Dagrun's plan; using the map to plot all of Tarmo Holt's properties and then start . . . something that wouldn't work.

Dagrun Lund's plan that Gustav Gunnarson seemed all too ready to follow.

But it wasn't *his* plan, and he was still Master Intelligencer. He'd come up with his own course of action, and since these two had excluded him from their plans, he was excluding them from his.

He'd had nothing to do but think in the last day. He was on the mend and needed less sleep, and it had been a relief to have Dagrun and Gustav gone so much of the time. That had left him alone with Arnor, who was so adept at getting him what he needed: food, tea, and peace and quiet.

And time to think. And the conclusion he'd come to was that as Master Intelligencer it was his responsibility to find out what Holt was up to and stop him. Not a couple of barely trained students. Dagrun Lund might have finished her training, but that didn't mean he considered her his equal. Not when he had decades of experience to her few weeks.

So, he'd come up with his own plan: one that relied on his Trait and skills and knowledge. And he would complete it by himself and demonstrate to everyone why *he* was Master Intelligencer.

The stew was still on the stove: it had thickened up overnight, but instead of adding more water, he put a few generous spoonfuls in a bowl and ate it standing over the pot. Once he was finished eating, he grabbed a scarf from the peg near the door, Gustav's, he thought idly, and left. He didn't bother relocking the door. He was going to resolve everything with Tarmo Holt today, so no one needed to stay in this crowded apartment if they didn't want to. And he, for one, did not.

The apartment was something else that he had established that Dagrun Lund, fresh from her very first low-level assignment, had taken over.

He'd planned it as a retreat, an escape where he could plot to keep the Fair Seas Treaty Alliance safe if it was ever under threat. And it had been that. But he'd had to share it with people whom he'd trained; people he'd lifted far above their ordinary expectations for their lives. People who, in the end, didn't appreciate all that he'd done for them.

Dagrun Lund even blamed him. How dare she? And Nadez Norup too. How dare these two who had no idea what it was like to steer an organization like the Intelligencers through the perilous politics of the Fair Seas Treaty Alliance, blame him for anything?

And what was worse, they'd made him doubt himself—doubt his skills and his leadership. As if Nadez Norup would have done anything different.

So now he was going to find out what Tarmo Holt was planning and stop him from causing more harm to the Fair Seas Treaty Alliance.

JOOSEP ENTERED THE narrow alley that contained the small door that led into the Hall. The key was just where it should be, and he unlocked the door and entered.

He crept along the corridor that led to Holt's office, counting on his Trait to keep him from being seen. There was a light in the outer office, and he heard a muffled cough: it seemed that Holt's assistant Mykol was at work, although the absence of voices made him think Holt himself was not.

He turned at the sound of a soft footfall behind him.

"Arnor? What are you doing here?" He grabbed his assistant's arm and pulled him down into a crouch.

"What are *you* doing here?" Arnor asked in a whisper. "You're not fully recovered and you left without telling anyone." He looked around. "And then you come here."

"I'm going to find out what Holt is up to," Joosep said. "It's my Trait, after all."

"But Dagrun's is stronger."

"I am tired of hearing about Dagrun Lund's Trait," Joosep said. "*I'm* the one with experience." Too late he realized that in his anger, he'd spoken too loudly.

"Who's there?"

"It's Mykol," Arnor said. "I'll distract him so you can run." He stood up, shaking Joosep's hand off him. "It's Arnor," Arnor said, stepping out into the outer office.

"Arnor. You shouldn't be here!" Mykol said.

"But here he is," a new voice said. "Joosep Sepp's assistant. Holt will want to talk to you."

"Let go of me!" Arnor yelled.

Joosep leaned around a corner. A guard held Arnor and had pulled his hands behind his back as Mykol stood by, his face averted.

"Stop!" Joosep rose and stepped into the office. "Let him go." Arnor frowned and shook his head at him, but Joosep ignored him. There was no way he was going to run and leave his assistant behind. "In the name of the Three, let him go."

"The Three," the guard said. "You don't speak for the Three, and even if you did, it wouldn't matter. I work for Tarmo Holt."

"You think you can capture us both?" Joosep asked. He stepped towards the guard, trying to gauge if Mykol would help the guard or him and Arnor.

"He doesn't have to."

Joosep's heart sank as he turned to see Tarmo Holt exit his office, flanked by two guards.

Now Joosep did try to run, but he only got a step away when he heard Arnor's shout of pain.

He paused and turned. The guard had a knife to Arnor's throat, and a trickle of blood seeped down his neck and pooled in his clavicle.

"Don't hurt him," Joosep said, defeated.

"You really are stupid," Tarmo Holt drawled as he stopped in front of him, staring at him, a small smile on his face. "Did you think your Trait would keep you safe? That it would somehow tell you how to defeat me?" Holt shook his head. "It's far too late for me to be stopped."

"I don't believe that," Joosep replied. "That it's too late to stop you."

"Who's going to do it?" Holt asked. "Dagrun Lund? A barely trained Intelligencer with no allies or resources whose twin is loyal to those who are loyal to me?"

"Yes," Joosep said, although even to him he didn't sound sure.

"If she's smart, she'll get on a ship and sail away," Holt replied. "Something you should have done." He looked at the guard holding Arnor. "There is no need for that one."

Before Joosep knew what that meant, the guard holding Arnor sliced the knife across his captive's neck. Red sprouted in a thin line, and then blood spurted out in an arc, leaving a bloody trail down the opposite wall. Arnor's eyes widened a moment before he crumpled to the floor.

Joosep gaped in shock. "Why did you do that?" Arnor! Blood continued to seep from the wound in Arnor's neck, but it no longer pulsed.

"So that you know I will not hesitate to kill you or anyone you care about in order to learn what you know," Holt said. "Take him."

The guard stepped past Arnor's body to grab him, and all Joosep could do was stare at the print the man's boot left in Arnor's blood. Only when his arms were pinned painfully behind his back did Joosep realize the mistake he'd made.

He was shoved roughly through the door and out into the

hallway and then was marched through the Hall: Tarmo Holt didn't even bother trying to hide the fact that he had taken the Master Intelligencer prisoner. Joosep kept his head down, not wanting to make eye contact with anyone they passed, his shame almost overwhelming him.

Arnor was dead because of him. Because instead of being grateful that Dagrun Lund had stepped up and taken control when he wasn't able, instead of helping her refine a plan that would save the Fair Seas Treaty Alliance, he'd been angry and petty and resentful that somehow she'd usurped his authority and had set out to prove her wrong.

And now Arnor was dead, and Holt had taken him prisoner.

The only thing he could do now, the only way to salvage anything from his terrible blunder, was to make sure that he didn't tell Holt about Dagrun's plans.

CHAPTER 15

DAG ROLLED OVER and stretched, wincing when her back ached. Sleeping on the floor in the apartment was safe but not very comfortable. She opened her eyes. It was quiet, far too quiet for daytime in an apartment that housed four people. She sat up, and Gustav nodded to her from where he sat at the table.

"Where are Joosep and Arnor?" she asked. She shoved the blanket off and got up, shaking the blanket out before folding it and then draping it over the back of a chair.

"I don't know," Gustav replied. "No one was out here when I got up, so I assumed they were still sleeping. About an hour ago I went to check on them, and they're not in their room."

"Huh. Did they leave a note?"

"Not that I found," Gustav said. "It looked like someone had a bowl of stew, but that was all."

"Probably Joosep," Dag said. Had he snuck out again to see Nadez, taking Arnor along in case he tired? "If they don't return in a couple of hours, I'll go check with Nadez."

"Sure, that's where I thought they'd gone too."

Dag headed for the stew. She scooped some into a bowl and sat down across from Gustav.

"I put everything I discovered yesterday on the map." Gustav pointed at three new marks.

"Thanks," Dag said around a mouthful of stew. "I saw that when I came in. I confirmed that these two are warehouses."

She jabbed her finger at two spots in South Tarklee. "And this looks like a guardhouse beside the second warehouse. By my guess, it can accommodate half a dozen guards."

"South Tarklee is still the main target?" Gustav asked.

"Yes. Clan Freeholder Timonis is expected to be the next Grand Freeholder. I think he'll be sympathetic." She wasn't sure if he was even in Tarklee: he'd been in Nurmi a few days ago. Should they try to send him a message? But who could they send?

"Do we wait for Joosep?" Gustav asked.

"No, I'll follow up with Nadez and Joosep, if he's with her. You stick to the plan." Gustav was going to spend the next few days with his cart, slowly spreading information and rumours. "If you have news for me and no one is here, just leave it in Arnor's cubby in the kitchen."

"All right." He stood up and frowned. "My scarf is gone."

"Will that be a problem?" Dag asked. Why would either Joosep or Arnor take Gustav's scarf?

"No. I'll just talk someone else into giving me another one," he grinned. "I probably won't be able to get back here more than every day or so." He nodded then left the apartment.

Leaving it quiet: too quiet. Dag felt the familiar itch between her shoulders. Something had gone wrong, or she'd missed a crucial piece of information. But what? She got up and paced the apartment, but nothing inside triggered her Trait.

She opened the door to the bedroom. One bed was tidily made while the blanket on the other was bunched up against the wall. But nothing here seemed to hide any secrets. She shut the door and returned to the table.

After staring at the map for a few minutes, she got up, pulled out the dried fish, pumped some water, and put the fish in to soak.

Whatever was going on, people would need to eat. She sat back down at the table to wait for the fish to soak—and for Joosep and Arnor to return.

THE LITTLE SAILBOAT skimmed across the water, and Calder shifted the tiller slightly, sending the boat in closer towards the shore.

He was approaching his mother's cabin, and so far, there had been no sign of the *Bright Breeze*. Had Ansdottir taken her farther out to sea, or had she gone south towards Langin? Should he have left his mother to her own fate in order to warn Langin about the pirates? He sighed: an impossible choice, and he'd made the one he'd thought best at the time, but if he saved his mother at Langin's expense, he would carry that guilt for the rest of his life.

At least the defences they'd created had kept Cutterstown safe: for now, anyway.

He had to assume that when Ansdottir learned that he was behind Cutterstown being prepared, once Inger told her about meeting him, the pirate captain would redouble her search for his family. The only bright spot might be that Ansdottir would be more intent on hurting him through his family than following Tarmo Holt's plans for destroying the winter food stores.

He rounded the point and sighed in relief when he saw his mother's camp. Nothing seemed amiss: fish were still drying on the racks and the buildings looked the same as they always did. Pirates had not been here.

Mindful of his mother's comments about lying in wait for the pirates, he tied up his boat at the north end of the pier.

"Mother!" he called as he stepped onto the pier. "I'm back to see if you need any help."

"Back to take me from my home is more like it." His mother stepped out of the trees to stand a few yards in front of him. "I'm not going."

"I didn't say I was going to take you anywhere." He'd hoped to convince her to go to Cutterstown, now that it was safe. "The pirates arrived in Cutterstown last night," he said. "We were able to prevent an attack, and they left. I was worried that they'd come here next."

"I told you I'd be ready for them," his mother replied. "And I am. So, you can go now."

"Aren't you even going to offer me a meal? Or at least listen to how we kept the pirates from landing at Cutterstown?"

"I don't care," she said. "Whatever worked there won't fool them again here, so what's the point?" She shook her head. "And you hate my cooking, so asking for a meal is just you trying to get me to do what you want."

"Yes," he agreed. "I didn't actually expect it to work." And he hadn't, but it was one of those times when not trying would have made her angrier than trying. "All right, I've seen that you're safe, I've offered you help and advice. I've even offered to eat your cooking." His mother snorted at that. "So, I will leave." He turned to head back to his boat. And stopped.

"Get to your cabin, Mother," he said. "Or wherever you planned to be when the pirates attacked. Now."

"What is it?" She stepped up to him and put a hand on his shoulder as she peered past him out to sea. "Is that a ship? You can see that far away?"

"Yes," he said to both questions. "And not only can I see it, but I recognize it. It's the *Bright Breeze*: the pirates are here." He untied his sailboat and was about to step into it but paused when he didn't sense his mother leaving. "Go now. I'll try to lead them away."

She turned to him with an odd look on her face. "I didn't think you were telling the truth," she said. "I thought you were just trying to scare me."

"You mean you didn't set any traps?" She shook her head, and his heart sank. All this time he'd thought that she'd at least had some protection. "Get in," he said more sharply than he'd intended. "Get in the boat, you're coming with me." For once, she didn't argue and simply did as he asked.

As soon as his mother had climbed in the boat, he pushed it away from the dock and jumped in after her. A moment later, he had the sail unfurled.

He studied the *Bright Breeze* for a moment before pointing the bow north. He'd lead them away from Cutterstown and Langin, up toward the White Wood. It wouldn't be too cold this time of year, he hoped. He sighed. At least he wouldn't have to wonder where his mother was. And she was as safe as he was. Unfortunately, that didn't seem safe at all.

They were just past the point when he saw the *Bright Breeze* change direction: they'd been spotted. The ship was going to chase them; it would catch them, eventually, unless Luck intervened.

GUSTAV PUSHED HIS cart down the narrow lane, his face mostly covered by his hat and his new-to-him scarf. This scarf was blue, or at least it once had been—now it was a muddy greyish colour. He'd wrapped it around his neck and pulled it up high enough to hide the shape of his jaw, making him a little less recognizable.

Not that he knew many people who might be on the streets of South Tarklee, but anyone who might recognize him would probably be dangerous.

A crowd had gathered up ahead, and he stopped when he reached them.

"Bits and bobs," he called out. "Trinkets for your love, cloth to patch your trousers. Best prices in the city."

A couple of women stared down at the small display of goods he had on his cart before moving past him.

"You been at this long?" someone asked. The crowd parted, and a man strode over to his cart. "You look young for it."

"My da's laid up with the gout," Gustav replied. "And I'm taking his place. I'm not very good at it yet, but if there's anything you need, I can get it."

"Best to try a richer part of town," the man replied. "Most folks here only have money for food. And sometimes not even that. Besides, there's some competition, I hear."

"Competition, huh," Gustav said. "I chose this part of town especially since there was no competition. Other carts, is it? And not enough trade for us all? I guess I should move on." He knew the people here had no money, that's why he was here. Desperate people he could tell about warehouses full of food.

"Nah, not other carts." A second man stepped forward. "Competition from the Freeholders. A shop has opened where anyone can buy goods, and all you have to do is sign a promise note saying you'll repay at a later date."

"A promise to repay, that's all?" Gustav didn't think that was all, but would this man realize that? "So, I could buy without paying today? When would I have to repay?"

"Oh, not for weeks," the second man said. "Plenty of time to get the coin together."

"What if I can't repay in a few weeks? All I have is this cart; my da's cart. Would they take that from me?"

"Yes," the first man said. He turned to the second man. "See? Even this lad understands what they're doing." He turned back to Gustav. "Don't go buying anything at this store. It's not here to help us."

"But it's the Grand Freeholder himself who's behind this," the second man said. "He's sworn to look out for us."

"He'll look out for himself no matter what he's sworn to do," the first man replied, and Gustav agreed with him. "I'm not buying anything from there, not unless I'm starving."

"I already bought," the second man said. "And if I can't repay then good luck getting anything from me. I got nothing to my name." He shrugged and walked away, and the other man shook his head.

"Sorry about your trade," he said to Gustav. "But folks with no money can't buy from you. You're best to find a better neighbourhood." He nodded and wandered away.

A few people stared at the building across the street that housed the new shop that was backed by the Grand Freeholder. One woman, her head down, left the group and entered the shop.

Starving people would take what was offered today, with no concern about future consequences. And who could blame them? He was pretty sure that Tarmo Holt was doing this in order to make people indebted to him. What he didn't know was how that benefitted Holt.

He pushed his cart past the shop towards another poor section in South Tarklee. He had a new mission now: find out just how many of these shops Tarmo Holt had opened up and where they were. People were desperate in different ways in different parts of town. How shrewd was Holt? He suspected he was very shrewd.

But so was Gustav. Each shop most likely had a warehouse close by that supplied goods to it. In a week or so, when the promises were expected to be repaid and weren't, these people might be ready to riot.

The third shop was very close to a warehouse he'd surveyed the day before. He parked his cart in the shadow of a building and watched as a steady stream of people entered the shop and others came out carrying parcels.

A crowd milled around in front, but unlike at the first shop, no one seemed to find this suspicious. Those exiting the shop were being congratulated by the ones watching.

Gustav settled his cart against a building and joined the

crowd. A woman holding up a sack grinned as she came out of the shop.

"Food for the next three days," she said to cheers. "And all for a promise." She hugged the sack to her chest and headed down the street.

Gustav nudged his way to the front. "Just a promise?" he asked. "That's it? Then someone gives you food?"

"That's it," a man beside him said. "A promise. I don't need it myself, not today, but I am happy to see my neighbours able to feed themselves."

"Happy, sure," Gustav repeated. Although this man's neighbours weren't exactly feeding themselves. Tarmo Holt was feeding them. He suspected that meant there would be a steep price to pay later.

"Do you think the food is from that warehouse?" he asked the man beside him. "I saw them loading it up a few days ago." He gestured behind him towards his cart. "I'm in the trade, so I was curious when I saw goods being stored there."

"Warehouse? What warehouse?"

"The one down that lane," Gustav replied. "With the double doors. It doesn't look like much, but I bet it can hold a lot of food."

A woman leaned over his shoulder. "Never seen anyone at that building, not in a year, but now they always got someone standing out front. You think that's where they're keeping the food for this shop?"

"I think it's full of food," Gustav said. Then he gave a big theatrical sigh. "I can't afford to give goods away on a promise, so this will take all of my trade. I'll need to find another part of town to do business in, one without a shop and a big warehouse supplying it." He turned away and edged to the back of the small group, whispers about a warehouse full of food following him.

He grabbed his cart and pushed it back the way he'd come. There was one more warehouse he wanted to visit; one more place where he thought Tarmo Holt might have set up a shop. One more rumour of a warehouse full of food to start.

Then he'd find a place to park his cart, hunt down something to eat and drink, and decide if he should try to contact Dagrun tonight.

JOOSEP KNEW THEY wouldn't kill him, at least not yet. Tarmo Holt had told him that he would live long enough to reveal all of his secrets. But he wanted them to kill him: he wanted to die of shame for losing his way so terribly that Arnor was dead and everything and everyone else was in jeopardy.

So, every time one of his tormentors hit him, or cut him, or burned him, he smiled.

They broke two of his teeth, and he smiled. They crushed his finger, and he smiled. He took all of the pain and agony and pushed it down, pushed it into his shame and horror at his own actions, and smiled.

Eventually one of these men would lose patience and kill him. That was the hope, that they would become so frustrated that one of them would lash out in anger and kill him. He was still weak from his first imprisonment, he didn't think it would take much.

A cup was lifted to his mouth, and water dribbled down his chin. He didn't want to drink: they put something in the water to try to make him want to talk, but he couldn't help swallowing. He tasted blood when he did.

"The Grand Freeholder wants to know what you know," one of his tormenters said. Joosep thought that this one was in charge: at least as in charge as anyone could be when doing Tarmo Holt's bidding. The man emptied the cup onto Joosep's head and tapped his forehead with it. "Everything in here has to come out."

Joosep didn't bother replying. Something he was rather proud of, when he had so little to take pride in today.

Arnor was dead, and Joosep had endangered the Intelligencers and the Fair Seas Treaty Alliance. Everything he'd worked for his whole life was now at risk because of his behaviour.

And all because he'd been jealous that Dagrun, and worse, his old rival Nadez, had been more competent than he had been. And because he was angry that they were right, he'd let Tarmo Holt become a threat to the Fair Seas Treaty Alliance, but he couldn't accept it.

He accepted it now. After seeing Holt casually order the death—the *murder*—of Arnor, he accepted it now.

Which is why he accepted the torture. It was nothing that he didn't deserve. In fact, he deserved worse.

He closed his eyes, knowing that his tormentors would cause pain in order to make him open them. The first blow came, and he smiled but kept his eyes closed. The second blow came, and he felt dizzy. Still, he smiled. This was good. They would either knock him unconscious, or they would kill him. Either outcome meant that he won. Either outcome meant he would be beyond telling them anything. A third blow landed.

DAG WATCHED THE entrance to the apartment. She'd left it an hour ago, but neither Joosep nor Arnor had entered it. She hoped they were with Nadez, otherwise she'd worry that they'd been captured. Or worse, that Joosep had betrayed them, perhaps unwittingly, to Holt.

She still didn't trust the Master Intelligencer. He'd never given an explanation for why he'd allowed Holt so much time and opportunity to consolidate his power. Holt must have been planning this from the day he took office as Grand Freeholder—maybe even *before* he took office.

And as someone with the Unseen Trait, she couldn't believe Joosep hadn't noticed things that worried him, that his Trait hadn't been triggered many, many times in the past few years. And yet he'd done nothing.

Even Gustav's theory that Joosep didn't trust his Trait didn't explain or justify his years of inaction. And now it might be too late to stop Holt's terrible plan.

Satisfied that Joosep and Arnor's disappearance hadn't compromised their safe haven, she stepped out of the doorway she'd been hiding in and on to the street. It was time to find Nadez and see if Joosep was with her.

She was a few streets from the Hall when she heard someone whisper the word murder. The itch between her shoulder blades was so strong that it was all she could do to keep walking normally. Usually when her Trait was triggered this intensely, she had some warning, or it was related to . . . she was going to see Nadez, was she the one who'd been murdered?

She edged closer to the whisperer, but someone else passed them, and they stopped speaking.

Dag turned down a lane, the itch between her shoulders

making it hard for her to concentrate. She was so worried that Nadez was dead that she wanted to run and find out, even though she knew she *had* to go slow in case it was true and Nadez's secrets had been discovered.

She knew of three of Nadez's safe places, but she decided to start with the one she'd followed Joosep to because Nadez hadn't invited her in.

The little stable looked abandoned and empty, but when she walked around to the side, Dag saw the small signs of footprints in the dirt. After making sure no one was watching, she ran her hands over the weathered wood. Her left hand snagged on something: it took her a moment to figure out how to work the mechanism, but then it opened easily. After a glance over her shoulder to make sure she hadn't been noticed, she ducked inside and slid the section of wood back in place.

She paused, waiting for her eyes to adjust to the darkness before following a short passageway to a small room illuminated by a window set high up along the back wall. A pile of blankets indicated that this was a place where Nadez felt safe enough to sleep.

A noise startled her, and she was about to hide when she recognized Nadez as she came through the opening.

Nadez slid the wooden planks back into place and glared at her.

"I saw you come in here," she said. "Putting me at risk at a time like this."

"What risk?" Dag asked. "I heard the word murder and it triggered my Trait. I was worried that it was you. Have you seen Joosep? He and his assistant are missing. Oh." If Nadez wasn't the murdered one, then it was one of the others.

"Oh is right," Nadez said. She brushed past Dag. "Since you're here, you might as well get comfortable. I've sent word for everyone to hide." She glared at Dag. "That includes me and now you."

Nadez sat down on the blankets, and Dag perched on an overturned bucket.

"Was it Joosep?" Dag asked. "Who was murdered?"

"No, although I almost wish it was. It was his assistant."

Dag closed her eyes. She'd spent the last few days confined in the apartment with Arnor, and besides being very efficient, he'd had a sly wit. And was totally dedicated to Joosep.

"Do you know how?" Dag asked.

"I know who," Nadez replied. "It was on the orders of Tarmo Holt, who then marched a bound Joosep through the Hall to some dungeon or other." She paused and stared at Dag. "But I don't know why. Why was his assistant killed, and what were he and Joosep doing in the Hall? They had a perfectly good place to hide, didn't they? It was well stocked and even had a water supply. So why?"

"I'm not sure," Dag said. The itch between her shoulders had subsided but hadn't disappeared, so there was more to learn. "They left while Gustav and I were sleeping. They had to practically step right over us and . . ." she paused. But Gustav had said that only one bowl was used for stew. "I think Joosep left, and Arnor followed him. He was probably worried that Joosep wasn't strong enough to . . . do whatever he was planning to do. He was taken from the Hall as a prisoner? Could Joosep have been caught looking for something?" Except she'd found his hiding places in his office, and Arnor had copied the records they'd needed.

Nadez sighed and relaxed. "I was hoping you knew. I have someone out looking for answers, so let's hope they are there to be found."

"I can find them," Dag said. "Using my Trait."

"No." Nadez's reply was immediate. "We cannot risk you. Or me. The two of us are the most senior and experienced Intelligencers. If we are to defeat Tarmo Holt, we need to stay alive and in control."

"Neither of which you think Joosep is," Dag said, and her back spasmed when her Trait intensified. "Control. It has something to do with control." She met Nadez's gaze. "Why Joosep left."

"*Skit.* I should have seen this coming. It's why I left the Intelligencers, after all."

"Over control?" Dag asked.

"Yes," Nadez replied. "Joosep is a big believer in the formal chain of command, and he hates to be second guessed. And he *really* hates when someone who reports to him disagrees with him. I tended to disagree with him often, so I quit."

"You think he let Arnor be killed and himself be captured

because he was mad that you . . ." she paused and thought about what she'd said to Joosep. "Because *we*," she amended, "disagreed with how he'd managed Tarmo Holt?"

"We did more than disagree," Nadez said. "We blamed him. And yes, I think it's very possible that he got angry and decided to prove that he was still Master Intelligencer and still in control."

Dag shook her head, not about Nadez's conclusion. The itch was gone, so she knew that this was the root of what Joosep had done. No, she shook her head because as an Intelligencer student, she would never have thought that her superior would react in such an irrational way. He had the same Trait as her: did that mean she might act just as irrationally?

Another thought struck her. "Everything is compromised now, isn't it?" Dag asked. "Because Joosep might have told Holt all of our plans."

"And all of our secrets," Nadez replied.

CHAPTER 16

THE SUN WOULD set soon and leave Calder and his mother at the mercy of the cold—and the *Bright Breeze*. Calder tucked a hand under his arm to keep his fingers warm.

"They're still there," his mother said. "Why aren't they coming any closer?"

"Because they don't have to," Calder replied. "We'll either need to land, at which point they will send a dozen men ashore to capture us." They'd probably kill them, but he didn't want to alarm his mother more than necessary. "Or we will get so far north that the cold and exposure will take care of us."

"You mean we'll die," his mother said. "Is that what they want?"

"Yes. At least that's what they plan for me." His mother was a good sailor, so he'd contemplated jumping into the sea to take Ansdottir's attention off her. Except that after Ansdottir either watched him tire and drown or picked him up and killed him, he didn't think the pirate captain would let his mother live.

"We need to make them pay then," his mother said. "Before we die."

He laughed, he couldn't help it. His mother had always been practical. "And here I was worried that you'd blame me for this."

"I do," she replied. "And I will, if we survive. But that's not going to help us, is it? And what the pirates on that ship don't know about me—about *us*—is that we're from the north. Cold is something we're used to, *born* to. If it's cold enough to kill us, then it's cold enough to put that ship in danger." She looked up at the sky. "The first storm of the winter would help." She looked over at him. "Any chance that Luck of yours can manage that?"

He laughed again. "I wish I could control it like that because that could cause them to founder." He had his father's blood too, but as a sailor, he'd always been able to work in the cold far longer than many other sailors could. He'd never before attributed it to being born in the north. "Ah, Mother, if this is our last day, we might as well enjoy it."

"I'm not sure we've ever enjoyed a day together," his mother said. "Not since . . . your brother died."

"I don't remember much before that day," Calder said quietly, "but I remember that." He'd often wished he could forget it, even though it was his only clear memory of his twin.

"I didn't mean to blame you for his death, but I know I did."

Surprised, he looked at his mother, but she stared ahead, not turning to face him.

"And I allowed your father to let that Intelligencer take you away because I knew that by blaming you, I would ruin you. But I couldn't seem to stop myself." She finally turned to look at him. "And then I blamed you for leaving me. I didn't mean to do that either, and I *hate* that I did: for a while I even hated myself, but wanting it another way didn't mean I could make that happen." Her eyes were clear, and he could see her sorrow, but there were no tears.

"I think, in some way, I always understood," Calder said. "But coming home to visit was uncomfortable."

"I know, for me too. And for that, I am truly sorry," his mother replied. "Because it meant you didn't grow up with Yakop and Berna the way you should have." She settled her hands in her lap and shrugged. "I came to terms a long time ago that I'm not perfect, and there are times when I've failed those I love. It doesn't mean I don't love the ones I failed, but that reality has a harder time getting through my self-recriminations."

"Thank you," Calder said finally.

His mother nodded and turned and faced forward again. She was a hard woman; he'd always known that, so he knew it was difficult for her to admit her faults to him, even if it was because they were facing death.

He sighed. The sun had almost set, and the sky was turning a deep indigo. The wind picked up, and he rubbed his hands together to keep them warm and supple.

"What's that?" his mother asked, pointing ahead and to starboard.

A light flickered. Had the *Bright Breeze* gotten ahead of them? He looked behind. The ship was still there, still following them. So, what was ahead?

A second light bobbed behind the first, and his focus narrowed: his Trait telling him what to do.

He steered the little sailboat towards the light. Whatever it was, it was friendlier than what was behind them. A few minutes later, he laughed.

"It's not a winter storm, Mother, but I think my Luck has provided." Now he could make out three ships: the three log haulers that he'd sent north with Jaak.

They were lined up facing them; facing the *Bright Breeze*. Calder's little boat was practically beneath the first ship when a lamp was swung over the side.

"Calder Rahmson, is that you?" Jaak leaned over the gunwale. "Get aboard, hurry, we're about to test out a little something me and the crew came up with."

Calder hurried to take the sail down while his mother caught the line that was thrown to them. The log hauler was carrying cargo and rode low in the water, so his mother just needed a hand to help her scramble up and over the gunwale. Once she was safe, he climbed aboard after her.

"Good to see you, Jaak," he said. "Your timing is excellent."

"Yours too," Jaak said. "Welcome aboard the *Oakhaven*. We sure appreciate you bringing Captain Ansdottir with you." Jaak grinned and slapped Calder on the back. "And who's this?"

"Jaak, meet my mother, Lauma. Jaak here's the one I sent north with these ships." He stared at Jaak. "To save them."

"That's what we're trying to do. Come watch." He hurried to where three people stood on the bridge. "Captain Eklund, we've found Calder Rahmson and his mother."

A man dressed in a thick overcoat turned. His glance skimmed past Calder and settled on his mother.

"Lauma Strauskas," he said. He smiled and gave a half bow. "Welcome aboard." His gaze returned to Calder. "And Calder Rahmson."

"Captain Eklund, thank you for helping us," his mother said. To Calder's surprise, she smiled at the older man and took his arm. "My son and I have gotten ourselves into some trouble. I appreciate the help."

"Of course," Eklund replied. "You are one of Cutterstown's Freeholders, so I am obligated, but I am also delighted to be of service."

"And it will be fun," Jaak interjected. "We're ready."

"Very good, Jaak," Eklund said. He peered out into the night. "I believe the *Bright Breeze* is close enough. Relay fifteen degrees east!" he called out. The order was repeated on board and then relayed across to the other two ships.

Calder hung on as the man at the wheel turned east: the ship lurched, and the wind caught in the sails.

"Come on," Jaak grabbed him and pulled him to the stern. "We want a good view."

"Are we trying to outrun the *Bright Breeze*?" Calder asked. The log haulers sat low in the water, which made them stable for carrying heavy loads but unable to travel very fast.

"Of course not," Jaak said. "These tubs aren't going to outrun the *Bright Breeze* even without Captain Ansdottir at the helm. We have other plans."

In the dark, the men who lined the gunwales of the stern were almost invisible, as were the logs that stretched across the deck from one side of the ship to the other at the stern. When he looked over at the next ship, Calder saw men standing along the gunwales near that stern too.

The *Oakhaven* finished its turn and now pointed due east. The *Bright Breeze*, a couple of lamps swinging in the darkness, followed them.

The three log haulers maneuvered until they were sailing side by side, just the width of a ship separating them.

Still trailing, the *Bright Breeze* centred itself behind the middle log hauler.

Captain Eklund's shouted order was quickly relayed across to the next ship.

"Ready crew," Jaak said.

"Now!" Eklund called.

Jaak repeated it. "Now!"

The sailors that lined the gunwales all stooped and picked up logs. The pair at the very stern lifted their log up and over the stern gunwale and tossed into the sea. The next log was handed down and was also tossed overboard.

The log hauler beside them was doing the same, and Calder assumed the third ship was as well.

Jaak laughed. "Let's see Captain Margit Ansdottir navigate her way out of that!" He cheered along with the rest of the sailors as the last log was heaved over the gunwales.

She would: Calder knew that somehow Ansdottir would get clear of this, but Jaak's enthusiasm was infectious.

"She won't have seen that coming," Jaak said.

"I agree." They were already far beyond the *Bright Breeze*. Calder stared across the dark sea at the *Bright Breeze*. "I think they've struck the sails."

"That was fast," Eklund said as he joined them. "They might not have taken any damage at all."

"But they know you're not afraid of them," Calder said. "The surprise and impact of being a ghost ship is gone."

"You think they'll attack," Eklund said. "Where?"

His mother came and stood beside Eklund. "Not here. They're done looking for us—your family. They'll go south."

"Yes," he agreed. "They'll go south. To Tarklee. So that's what I must do too." Dag was there, and Tarmo Holt still needed to be stopped.

"I can take you there," Eklund said. "But if we want to try to keep up with the *Bright Breeze*, we won't have time to drop Lauma off at Cutterstown."

"I haven't been to Tarklee in a while," his mother said.

GUSTAV VISITED TWO warehouses and found that both of them were near stores selling goods to people for promise-to-pay notes. Now he had just one more place in South Tarklee to visit.

Wondering if the store would be closed for the night, he pushed his cart through the streets towards the warehouse. Even if it was closed, he might be able to learn if it was the same set up as the others. And if not, he'd be there to see it open in the morning.

When he was within sight of the warehouse, he found a spot along a wall, positioned the cart with a view of the roads near the warehouse, and slid underneath.

A lamp was burning outside the door to a building down the road, and someone was standing underneath it. A couple went past the person and entered the building. A few moments later they came out carrying a bundle.

It had to be a store—with a guard outside it. Gustav pulled his scarf up over his nose to keep the dust away and stared out at the store.

"Traded for a half a dozen tankards of ale, is what I heard."

Gustav jerked awake. It was dawn, and two pairs of booted feet were so close to him that he could have touched them. The cart jostled as someone leaned against it.

"Maybe I'll try my luck at that instead of signing a promise note," a second man said. "I could manage enough coin to pay for watered-down ale if someone wanted to trade me a couple days' worth of food for it."

"I heard it was a week's worth," the first man said. "No doubt Alf's wife'll have a few words for him this morning."

"Most any wife would," his companion agreed. "Look, he's here already. And don't even seem proper awake yet. Alf!" he called. "Get any sleep?"

Gustav looked past the boots to see a man in rumpled clothing gesture towards the two men, which only made them laugh.

One pounded on the cart. "I want to see this," the second man said. "Alf'll get right mad when they don't give him anything else."

"You sure they'll cut him off?"

"Won't give you anything until you pay off the first promise note," the man sad.

The men moved away from the cart and headed across the street. When they were far enough away that he could see that they had their backs to him, Gustav crawled out from under the cart.

He was curious to see what happened when Alf was told he had to repay the first promise note before he could get anything else from the store.

Alf entered the store and a few minutes later, was escorted out by the guard, followed by a second man who yelled at Alf to not come back until he could pay what he owed.

A crowd had gathered to see the spectacle of Alf pleading, begging, cursing, and finally threatening the man in charge of the store, and many laughed at his increasing desperation.

Gustav thought that was very short-sighted of them since any of them, any of the people who had signed a promise to pay, could end up just as desperate as Alf.

It bothered him that he too was going to take advantage of Alf, but this was what he and Dagrun had planned: to take advantage of the desperate and hungry and encourage them to riot.

A few stragglers continued to heckle poor Alf, who stood with his head down in front of the store. The guard stared at him for a moment before stepping out of sight and inside the building.

Alf shook off the hand of a woman who actually seemed to be trying to help and stumbled down the street towards Gustav's cart.

"Terrible what they done to you," Gustav said as he joined Alf in the street. "Them havin' all that food, and you and yours going hungry."

"Can't go home," he said. "She told me not to come home without it." He shook his head. "Didn't mean to trade it all for a drink. It were just a drink, a man has a right to a drink every now and then, don't he?"

"You have the right of it," Gustav said. "Sometimes you need a drink to feel like a man."

"That's it exactly." Alf poked Gustav in the shoulder. "That's what the wife don't understand. I deserve a drink every now and then. I deserve it!"

"A man deserves to eat too," Gustav said. "Except those who have, don't like to share with those who have nothing." He leaned closer. "I know where all the food is. For the store." He peered around to see if anyone was watching them, but no one seemed to be. He leaned towards Alf's ear. "A warehouse full of food is just down that lane." He pointed to an alley. "In a big building made of stone with green doors."

"And it's full of food?" Alf asked.

"Aye, to the rafters. I should know since I helped carry it all in," he lied. "Bags of flour and sugar and barrels stacked three high with dried fish and ale."

"Ale?" Alf asked. "They have ale too?"

"That's what I saw." Gustav nodded. "It's being guarded by men who live in the house three doors down. Six of them, I think." He grinned. "Although, if I was them, I'd be into the ale in the middle of the night. A man deserves a drink, after all."

"A man deserves a drink," Alf repeated. "Warehouse with green doors, you said?"

"Yes, at least they were green at one time," Gustav replied. "The paint's mostly peeled off, but you can still tell." He slapped Alf on the shoulder. "I'm off. I have to get my cart to a different part of town. All these stores allowing promise-to-pay notes means I can't make a living around here."

He pushed his cart past Alf and waved, but he didn't think the man noticed him. He was still staring down the lane towards the warehouse.

When Gustav arrived with his cart at New Bridge, it was crowded. He slipped in behind a woman driving a wagon, and when she stopped suddenly, he accidently pushed his cart into the back of her wagon. She turned and glared down at him from her seat but didn't say anything.

A guard wearing Swyford colours travelling in the opposite direction tried to squeeze past him.

"Is there trouble ahead?" Gustav asked the guard. "Would I be better staying in South Tarklee?"

"Trouble ahead, yes," the guards said. "Tarmo Holt has called a halt to this year's election for the new Grand Freeholder."

"Wasn't it supposed to be someone from Swyford?" Gustav asked. "I heard it was going to be the Clan Freeholder from Lavais."

"My Clan Freeholder," the guard said. "It was supposed to be. That's why I came, so I can notify him about the announcement. I didn't think it would mean he wasn't getting the task."

"Did he say why?" Gustav asked. "Tarmo Holt, did he say why the election isn't being held?"

"He told a bunch of lies, if that's what you mean." The crowd surged, and the guard was gone before Gustav could ask anything else.

Eventually, he made it across the bridge and into North Tarklee. Once off the bridge, he headed closer to the apartment. Joosep and Dagrun needed to hear this news right away.

"SHE'S HERE, FINALLY," Nadez said, and Dag stepped away from the front door of the little stable and joined Nadez in the back.

They'd spent a wary night and morning taking turns keeping watch and sleeping while waiting for a student to report. Nadez didn't want to lose touch with Kaja, the student, since she'd been the conduit between Nadez and the handful of Intelligencers, instructors, and students still in the city.

"The Grand Freeholder just—" the young woman who stepped through the opening in the wall stopped speaking when she saw Dag.

"There's a reason why you need to wait until I ask for your report," Nadez said. She put the boards back in place and stared at the girl, her hands on her hips. "Come on, meet Dagrun Lund, Intelligencer." Nadez edged past the girl and sat down. "Dagrun, this is Kaja Haugen."

"Ah, from Gustav's training group," Dag said. "You're the one with the excellent Memory." She ignored the girl's open mouth and turned to Nadez. "Now I understand why you picked a student for this task."

"Dagrun Lund," Kaja said. "Twin sister is Inger who is not an Intelligencer. You've had one assignment since completing your training?"

"That's right," Dag said. Was Kaja trying to impress her or intimidate her? She stared at the girl, who finally looked away. She didn't seem to be hiding anything other than pride that she was doing such an important task. "And for your information, my Trait is Unseen. I discover secrets."

"Oh, so that's how you knew my Trait," Kaja said.

"Yes, but Gustav also confirmed it. We need to know what tools we have to use against Holt. What has the Grand Freeholder done that we need to know?"

Kaja looked at Nadez, who nodded.

"Tarmo Holt made an announcement this morning that the election of a new Grand Freeholder has been postponed."

"Did he give a new date?" Nadez asked.

Kaja shook her head. "But he gave a reason. He said that the process has been manipulated: that he'd heard that the person who was expected to be next in line was somehow a threat to the Fair Seas Treaty Alliance."

"Was anyone standing with him?" Dag asked. "Especially anyone from Swyford?"

"Not that I recognized," Kaja said. "But there was a guard in Swyford colours. He left right after the announcement."

"Did you see Joosep?" Dag asked.

"No." Kaja seemed surprised by the question.

"You think Holt would put him on display," Nadez said.

"I think that if Tarmo Holt wanted to convince people that there was trouble with the election process, or the man who is the most likely to be the next Grand Freeholder, he would want the Master Intelligencer there," Dag replied. "So yes, I think he would put Joosep on display." She shrugged her shoulders as her Trait activated. "So why wasn't Joosep there?"

"Holt won't trust him," Nadez said.

"He doesn't have to," Dag said. "He could easily have him placed where he can't do any harm and yet can be seen. Even if all he did was mention that the Master Intelligencer had uncovered these irregularities and then point to him, it would have been enough to validate Holt's position."

"Unless he doesn't have to validate it," Nadez offered. "Because it's true?"

Dag shook her head. "The only person manipulating anything is Tarmo Holt. My one assignment was in the household of Clan Freeholder Timonis. That man has the respect and trust of his fellow Swyford Freeholders. Besides, my Trait would have uncovered any hidden threat Timonis posed. No, if Joosep wasn't at Holt's announcement, it must be because he couldn't be."

"Maybe Joosep has already been killed," Nadez said. "Kaja, tell me again what the person who saw Joosep alive said."

"There was blood," Kaja said. "They saw a lot of blood. Joosep was between two guards, and he was being dragged by them—"

"Dragged?" Dag asked. "They said he was being dragged by guards? That doesn't sound like he was willing. At least not at that point in time."

"Yeah, they said he was being dragged," Kaja said. "And that he was splattered with blood, but he didn't seem hurt."

"Hmm." Dag frowned. "He didn't seem hurt, or he didn't seem to be bleeding? They are two very different things."

"They said he didn't seem to be hurt, but they could have meant that he wasn't bleeding," Kaja said. "I didn't think to ask. Sorry."

"Don't be," Dag said before Nadez could say anything. "You've done very well. And you're only half way through your training." And was still little more than a child, Dag thought, about Gustav's age: another student doing remarkably well. But then Calder had been a full-fledged Intelligencer at the age of sixteen.

"I don't think we're compromised," she said. "I don't think Joosep has told them anything. At least not yet."

"You're sure?" Nadez asked.

"As sure as I can be," Dag replied. "I'm not suggesting we keep using any of our current safe places, just that I think we have time to remove anything of value." Or anything that would tell Holt their plans. "I'll go see if Gustav has returned. Should Kaja come with me? She can look at the maps we've marked."

"Kaja?" Nadez asked. The girl nodded. "Good, when you return you can tell me what Dagrun and Gustav have been up to. At nightfall, I'll meet you where I first found you."

Dag left the little stable with Kaja at her back.

The streets were busier than usual, and many small groups of people clustered on corners talking in low voices. Dag and Kaja paused in the shadow of the building across from the apartment. A couple passed by them, whispering about Tarmo Holt's announcement.

It took almost an hour, but eventually the street in front of the apartment emptied, and they made their way inside.

Dag locked the door behind Kaja.

"Gustav!"

Dag turned to see Kaja launch herself at Gustav, who looked up bleary-eyed from the maps.

"Kaj, hey! You're safe. Dagrun? I thought you might be Joosep and Arnor. Any news?"

"Yes, and it's bad," Dag said. She headed to the stove. "Good, you made soup." She'd left the fish soaking yesterday and had expected to have to cook it. She was grateful that Gustav had done that task. She pulled out three bowls and started filling them.

"Arnor is dead, and Joosep is with Tarmo Holt," she said to Gustav. "And we don't know what secrets Joosep has already, or soon will, disclose, so we need to abandon this apartment."

"What?" Gustav asked.

"Nadez and I think Joosep somehow convinced himself that he needed to work around us or that he needed to fix this himself." She placed the bowls on the table on top of the maps. "Arnor either went with him to help or followed him to try and stop him."

"I'm sure Arnor was trying to keep Joosep safe," Gustav said. "He would never have helped Joosep do anything dangerous."

"We may never know exactly why," Dag said. "But the end result is that Arnor is dead and Joosep has been captured by Holt." She made it sound as though the why didn't matter when it did. But finding the answer to that question wouldn't help keep them safe: not in the immediate future, anyway.

"It's true," Kaja said. "I spoke to a few people who saw Arnor and Joosep. Shall I recite what they told me?"

"No." Gustav seemed to sag.

"But Joosep is still alive," Dag said. "Which means this secret," she gestured to the apartment, "may not remain a secret for much longer. We need to be gone by dusk. So as soon as we've eaten, you need to tell me and Kaja what all this," she waved at the maps, "means."

The small room was silent as they sat down and ate. Dag refilled her own bowl again, as did Kaja and Gustav. Finally, she put her empty bowl aside and sat down at the table.

"Eat more if you want," Dag said. "Who knows where the next meal will come from."

Gustav refilled his bowl, but Kaja pushed hers aside and stared down at the map. Dag picked the bowls up off the maps and put them near the stove.

"I'm ready," Gustav said, placing his bowl with the other two.

"Then let's hear what you learned," Dag said, leaning over the maps.

It took almost an hour for Gustav to tell her what he'd done. He pointed out on the map which warehouses he'd disclosed to people nearby. When he described the man who'd been refused a second promise-to-pay note, her Trait activated.

"Wait," Dag said. "That. What happens to those who can't repay their debt?"

"No one I spoke to knows," Gustav said. "Other than that they cannot get more goods, as Alf found out."

"But he is now in debt to Tarmo Holt," Dag said. "That might be all Holt wants: people who owe him. This Alf still has a few days before he has to repay. If you can, find out what happens then."

Dag sighed. It was getting late. "We need to destroy anything that can give away our plans to Holt. Kaja, have you memorized everything you've seen?" She nodded. "Good. You two leave now. I'll clean up here." She turned to Gustav. "You have a safe place to go to?"

"I'll stay with my cart," Gustav said. "It's not much different from our original plan. Who will I contact with information?"

"Kaja," Dag said. "She's already doing the same for others."

"What about you?" Gustav asked. "Where will you go?"

"I'll hide," Dag said. "And try to find out more about Holt's plans for his ships." And she'd be at the harbour, in case Calder returned.

The other two left, and Dag studied the room. The maps and list of Intelligencers and Traits went into the fire in the stove: she knew most of that already, and any detail that she forgot, Kaja would remember.

She opened the door to the small bedroom. She hadn't spent any time in it, and it didn't seem to hold any of Arnor or Joosep's personal items.

She did find a small compartment hidden behind the bed. It held a handful of coins. Dag pocketed them and headed back to the main room.

She was tempted to set the whole place on fire, but that would cause undue scrutiny and put the neighbourhood at risk.

No, the best option was to leave it as it was. She made sure the fire in the stove was out, and then she stepped out into dusk. After putting the key behind the stone, she walked out into the city.

CHAPTER 17

CALDER STARED OUT across the sea. The sun was setting, and the reds and golds and oranges gave the water under the *Bright Breeze* the appearance of being on fire.

Margit Ansdottir had caught up with the three logging ships hours ago, and instead of trying to cut them off or destroy them, she'd been content to follow them. Which made Calder think that her plan was to herd them into Tarklee Harbour. Once trapped, they'd be easier to set on fire.

He swivelled his head to watch the city come into sight. As dusk crept across it, lights flickered to life along the dock area and above, on the high wall of the Hall.

Was Tarmo Holt up in his apartment watching? Had he already sent a message with orders to stop and confiscate, or set fire to, any ships arriving in the harbour that did not belong to him?

He headed to the bow and joined Captain Eklund and Jaak.

"It's time," he said.

Eklund nodded and shouted an order, and the Second Mate ran a yellow flag up the mast. Sailors in the rigging scrambled to lower the topsail, and the ship started to slow.

"You're sure, Jaak?" Calder asked as the younger man followed him to the port gunwale.

"I wouldn't miss it," Jaak said with a grin. "These log haulers aren't the daintiest ships, but they're solid. Besides, I may never get another chance to be First Mate on anything."

"I'll call you captain if you want," Calder said. "It's a title I've

215

had more than once in my life."

"I'd like that," Jaak said. "Although I'll be sure to run all my decisions past First Mate Rahmson."

"As you wish," Calder said. The smallest of the log haulers, *The Mischief*, pulled alongside them, and Calder jumped up onto the gunwale and crossed over to it.

"Welcome aboard, Captain," he said when Jaak joined him.

"Thank you, First Mate."

"I take it Captain Eklund's plan is now underway," a man said. "I was hoping he'd changed his mind."

"I'm afraid not, Captain Sorensen," Calder said. "Is everything ready?"

"Yes," Sorenson replied. "I have followed my orders. But I'm not happy; my ship deserves better."

"We all do," Calder replied. "Captain Eklund is waiting for you to join him. No doubt he will listen to all of your concerns." As senior officer of the small fleet, Eklund had the final decision about their strategy, so Sorensen's unhappiness was his problem.

"I'd say take good care of her," Sorenson said. "But that's not the plan, is it?" He frowned before he stepped past them to join the rest of his crew as they crossed over to the *Oakhaven* and Captain Eklund's command.

"I'll take a quick look below deck," Calder said. "If that's all right with you, Captain?"

"I need a report anyway," Jaak said. "I'll be at the wheel."

Calder's smile faded as he made his way down the stairs. Jaak was taking this all in stride, but this might be his only chance to be a captain; it was possible neither one of them would live through this.

As for him, he couldn't ask someone else to do anything this risky, not when it had been his plan. Besides, he had Luck on his side.

As he walked through the narrow passage to the prow, he could feel how steeply the ship tilted towards the bow.

Any timber and logs that hadn't been used to slow Ansdottir down had been layered at the very front of the ship. It was tightly packed; the crew of *The Mischief* had taken time to carefully wedge each log in tight. Skit, the logs were so well packed that the ship might not even take on water for a few minutes, which could give Jaak and him enough time to jump ship and get clear.

He headed back up to the deck. All they needed now was a little Luck. *The Mischief* would be unwieldy with the load stowed the way it was. And Margit Ansdottir was too smart a sailor to not notice.

"Any orders, Captain?" he asked when he joined Jaak at the wheel. The other two log haulers had already left them behind. They would stay just outside of the harbour until they knew the outcome.

"Get ready to come about," Jaak said.

"Aye aye, Captain." Calder headed up into the rigging as Jaak swung the wheel. Slowly, they turned until they were pointing directly at the *Bright Breeze*.

Calder thought he caught a glimpse of blonde hair on the deck of the other ship. He heard an indistinct shout and a chorus echoing it as sails were lowered and the pirate ship slowed.

So that she knew where to find him, Gustav led Kaja to the place where he usually left his cart. The streets near it were busy: too busy for this late in the day. He headed into the lane, grateful to see that whatever was occurring, his cart hadn't been disturbed.

"I should find out what's happening," he said to Kaja.

"*We* should find out," she replied. "I'll come with you. Then I can pass that information on."

"Stay close." He'd been training with Kaja long enough that he hadn't expected anything else. Vilis had been the one of the three of them most likely to wait to be told what to do.

They returned to the main street and joined the crowd that was slowly making its way towards Key Bridge.

"Has something happened?" Gustav asked a man on his left, "because of the Grand Freeholder's announcement?"

"You could say that," the man replied. "I heard he's been keeping all the food to himself, and selling it at shops he owns. But that's our food, and we're going to take it back."

Gustav turned to Kaja.

"We should stay out of this," he said. "If we can."

The crowd was pushing now, and people were yelling about

Tarmo Holt and his warehouses of food. People surged forward, and Kaja was pressed up against him.

"I don't think we can get off the bridge," she said. "We'll have to wait and try to get free once we cross over into South Tarklee."

They were near the stone railing of the bridge when the crowd shifted to the right. Gustav watched in horror as a woman was squeezed over the railing and off the bridge. The shouts and curses from the crowd drowned out the woman's screams as she fell to the river below.

Gustav and Kaja huddled together as they were pushed forward. They were almost at the crest of the bridge, and the crowd was even more tightly jammed together. Someone stepped on his heel, and a body crowded into him. If Kaja hadn't been holding on to him, he might have fallen and risked being trampled.

The crowd surged again, and then they were being pushed down the slight slope of the bridge towards land. Higher than the heads in front of him, he could see to the end of the bridge: night had fallen, and torches bobbed up ahead, illuminating the seething crowd.

Finally, they reached the end of the bridge. A couple on their right veered away as soon as space allowed, and Gustav and Kaja followed them.

They stood at the side of the bridge, staring at the mass of people still making their way through the streets.

"It's ahead of schedule," Gustav said. "But the riots have started. I didn't expect it to be like this." He'd known it would be dangerous to be out in the riot, but he'd thought the danger would be centred around the warehouses; that as long as he stayed away from the places he'd marked on the map, he'd be safe. Now he wasn't sure anyone was safe.

Certainly, Tarmo Holt wasn't safe, not with a crowd this angry.

People might die tonight, because of his actions, his rumours, his intelligence.

People might die. And just because some of them were complicit in Tarmo Holt's scheme, it didn't mean that they deserved to lose their lives.

"Come on," Kaja said. "The crowd's thinned out enough to

head back across." She tugged at his arm, but he stood rooted on the spot.

"No, I need to see the damage," he said, "so I can report it." He needed to see the havoc the mob visited on the warehouses he'd revealed to people. He needed to try to tally up the deaths caused by his actions. And see if he could maybe prevent a few.

Kaja nodded. "I'll find you later," she said, and then she slipped away, back across the bridge.

THE MERCHANT ADVENTURERS' office was dark when Dag arrived at the harbour. She peered in the window, but there was no sound or signs of movement from inside.

The door was locked, but she found a window that faced onto the harbour that was unlatched. She opened it and climbed inside. When she turned to make sure no one had seen her enter, the telltale itch between her shoulder blades made her stop and stare out at the harbour.

There should only be three ships in the harbour; the rest had been destroyed by the fire. Now lamps illuminated two smaller ships that hovered at the mouth of the harbour. And there! The whitewashed ghost ship was just behind a third, even smaller ship.

Were they from Cutterstown? Was Calder out there in the harbour, on board one of those ships?

The two smaller ships near the mouth of the harbour dropped their sails while the third one turned to face the ghost ship. It had to be Calder: who else would challenge Margit Ansdottir?

Inger would be on the ghost ship too, with the captain of the pirates. A cloud skidded across the moon, hiding the harbour from her.

She shrugged her shoulders, but the itch was still there; her Trait was still activated. But she couldn't think of anything she could do to help either Calder or her twin.

She turned back to the office. She'd found information about Holt's ships here before, and although she didn't expect to find anything else, it was a starting point.

Dag found a hidden compartment in a small closet that held a broom and bucket, but it was empty.

Out in the harbour, the ghost ship still faced off against the smallest ship, but now the remaining two ships were positioned in the mouth of the harbour, blocking it.

Her gaze swept over the three ships already at anchor: the three ships belonging to Tarmo Holt that had survived the fire.

The itch between her shoulders intensified: *that* was what her Trait was telling her to look at. It wasn't about Calder and Inger, it was about something hidden on one of the other ships.

She unlocked the door and ran down the path and onto the pier until she was close enough to read the names of the ships. The *Tazeyar* was on the list she'd found and belonged to Holt, the *Neas* . . . she stopped. Holt's personal ship: the ship he'd sailed to Strongrock when he'd met with Margit Ansdottir.

The ship most likely to be where he kept his deepest secrets.

She studied the ship. Lamps were lit at the stern and the bow. How many people would Holt have on board? Would they be guards or sailors?

Nothing moved on deck. After a few minutes, she made her decision. A barge was tied up at the pier, and a rope ran from it to the *Neas*. That was her way onto the ship.

She felt exposed the whole time she was climbing the rope, but no one shouted an alarm. Once she'd swung herself over the gunwale and onto the deck, she understood why.

Five men stood with their backs to her, staring out at the harbour.

"That log hauler's going to win," someone said. "The white ship doesn't stand a chance."

"What's winning if you go down with your ship?" another voice asked. "Don't see no way for the little ship to ram the big one and not go down."

"They're moving!"

Dag ignored the spasm of fear that coursed through her. *I can't help Calder or Inger*, she told herself as she forced her feet in the direction of the door that led below deck.

Lights lined a narrow passageway, and because she had no desire to be trapped deep in the ship by an off-duty crew member, she cautiously opened each door as she came to it. Every cabin she looked in was dark, and the light spilling from the passageway showed small spaces filled with cots and hammocks. They were all empty. It looked like everyone on board was on deck.

The passage ended at a door at the stern. When she opened the door, this room was dark as well, but the light from the corridor shone on a lamp and flint on a desk beside the door. In a moment she had the lamp lit and was surveying what had to be Tarmo Holt's private quarters.

A small desk and chair sat beside the door, and a larger desk ran along one wall, facing inward. A sturdy chair and a low shelf were behind the desk. A quick search of every piece of furniture in view yielded an account ledger and some rolled up maps.

A round table and chairs sat below a window that stretched across the stern. A small door on one side opened onto a sleeping chamber, the bed hanging from the ceiling by ropes.

Dag closed her eyes. Tarmo Holt must have secrets here. She tried to focus on her Trait, on seeing the Unseen, on finding what was hidden.

When she opened her eyes, her gaze landed on the wall between the round table and the sleeping chamber. Unconsciously, she scratched between her shoulder blades even though it would do nothing to relieve the itch caused by her Trait.

She ran her hands over the wood of the walls, but they were polished smooth: she didn't find any hidden levers that might open a secret compartment.

She wedged into the space between the bed and the wall and did the same on the sleeping chamber side but still found nothing to indicate any hidden compartments. She stood in the doorway with her back against one door frame and tried to look at both walls at the same time to see if there were any indentations she'd missed, but the wall was too thick.

Frowning, she turned towards the door frame she'd been leaning against and placed her hand on it: the wood was three fingers thick. On the opposite side, her whole hand fit against the frame. There was an extra two to three inches of width; plenty of room to hide some secrets.

Just above eye level, built into the door frame, a piece of metal had been inserted into the wood. She pushed it and one end flipped up, and with a soft click, the entire wall shifted out into the main cabin.

She tugged at the wall until there was enough room for her to step in behind it.

Documents were layered against the wall, slipped behind taut lines of string that kept them flat. Dag retrieved the lamp to get a better look at what Holt had hidden.

With the lamp in one hand, she rifled through the corners of the papers, hoping that one would jump out at her.

But her Trait didn't single out any one paper or group of papers: they were all important. But there was no way she could take everything *and* climb down the rope to the dock.

A small notebook with a familiar binding caught her attention: it was a mate to the ledger she'd already found, so she grabbed it.

She had just pulled out a stack of papers that seemed to be cargo manifests when she heard shouting from the deck above. Had someone noticed her light?

She blindly grabbed another sheaf of papers, stepped out from behind the wall, and pushed it back into place. She turned the lamp down low and set it back on the desk near the door.

More shouts drifted down to her, but they seemed no closer than before. Should she assume she hadn't been discovered and try to find more information?

When the shouting turned to cheering, Dag rushed to the window. She didn't have the best view, but she could see enough to tell that the ghost ship and the smaller log hauler were both well into the harbour.

She grabbed a pack that had been slung across the back of a chair, shoved all of her discoveries into it, settled it across her shoulder, and went to the door.

She turned the wick on the lamp down and extinguished the flame before she opened the door and stepped into the passageway.

The five men at the gunwale were so consumed with the spectacle they were watching that they didn't notice her sneak past them, climb back onto the rope, and slip back down it to the barge.

As soon as her feet touched the barge, she sprinted across to the pier and headed for the shore. From there she made her way to a vantage point where moonlight revealed the events in the harbour.

Where the two people in the world she cared about the most were in danger.

CHAPTER 18

CALDER WRENCHED THE sheet and the sail fluttered slackly for a moment before the wind caught it, and the ship surged forward.

The bow of *The Mischief* was pointed directly at the *Bright Breeze*, this time at its port side. He scrambled down from the rigging and jogged along the deck to join Jaak at the wheel.

"I think we have her this time," he said. Ansdottir hadn't used the cannon, and Calder wondered why. The log hauler was slow enough that a captain with Ansdottir's skills could easily hit them. Was she so sure of herself that she didn't think she needed to use it?

"The wind's changing," Jaak said. "In their favour."

"It won't be enough." Calder stared out at the *Bright Breeze*. The moonlight revealed sailors in the rigging, trying to execute Ansdottir's orders in time to do . . . "Are they trying to outrun us?" He shook his head, Ansdottir wasn't someone to turn and run; this was part of a plan.

"They're trying to line us up with their stern," Jaak said. "And the cannon."

"You're right," Calder said. "But it's too late for them."

The *Bright Breeze* slowly turned, and then suddenly the wind died. Calder could see pirates scrambling on deck as they tried to react to new orders.

He looked up: their own sails were still catching enough wind to allow them to close the distance between the two ships.

More Luck? His focus narrowed to the stern—and the captain's cabin.

"Aim for the port stern," he said to Jaak. "And then tie off the wheel." He grinned. He and Jaak just might make it out of this alive.

The other two log haulers were still near the mouth of the harbour. He grabbed a lamp and took it to the stern and swung the light back and forth, once, twice, three times.

A moment later, the ship on his port, the *Oakhaven*, returned the signal. Calder headed back to Jaak.

"They're ready for survivors," he said. "Let's make sure that includes us." They'd decided not to use a dinghy, thinking that it would be too easy for them to be overrun with pirates from the *Bright Breeze*. Instead, they were going to swim.

"She's all tied off," Jaak said. He patted the wheel. "It's too bad, I really like this little ship. *The Mischief*," he laughed. "More like trouble."

Calder followed Jaak to the stern. They both turned to watch as their little ship closed in on the *Bright Breeze*.

The other crew was scrambling to get their dinghies ready. Calder saw a flash of blonde amongst the darker haired Pilalian crew and desperately hoped that Inger made it to safety.

Now they were only a half a dozen lengths from the *Bright Breeze*, and a direct hit was unavoidable.

"Hang on or jump ship now," he said to Jaak. "I'm going to wait until we hit." He wanted to see where—ah, there she was. Taller than anyone else, Margit Ansdottir strode along the deck. They were close enough that he could hear her shouts, although he couldn't decipher her words. Ansdottir grabbed Inger by the arm and pulled her to a dinghy that was ready to launch.

Another non-Pilalian ran up to them: it was Charis, apparently responding to an order from Ansdottir. He argued with the captain for a moment, but at her emphatic head shake, he joined the sailors and helped launch the dinghy.

Ansdottir strode to the main mast and stood staring out at *The Mischief.* Calder knew the moment she saw them. He waved an arm over his head. He wanted her to know that she'd been bested. That *he'd* bested her; he and Jaak.

"Jaak, you ungrateful *skit*," she yelled. "I should have drowned you years ago."

The Mischief slammed into the hull of the *Bright Breeze*, the log-laden prow splintering the larger ship's hull. Calder held onto the gunwale as the ship shuddered to a stop. Then the wind picked up, and the sails billowed out, forcing the log hauler deeper into the side of the *Bright Breeze*.

A few lamps had been lit on the *Bright Breeze*. Ansdottir was on the deck, her arm wrapped around the main mast, the only still form on the ship. The rest of her crew scrambled to the bow. The dinghy launched, and with relief, Calder saw Inger's blonde head in it.

The deck he was standing on bucked, and he had to grab the gunwale in order to stay on his feet. When he looked up, the *Bright Breeze* was listing at the stern and taking on water. Ansdottir hadn't moved.

"I'll abandon ship when you do, Rahm," she yelled at him.

"You go, Jaak," he said. "I'll stay and keep an eye on Ansdottir." Her Traits made her a dangerous prisoner if she was caught. He needed to see where she went so he could make sure she didn't cause more trouble.

"I'll look for you," Jaak said.

Calder kept his eyes on the captain, but he heard the splash when Jaak hit the water.

"I'm not leaving until I see where you go," Calder called to Ansdottir.

A sailor approached her, but she brushed him off. The deck of the *Bright Breeze* was angled down towards the stern now, making it hard for the remaining sailors to get to the bow.

A few Pilalians jumped overboard, and then the wind gusted and wood groaned and snapped as the prow of *The Mischief* was pushed even further into the *Bright Breeze*.

The deck tilted away from Calder, and he knew that the hull of *The Mischief* had been breached.

"Which ship goes down first?" Ansdottir called out to him. "Which one of us abandons our command first?"

Calder didn't answer her: he wasn't interested in her games. All he wanted was to see where she went.

"You're destroying two ships," Ansdottir said. "And you don't even realize how important they are going to be."

"This one can't sail to the Sapphire Sea," Calder said. "And I'm happy to take the *Bright Breeze* away from Tarmo Holt."

"I knew you were smart," Ansdottir replied.

Both ships shuddered, and Ansdottir lost her grip on the mast and stumbled into a mass of twisted rope. Wood squealed and split, and Calder almost lost his balance as the deck under him pitched towards the bow.

When he regained his footing, he saw Ansdottir trying to stand up as the *Bright Breeze* started to sink. Then he saw the line that had tangled around her feet and her desperation as she tried to get free.

Her hands went to her waist, maybe for a knife that was supposed to be there. "Skit, skit, skit," she cursed. She kept working at the ropes, but the ship started to roll onto its port side, and the ropes tightened around her ankles.

The deck and mast of the *Bright Breeze* loomed over him as the deck of *The Mischief* started slipping down toward the sea.

Calder got ready to jump. He took one last look at Ansdottir. She was flat against the deck as the *Bright Breeze* rolled towards *The Mischief*.

He jumped, hitting the water a second later. As soon as he surfaced, he swam as fast as he could, away from the two sinking ships.

Every time he came up for air, he heard the crashing and splintering of wood, along with the calls and shouts of pirates.

Eventually, he lifted his head to get his bearings, and his focus narrowed on a light that bobbed north of him. Letting Luck tell him where to head, he swam for it.

As always with his Trait, he never knew if it was sending him to friend or foe, so it was with relief that he recognized the silhouette of one of the log haulers.

THE GUARDS DIDN'T arrive until the fire was well under way. Gustav watched as many of the same people who had broken into the warehouse and carted off crates, returned and helped extinguish the flames.

Had there been some agreement between the rioters and the Swyfordian guards? Had the Clan Freeholder decided that Tarmo Holt's warehouses weren't worth guarding and allowed his people to empty the warehouses unchallenged? Gustav wanted to think that the Clan Freeholder had facilitated this small aggression against Tarmo Holt, but he had no proof.

Perhaps the guards had decided this on their own, or maybe it was nothing more than a coincidence.

Curious, he decided to find out if the same thing had happened in North Tarklee, in Nordmere, where Tarmo Holt commanded the guards.

He stepped out into the street and was walking away from the fire when he heard a commotion.

"Get out of my way!" a voice Gustav recognized called.

He pulled his scarf over the lower half of his face and turned his head as Tarmo Holt, Nordmerian guards clustered around him, barrelled through the crowd.

"This is Swyford territory," a guard in Swyford colours said. "Nordmere has no jurisdiction here."

"Do you not recognize me?" Holt asked. "I am the Grand Freeholder, and these men are my personal guard. Let me through, I must check on my property."

"You're to blame," a woman called from the crowd. "You're the one we've been signing notes for, promising everything for a day's rations." Others in the crowd muttered angrily, and the guards around Holt unsheathed their swords.

"You dare to draw your weapons in Swyford?" The Swyfordian guard was joined by half a dozen others, and the crowd lined up behind them. "I will make a formal complaint to the Fair Seas Treaty Alliance."

"Which I am the head of," Holt said. "Tell me what happened to my warehouse? Tell me!" No one from the crowd stepped forward, and Gustav edged into the shadow of a building.

Another guard rushed up to Holt's group from behind, the rest of the guards parting to allow him to reach Holt.

"What? When?" Holt asked. The answer was too low for Gustav to hear, but suddenly, Holt turned to leave.

"Keep asking questions," he said to one of his guards. That guard tapped two others, and they faced the crowd as Holt and the rest of his men headed back toward the river.

"Get away with ye," a man in the crowd called. "Ye don't belong here!"

"We want answers," the Nordmere guard said. "And we won't leave until we get them."

The two groups stared at each other for a few moments. Once Holt was out of sight, Gustav stepped out of the shadow and into the middle of the street.

"I can give you some answers," he said, trying to imbue his words with Charisma. "No need for anyone to be hurt. And certainly not if you're willing to pay me." He turned to the crowd and winked. "And my friends."

"We're not paying you," the Nordmere guard said. "Why should we?"

"Then you'll hear different stories from each of us, isn't that right, my fellow Swyfordians? And who's to say which tale is the truth?" Cheers and laughter followed Gustav's statement, and even the Swyford guards looked amused.

"But I," he flourished a bow, "have a proposition. If my fellow Swyfordians agree, I will tell you what happened if you," he paused, "agree to invalidate every single promise note signed by a Swyford citizen." As another cheer rose, Gustav wandered towards the Nordmere guards.

"I am trying to help you live through this," he said quietly. "So say yes." He met the gaze of the guard and called on his Trait, hoping it would be enough. The guards didn't know that this crowd had just stolen and then burned their master's property. Would harming these two really be that much of a stretch for this angry crowd?

Finally, one guard nodded. "All right," he called out. "All promise notes signed by Swyfordians will be destroyed. Come on." He grabbed Gustav by the arm and pushed him in front of him as they headed away from the crowd. They crossed at the Key Bridge into Nordmere and stopped just on the Nordmere side of the river.

"Now talk," the guard said, stopping in the square. "What happened?"

"When the stores opened, the rumour started," Gustav said, not mentioning that he himself had started those rumours. "About warehouses full of food."

"So?"

"Well, people didn't like the idea of all that food just sitting there." He sat on the edge of the fountain trying to force his Trait into every word and gesture. "Grand Freeholder Holt had a very nice coat. Does he live near here?"

"Huh," another guard said. "Houses here aren't nearly fine enough for the Grand Freeholder."

"Quiet," the first guard said. He turned back to Gustav. "And? What else?"

"What else?" Gustav asked. "They took it upon themselves to liberate all that food from the warehouse. And then the fire started." He leaned in. "I don't think it was set deliberately and the folk banded together to put it out." He straightened. "In fact, they saved Tarmo Holt's warehouse. I don't see any other way to look at it." He shrugged.

"After they set it themselves?" the guard asked.

"I told you, I think that was an accident." Gustav glanced up at the sky. The stars were starting to dim; dawn wasn't far off. "I'm very disappointed that I couldn't tell this to Grand Freeholder Holt himself. It must have been very important news to take him away from hearing this."

"It was," the guard said. "So, remember that whatever you have to say, it wasn't even the most important issue he had to deal with tonight."

"Now I am curious," he said. "What is more important than his warehouse?"

"His ships," one guard mumbled under his breath, "and his family."

"Hush," the first guard said. "What's your name, so I can follow up with you if I need to?"

"Arnor," Gustav replied. "My name is Arnor. I can usually be found near New Bridge, with my cart." He tried to sound as though he had all the time in the world, but really, he needed to leave. Tarmo Holt's ships and family had drawn him away tonight. Gustav wanted to know what had happened to do that.

And he needed to find Kaja and have her take him to Nadez.

CHAPTER 19

DAG SHIFTED THE pack and stared out at the harbour. Soft moonlight had cast enough light for her to see the two ships collide. A split second later, the horrible sounds of shattering wood had echoed across the harbour. Now, the sky was starting to lighten, showing the extent of the destruction.

She sucked in a breath. The smallest ship had rammed the ghost ship with such force that it looked as though the white ship had two sterns. Where they met, the decks tilted towards each other. The mast of the smaller ship cracked; the sound of splitting wood loud in the quiet of pre-dawn. The mast slowly toppled onto the ghost ship, crashing into the sails and sweeping them down into the sea.

Dag scanned the two ships, hardly daring to breathe, hoping her Trait didn't show her any familiar figures in danger. The stern of the smaller ship lifted up out of the water as the bow sank down into the sea, pushing the ghost ship down with it.

No one was visible on the smaller ship: if Calder had been there, he wasn't now. The ghost ship seemed deserted as well, with no sign of Inger.

She closed her eyes in relief: she had no proof that Calder and Inger were safe, but at least she wouldn't be forced to watch them perish while helpless to do anything to aid them.

The itch started between her shoulders, and she opened her eyes in fear. Was her Trait telling her she was wrong? That

Calder or Inger were still out there and in danger?

The sails of the ghost ship fluttered, and for a moment, she had a clear view of the deck. There *was* someone there, but it wasn't Inger. Even from this distance, Dag recognized the height and bulk of Margit Ansdottir.

Was she planning on going down with her ship? That didn't make sense: the ghost ship was stolen, and Ansdottir had her own ship, the *Vassan*. Why wouldn't she abandon this one? Unless! And then the terrible thought struck her that Inger might still be on the ship too.

The wind whipped the sails around, obstructing her view. Not caring if she was seen, Dag left her hiding place and ran along the pier, searching for a better view.

The *Neas* was closer to the wreckage and offered a higher vantage point: she'd be able to see what was happening from its deck. With fear for her sister driving her, she scrambled across the barge and back up the rope to the deck of the ship. The five sailors hadn't moved from the gunwales.

In the stern, Dag crouched down beside a dinghy and peered out between the railings of the gunwale.

From this angle, she had an unobstructed view of the deck of the ghost ship. She could clearly see that going down with this ship was not Margit Ansdottir's choice.

Ropes crisscrossed the captain's legs, trapping her on the deck. Ansdottir was pulling frantically at the ropes, trying to free herself.

Suddenly, the smaller ship plunged a few feet lower, and the ghost ship seemed to groan as it was pushed deeper into the sea. The deck tilted more, and Ansdottir cursed; her voice carrying across the sea.

She was still cursing as water gushed up and covered her, and the two ships sank below the surface, taking the captain with them.

"*Skit!* Never seen the likes of that," one of the sailors said.

"Nor hope to again," came a reply. "I see a few dinghies. Must be survivors."

"Any coming our way? They'd be our people."

"They're not our people. They're pirates."

"Who are allies of our Freeholder: we'll welcome them aboard if they make it this far."

Dag scurried to the other side of the dinghy for a better look. There were a few smaller boats in the water, as well as the two small ships that were still near the mouth of the harbour. Those ships raised their sails and headed into Tarklee Harbour.

A couple of black dinghies were being rowed out towards the two log haulers, and closer to the pier, fishing boats and barges headed out from shore. A few of them reached survivors and began plucking them from the water. One more black dinghy was coming straight toward the *Neas*.

"On deck sailors, the Grand Freeholder is coming aboard," someone called from the pier.

Startled, and angry at herself for being distracted, Dag scrambled under the dinghy. In her fear for Inger and Calder, she'd forgotten that she was on Holt's ship. Of course, Tarmo Holt would get news of the ghost ship being attacked in the harbour. And of course, he would want to see what happened.

More booted feet were on deck now: Holt and his guards.

"Papa, can I stay here and watch?" a girl asked.

"No," Holt replied. "I need you to stay below with your mother."

What was Tarmo Holt's daughter doing here? And his wife? Dag eased out from under the dinghy. If Holt had his family here, did that mean he was planning on sailing away? She had to get off this ship before that happened.

She climbed over the gunwale and clung to the side of the ship. She could drop into the sea and swim to the pier. It might be her best chance of getting off the *Neas* even if she was noticed. Would they shoot at her?

"What about this one?" someone asked. "Should he be taken down into the hold?"

"A dinghy is coming alongside with survivors, Grand Freeholder, from the *Bright Breeze*. Shall I let them board?"

"Yes. Is Ansdottir with them?" Holt asked.

"No sir, she went down with the ship."

"That's inconvenient," Holt said. "Bring whoever is in this dinghy to me," Holt said. "Line them up on deck; I want to make sure none of my enemies are hiding among them."

"And this one? He's starting to regain consciousness."

"One thing at a time," Holt said. "I'll deal with him after I've seen who these survivors are."

Dag inched along the gunwale, keeping her head as low as she could until she could see Tarmo Holt, who stood on deck with a couple of guards at his back.

A body was stretched out on the deck. It wasn't until it moved that she realized that it was a man, and that he was alive. A bloodied hand flailed in the air, and the man heaved himself to his side. And stared right at her.

Dag ducked lower: it was Joosep. He was alive, barely, and he'd seen her.

She took another look and met his gaze. He raised his hand again, this time making a deliberate signal, telling her that he would keep her presence a secret.

Then the bedraggled survivors from the ghost ship were herded into view. And she saw Inger.

AGONY COURSED THROUGH him as he rolled over, his eyes fixed on the sky. It was her; it was Dagrun Lund. Somehow, for some reason, she was the one who would witness his end. Because he knew that Tarmo Holt didn't plan on keeping him alive. He could only surmise that he'd been brought on board this ship because Holt didn't want his body found in the city.

But Dagrun Lund would know what had happened to him. He sighed. After all the mistakes he'd made and his recent anger and resentment for those who had criticized him, it was fitting that it was her. He turned his head towards the sound of feet on the deck. His Trait focused on one person in a line of half a dozen.

Of course. Inger Lund was here at the end as well. Why shouldn't she be?

People were talking above him, but he didn't pay attention; he couldn't pay attention. Until his Trait made him listen.

"I wanted her, but that was before she became Ansdottir's pet," Holt said. "Charis, you were second in command. What do you think?"

"Yes, sir, I was acting captain when Ansdottir wasn't aboard. I can vouch for Inger Lund. She has never been anything other than loyal."

"Has she," Holt said. "Her Trait has proven useful. But can I trust her? She does have that sister." Holt looked over his shoulder at Joosep. "You're the expert, Master Intelligencer. I've been told that this one can't lie. Is that true?"

"Yes," Joosep said. His voice was raw and it hurt, but this was important. This could save Inger Lund's life and maybe help make up for some of the mistakes he'd made with her and her sister. "That's one of the reasons why I didn't bother to train her."

Holt stared at him, and he wondered if he'd made too strong a case.

"I can continue to be useful," he said knowing that it wouldn't change Holt's mind about keeping him alive, but that it might make him trust what he said enough to save Inger. "I know a lot about Traits."

"You do, but this is the last time I'll need your help," Holt said. He turned back to Inger. "You swear to be loyal to me?"

"Yes, Grand Freeholder," Inger said. "Of course, I do."

"All right, you're now part of the crew. But there will be no special privileges unless they are earned. And Charis, you will be held accountable if she or any of these pirates cause me and my ship any trouble."

"Understood," Charis replied.

"Then let's get underway." Holt looked back at Joosep. "As soon as we're far enough from shore, you can dump this one in the harbour."

Joosep closed his eyes. He heard Holt walk away, and then orders were called out as the ship got ready to sail. He rolled over and opened his eyes, searching for Dagrun.

She was still there, clinging to the ships railing, and part of him was relieved that he hadn't imagined her. She signed that she would help him, and he shook his head, but she didn't leave.

He refused to allow Dagrun Lund to sacrifice herself to try to save him. The guard that had been left to watch over him was called to help move something, and Joosep surged to his feet and launched himself over the railing.

DAG ALMOST YELLED when Joosep went over the gunwale. Then she realized that she might not have another opportunity to leave the ship unnoticed. While most eyes were turned to where Joosep had entered the sea, she dropped into the water on the opposite side of the ship.

The *Neas* was already under way, and it quickly left her

behind. The pack of documents she'd stolen from Holt floated near her face, and she shifted it around to her back, hoping everything survived the seawater.

Anticipating a swim to shore, she was about to turn towards the pier when the retreating ship revealed a black dinghy. It bobbed on the waves, left behind by those who had used it to escape the ghost ship.

It was the dinghy from the ghost ship that had brought Inger to the *Neas*. In a few strokes, Dag reached it; she sheltered behind it, hiding, as the *Neas* sailed towards the mouth of the harbour.

When the ship was far enough away, she pulled herself into the small boat and scanned the sea around her. She didn't expect to see Joosep: he'd looked hurt and barely conscious, but she didn't want to have any doubts that she'd missed a chance to save him.

But he was gone: Joosep was dead. He'd helped Inger in the end, whose lie to Tarmo Holt had been believed because of him. Then Joosep had jumped, creating the distraction she'd needed in order to get off Holt's ship unseen.

She'd drifted for a few minutes, staring at the retreating *Neas*, before picking up the oars and setting them into the oarlocks. Once she had the dinghy pointed towards the dock, she looked out towards the mouth of the harbour. The two smaller ships were already too far into the harbour to block the *Neas*, and it sailed away. But the log haulers were closer to her than the pier.

Changing direction, Dag awkwardly started rowing towards the two ships, hoping that Calder was on one of them.

CHAPTER 20

HIS MOTHER HANDED him a mug, and Calder gratefully sipped the tea, the warmth of it chasing away the chill of his wet clothes. When he'd climbed aboard the *Oakhaven*, he'd immediately joined Captain Eklund to watch *The Mischief* finish sinking the *Bright Breeze*.

"You should find something dry to wear," his mother reprimanded him before she moved off to supply tea somewhere else.

Jaak had made it to *Tove's Folly*, the other log hauler. The two ships had tried to regroup when they'd noticed the *Neas* raising her sails, but Captain Eklund had determined that they were too far away to cut off the *Neas'* path out of the harbour.

"Should we try to follow?" Eklund turned to Calder. "What would you do?"

"I'd let him leave," Calder replied. "Something must have happened in the city for Holt to run."

"He lost out here," Eklund reminded him. "His pirate ship has been destroyed. And he doesn't even know that the north wasn't compromised."

"Wasn't it?" Calder asked. "There may not have been any towns destroyed, and none of their stored food was ruined, but without the shipyards, there is no need for timber, so there will be no work. And there will be no other food shipments to help them get through the winter. The north will be focused on survival, which might be all Holt wanted." He glanced away and watched his mother as she distributed tea to the survivors of the *Bright Breeze*. She'd been married to a Pilalian and spoke it fluently, a fact that he was certain the Pilalian pirates would not expect.

And perhaps Holt knew he couldn't win against that: people like his mother, people who were suspicious of outsiders and who would use any means they had, including tea and a middle-aged woman who could understand their conversations. Perhaps Tarmo Holt realized that about the north, so all he had planned was to create chaos and to have them stay out of whatever was coming.

Because even though Tarmo Holt had left, Calder didn't think the man had given up on his plans for controlling the Fair Seas Treaty Alliance.

Eklund gave the order to keep the ship out of the *Neas'* path. Calder finished his tea and decided that it was time to head below and finally scrounge up something dry to wear.

"Another dinghy, Captain," a sailor called from above. "A black one with just a single survivor."

Frowning, Calder headed to the port gunwale. A single person in a dinghy didn't make sense, not unless by some trick of fate Margit Ansdottir had survived the sinking of the *Bright Breeze*.

But it was blonde hair he saw, and at first, he thought it was Inger, because Inger should have been the only Lund twin in a dinghy from the *Bright Breeze*.

His heart recognized her before his head did. And then Dag looked up. When she spotted him, she smiled and waved.

"So, that's the one," his mother said from his side. "Well, you better go fetch her. I want to meet her, once all the chatter is done."

Dag didn't need him to fetch her, as his mother termed it. As soon as the dinghy was close enough, a rope was thrown down to her. She looped it around a strut on the little boat and was pulled in.

She scrambled up onto the deck and stood staring at him, a grin on her face.

He knew he was grinning back at her. He also knew everyone was watching, but he didn't care. He scooped her up into his arms.

"You are not who I expected to see out here," he said. He released her and studied her, trying to see if she was hurt. "Are you all right?"

"Me? I'm fine." Dag looked around at the people crowded around them. "But we need to talk. In private." She patted a wet pack that was slung across her shoulder.

"Yes." He turned to Captain Eklund. "We'll give you a report as soon as we can. This way." He tugged her through the crowd towards the door that led down to the cabins. He spotted his mother standing off to one side, a pot of tea in her hand.

"Can we use your cabin?" he asked her. She nodded, and he turned to Dag. "Dag, this is my mother, Lauma Strauskas. Mother, meet Dagrun Lund."

"Very nice to meet you," his mother said. "Come on, Calder spent most of his time on deck. I'll show you to my cabin." She led the way through the door and down a few steps.

Calder shrugged at Dag's questioning look. "I will tell you all about it," he said. Dag followed his mother, and he followed her.

His mother's cabin was small, but it was private. A single bunk swung from ropes fastened to the ceiling, and a compact desk jutted out from the wall.

"I'll get some fresh tea," his mother said. "And some dry clothes for both of you." She gave him a long look and then, thankfully, she left.

"Your mother?" Dag asked. "Does that mean the towns in the north are—"

"They're safe," he interjected. "The ghost ship tried to land, but the pirates didn't take more than a few steps on land. The people of Cutterstown made sure they couldn't get any farther than that. They caught me and my mother at sea and we headed north, where I met up with Eklund and the three ships. Ansdottir followed us back here, and we made a stand."

"That was you who rammed her?" He nodded. "I saw her. I saw Ansdottir go down with the ghost ship. I was on the *Neas*."

"What?"

DAG SHRUGGED AT him. "I was on the *Neas*," she repeated. "Finding these." She fumbled the pack open and pulled out the soaking papers and the two ledgers. Carefully, she pulled pages apart and laid them out on top of the bunk. "My Trait led me to them, and then I saw the ghost ship and was worried. About Inger." She paused. "And you."

"Yeah, well, I would have been worried about you if I'd known you were on the *Neas*," Calder said. He glared at her, and she shrugged again, too tired to argue.

"Joosep is dead," she said. "And Inger left with Holt."

"What? How?"

There was a knock on the door, and Calder's mother, Lauma, poked her head in.

"Dry clothes and hot tea," she said. "Out in the hall with you," she said to Calder. "Hold this." She pushed a pile of clothes at him then entered the cabin. Tea and mugs were placed on the desk, and a second bundle of clothes was handed to her.

"I'll be outside with my son. Let us know when you've changed." Then she backed out of the room, leaving Dag staring at the door.

The room felt larger with Calder gone. She quickly peeled her wet clothes off and pulled on the dry ones. The trousers were too big, and the shirt sleeves were too long, but she was dry and already feeling warmer.

She opened the door. "Your turn," she said to Calder. She squeezed past him and stood in the hall with his mother.

"You're an Intelligencer too," Lauma said. "Like my son."

"Yes, although I have a different Trait."

"Traits," she said, "have taken much from me, but my son embraces his. As I think you do."

"The tricky part is figuring out how they can work together," Dag said.

"That's true about everything," Lauma said. "Especially people."

The door opened. "Thank you for the tea and clothes, Mother," Calder said. "Is there anything else I should know about?"

"He means have I heard if the Pilalian pirates are plotting to take over the ship," Lauma said to Dag. "Not that I've heard. I think they really just want to go home." She looked at Calder. "I like her. Be nice." Then she left.

"I like her too," Dag said and grinned as she stepped past

Calder. "But I would love some tea."

By the time they'd each had two mugs of tea, Dag had finished telling him everything that had happened since Calder left Tarklee to go north.

"And Joosep?" Calder asked.

"By jumping overboard, he created a diversion," Dag said. "And that helped me get off the ship unseen." She didn't want to think about anything else he'd done when his last act had been to help her.

She picked up a sheet of paper from beside her on the bunk. It was still damp, but thankfully it was legible. The ledgers would need more time to dry out, but hopefully they too could be salvaged.

"And he was able to vouch for Inger," Calder said. He set his mug on the desk and sat back down on the chair. "At least she's safe."

"She's not safe!" Dag said. "Holt doesn't trust her, no matter what Joosep said. She'd only be safe if she was here, with me."

"No, she wouldn't be," Calder said, and she looked over at him and frowned. "It will be hard to prove that the part she played in the destruction of Lavais and Nurmi wasn't voluntary. She'll be considered an enemy of the Fair Seas Treaty Alliance."

"But she's not," Dag said. "Not really." She sighed. "Yes, she is until we can prove that she was forced. That Traits, hers and other peoples', made her do what she did. And that will be very difficult." Especially now that the Grand Freeholder had fled.

"But not impossible," Calder said. "Not for us."

"Not for us," Dag agreed, sending him a grateful smile.

"I still don't understand why Holt would leave Tarklee," Calder said. "We need to talk to Nadez and find out what she's learned."

"And decide what to do about Holt," Dag agreed. "Because leaving and taking his family with him does not make sense. Unless the destruction of the warehouses was the catalyst?" The itch started between her shoulders. "*Skit*, my Trait just activated. Something about the warehouses. Wait." She leaned over the papers on the bunk. She'd seen something on one of them. She grabbed one and stared at it. Was this it? Was this why Holt left? "Here," she got off the bunk and showed the paper to Calder. "Instructions to keep every warehouse only partially full: there was never enough food for the whole city. Not in Holt's warehouses. I think he left because he knows the city will face starvation this winter sooner than expected. Once the warehouses are empty, people will realize that there will be food shortages."

"He's trying to avoid blame," Calder said. "But there's still time to ship food. As long as there's coin to pay for it."

"And ships to carry it," Dag said.

"I still don't understand why," Calder said. "Maybe Nadez will have an idea." He looked up at her, and Dag's breath caught. "I never did tell you how glad I am that you're safe."

"Me too," she said. "About you." Then she leaned into him, and his lips met hers. Heat spread from where their mouths met along her body. She sighed and pulled away, staring into his eyes. "We need to go," she said sadly.

"Yes." Calder sighed. "We do."

Reluctantly, Dag stepped away to stack the papers and the ledgers and put them back into the still-damp pack. By the time she was done, Calder already had the cabin door open. She followed him along the passageway and up the stairs to the deck and Captain Eklund.

CHAPTER 21

GUSTAV ROLLED OVER and covered his head with his blanket. Near dawn he'd finally found Kaja, and she'd led him here, to what she said was one of Nadez's safe places, but she wouldn't lead him directly to Nadez.

And as much as he hated the need to wait for Kaja to find Nadez and tell her that he had news, in light of Joosep's defection, it was wise.

He heard a noise and lifted his head. Nadez crawled into the small room, followed by Kaja. Gustav rose, dropping the blanket onto the narrow cot.

"You needed to see me?" Nadez said. She stood up and brushed dirt from her trousers.

"Tarmo Holt has left the city," Gustav said. "With his family. It happened right after the riots started."

"You think they're connected?" Nadez paced the small space.

"Yes." Gustav had been puzzling this over for hours. "I don't think he planned to leave, certainly not right now. He'd just announced that the election to replace him as Grand Freeholder had been postponed. Leaving compromises his position."

"I agree," Nadez said.

There was a noise from the low passage that led outside, and Gustav froze. Then a blonde head poked into the room.

"It's me." Dagrun Lund crawled through the opening and grinned at them as she stood up. Gustav's answering grin faded when she stepped aside to let a second person through.

"Calder!" Nadez hugged him. "This makes up for you finding this place on your own."

"We have news," Dagrun said. "Holt has left the city."

"We know," Gustav replied. "He took his family."

"We think we know why," Dagrun said. "Joosep is dead, as is Margit Ansdottir, the captain of the Strongrock pirates." Dagrun paused. "And my sister left on Holt's ship."

"All right," Nadez said. "Kaja? Please make sure no one else surprises us. Everyone else, come this way. I need a full report."

Gustav thought it was close to midday before Nadez was satisfied that she had heard each report completely. His mind was racing with the implications of what he'd heard. Joosep was dead, and Holt had fled. A plot to deliberately starve the city over the winter. He hated that idea, but it sounded right.

"Why would he want so many to die?" Gustav asked. "These people already have so little." And yet the ones he'd met had been willing to help him, give him some of their very little because they thought he had less. Why would Holt deliberately hurt them?

"People like Holt," Nadez said, "don't care about anyone else. We're all just tools to be used as they gain power. And if we can't be used, then we better not be in the way."

"It's easy to control people," Calder said. "When they are worried about feeding their families."

"That's what the promise notes were about too," Gustav said. "Controlling people. Making them too indebted to him to dare oppose him. Disgusting."

"Yes, but we've forced his hand," Dagrun said. "*You* forced his hand by starting the riots."

"Now what?" Gustav asked.

"There's still some time before winter sets in," Calder said. "I'll go to the Sapphire Sea and try to buy more supplies."

"You said that two of Holt's ships are still in the harbour," Nadez said. "Who will crew them?"

"There are plenty of sailors without ships because of the fires," Calder said, then he grinned. "And my mother overheard the Pilalian pirates. All they want to do is go home. I can help them."

"I'll contact Clan Freeholder Timonis," Nadez said. "And tell him everything we've discussed. I will formally take over the Intelligencers. We also need to have someone appointed Acting Grand Freeholder in Holt's absence."

"My mother is the one to organize the Freeholders," Calder said. "And the best choice for Acting Grand Freeholder. She's the largest landholder in Byholt, and that country is neither relinquishing the position of Grand Freeholder, nor hoping to claim it in a few months."

"Your mother?" Dagrun asked, looking at Calder. He shrugged.

"She owns the land, and my brother manages the freehold," Calder said. "She won't appreciate that I volunteered her, but she'll be able to handle the other Clan Freeholders."

"Perfect," Nadez said.

"We still need to find Holt," Dagrun said. "He has more secrets to uncover."

"I'll never catch up to him," Calder said. "By the time I get a ship and crew sorted, he'll be through the Frozen Pass and safely past Strongrock and out of the Pale Sea."

"Would he stop at Strongrock?" Dagrun asked. "Would he want to take the *Vassan* with him as well?"

"He won't take the *Vassan*," Calder said. "Ansdottir is dead, but that's still her ship. But if he doesn't want to risk a mutiny, he'll probably drop off any pirates who made it to his ship after the *Bright Breeze* went down."

"Then we can catch him," Dagrun said. "If I come, *we* can catch him."

When Calder started to laugh, Gustav didn't understand the joke.

"All right. We will go after Tarmo Holt. At the very least it will keep him running. And we might find out that he has something useful stored on Strongrock."

"You think he'll stay on Strongrock and wait for you?" Nadez asked. "He's not stupid."

"If all goes well, we'll be in Strongrock before Holt is," Dagrun said. "Once I've navigated us through the Teeth."

THE END

Acknowledgements

As always, thanks to the crew at Tyche Books – especially my editor Karley Hauser and publisher Margaret Curelas.

Biography

Jane Glatt loves that along with creating original worlds, writing fantasy allows her to indulge her curiosity about an eclectic group of subjects. So far she's researched synaesthesia, medieval guilds, tidal rivers, cities atop bridges, pirates and privateers, plants used for healing and the history of spying. For that last one she blames a visit to the International Spy Museum (yes it's a real place), in Washington D.C.

For news on Jane's future releases visit her website http://janeglatt.com/index.html and sign up for her newsletter

www.ingramcontent.com/pod-product-compliance
Lightning Source LLC
Chambersburg PA
CBHW060927190726
48286CB00002B/667